COMING HOME

ALEXA ASTON

OLIVERHEBERBOOKS

CHAPTER 1

FEBRUARY—LOS ANGELES

Jackson Martin parked his sedan in the parking garage and grabbed his briefcase before locking his car. His gut churned. A general uneasiness filled him. Today, the jury would hand down the verdict in the Gerard McGreer trial.

And for the first time since he began practicing law, Jackson wanted his client locked up.

He had served for three years in the DA's office before making the switch to the other side of the table. Criminal law could be quite lucrative. It also could be incredibly expensive putting on a defense case, especially one in which their client had been indicted for rape and murder. Hours of manpower went into pre-trial preparations, including hiring private investigators to comb through their client's background—and that of the prosecution's many witnesses. Pre-trial motions had to be carefully written and filed. Strategy sessions with his law partner and their paralegal, lasting late into the night, where they crafted questions for each witness.

The culmination of all those months' work would be seen today. He'd given his closing argument at the end of Tuesday, as had the prosecution. The jury had deliberated all day Wednesday and Thursday, calling for various pages of transcript from the court reporter and a few key pieces of evidence. It wasn't unusual for a jury to take this long to determine guilt or innocence of a defendant when murder was on the table. The bailiff had called Jackson an hour ago, telling him it looked as if the jury might be wrapping up their deliberations this Friday afternoon. That's when he'd headed to the courthouse.

Dread filled him, knowing he would be expected to wait with the accused, Gerard McGreer. McGreer would be brought to the courthouse and allowed to change from his jail jumpsuit into street clothes. His client had been very specific about the combinations of clothes he had worn during the lengthy trial, even keeping a record of the outfit he wore each day. Before the trial, McGreer had been in IT—information technology—and was meticulous. Based upon McGreer's employment records and the things their private investigators had found, McGreer had worked with both software applications and computer hardware. Where most IT workers specialized and became either computer scientists, engineers, programmers, or systems analysts, McGreer had been involved in all four areas since his graduation from college a dozen years ago.

Jackson reached the entrance used by attorneys and other court personnel and went through the metal detectors, making small talk with the security guards on duty, whom he saw frequently since he was a trial lawyer. With the McGreer case, he had been at the courthouse every day for weeks, the only break coming when his client had developed a bacterial infection that was going around the jailhouse. The trial had been postponed for a week, allowing McGreer time to recover. Jackson should have pursued other cases during that time. Instead, he had been paralyzed, not wanting to move forward.

It was during that week that he made his final decision.

He was leaving LA and his law practice—and heading to the Cove.

Maple Cove had become his home when his parents had died in a freak avalanche while skiing. Jackson had been six, while his sister Willow was only three. Boo, their paternal grandmother and a renowned sculptor, had taken in the pair, raising them with plenty of love and an emphasis on education. Growing up in a small, coastal town in Oregon had made for an idyllic childhood, but Jackson had wanted to stretch his wings. After graduating from the University of Southern California in an accelerated Bachelor/J.D. program, he had accepted a job in the L.A. County District Attorney's office.

Over time, though, he had begun to miss the quiet life of the Cove, even more so after he left the DA's office, which had sucked the life out of him for very little compensation. The move to criminal law had been more glamorous at first, but the hours were brutal, especially during a case such as McGreer's. The stakes were high. The pressure tremendous.

Worse, for the first time in his career, he believed his client should be found guilty of the charges. Though he suspected previous clients had been guilty, McGreer was different. The man was beyond cold and calculated. Jackson was actually afraid of McGreer. He had never let his fear show, but he suspected his client knew of his attorney's feelings and was amused by them.

He entered the small room where McGreer would

be brought and took out a legal pad, scribbling a few notes on it that had nothing to do with the case. Instead, it was a series of questions to ask Clancy Nelson, the retiring attorney who had offered to sell his practice to Jackson when he'd returned to the Cove for Boo's funeral. Clancy was still sharp at eighty-five and had practiced law for six decades, serving all of Barton County. His practice was located in the Cove, where Jackson's sister now lived with her new husband, the local sheriff. Willow had chosen to move into Boo's house after their grandmother's death and had reconnected with her high school sweetheart. She and Dylan Taylor had admitted they never stopped loving one another, despite being separated during the last dozen years, both living in various countries across the world. They had married before Christmas, and he suspected they would soon start a family.

Clancy's offer had been interesting to Jackson, and he had begun to seriously consider it during this current trial. Suddenly, the sordid nature of this case—as well as dozens of others he had taken on over the last few years—caught up to him. While Jackson believed he had put on the defense of his life, he worried he had been too good—and that the jury would find enough reasonable doubt to let Gerard McGreer go.

His heart told him it would only be a matter of time before McGreer raped and killed again.

The door opened, and a deputy escorted his client into the room.

"Gerard," Jackson said crisply, nodding his head and then going back to his legal pad, not wanting to engage in conversation with his client.

"They tell me the verdict is imminent," McGreer said as he began shedding the prison jumpsuit.

"I believe so," Jackson said, keeping his eyes on the

page before him because he did not want to look into the cold stare of the man he was defending.

"You did an outstanding job. You know I'll be found innocent."

Jackson stopped writing, forcing himself to make eye contact with McGreer, who donned a white dress shirt. "The verdict is either guilty or not guilty. Innocence doesn't come into play legally." He went back to writing.

"You know what I mean, Jackson. But I like how precise you are. I'm that very way. We are a lot alike."

He swallowed, tamping down the words he wished to shout. That he was nothing like the man sitting across the table from him.

"I think the navy blazer was a good choice, don't you? And I always think a red tie makes a strong statement. I can't wait to talk to the reporters." McGreer began tying the tie, forming a perfect Windsor knot.

"I'd advise against that, Gerard."

"Why shouldn't I proclaim my innocence? I've been caged like an animal for almost a year now. No bail. Living for months in a dirty cell with inferior scum."

"If you are found not guilty, the best thing to do is take the high road and refrain from commenting. Remember, the victim's family is still out there. And hurting."

McGreer snorted. "Well, I'm hurting, too. Living in cramped conditions with common criminals. Having my freedom curtailed." He let out a long breath. "I cannot wait to sink my teeth into a rare steak and wash it down with a cold beer."

Jackson put down his pen. He had tried to prepare McGreer for the jury returning a guilty verdict. Yes, he had done an excellent job, tearing witnesses apart and creating doubt regarding the evidence. But juries were made up of humans. They mostly thought with their hearts and not their heads, especially when a violent murder had occurred. Most jurors saw the bloody photographs submitted into evidence and instinctively linked them to the person sitting at the defense counsel's table. He knew most jurors subconsciously thought there had to be a reason the accused was already sitting in court.

"I know you have high hopes, Gerard, but you need to prepare yourself in case the verdict comes back against you."

His client's dead eyes bore into Jackson's. "And I've told you I'll be walking out of this building later today. You put on a brilliant defense, my friend."

He didn't protest at being called *friend* simply because he did not want to be on McGreer's bad side. The man had made enough statements to let Jackson know he was quite vindictive—and he had a long memory.

"We should talk about your appeal, Gerard. Just in case."

Though Jackson did not want anything to do with that process, knowing it would only delay him from leaving California and heading back to Oregon, he still owed it to his client.

"That won't be necessary," McGreer insisted. "But... in case I ever *do* need an attorney again, I assume you would take my case."

Jackson shuddered inwardly. "That would depend on my current case load, Gerard. If I were knee-deep into another trial, whether in pre-trial motions or currently trying a case, you'd have to go somewhere else. You've met my partner, Bill Watterscheim. He's an excellent lawyer and would do a fine job of defending you. If Bill were also tied up, I have two or three other attorneys I could recommend to you."

He paused. "But on the chance you are found not guilty today, Gerard, you should aim never to darken the doors of this courthouse in the future."

McGreer smiled, slipping into his jacket. "Oh, you mean I shouldn't get caught again."

A chill ran through Jackson at his client's words. In that moment, he knew McGreer was guilty not only of the rape and murder he was now on trial for—but for others.

The door opened again, preventing him from replying.

"The jury's coming back, Mr. Martin. They're ready for you."

"Thank you."

He waited for the two deputies who would come to escort Gerard McGreer to the courtroom.

"I think I'm going to change my name," his client said dreamily. "My picture and name have been splashed across the media for a year now. "I've always admired Anthony Hopkins' work. I think Anthony would suit me. And I do like alliteration. Hmm. Anthony Adams. Anthony Arnold. Anthony Abbott. Yes, Abbott. Anthony Abbott. I like that. Do you like it, Jackson?"

The deputies entered, cuffing McGreer as Jackson returned his legal pad to his briefcase and closed it.

He fell in step behind them as the deputies led Gerard McGreer to the courtroom.

"Will you help me change my name legally, Jackson? Can we start after the verdict is read?"

"You won't need me for that, Gerard," he informed McGreer, deciding to detail the process and hoping McGreer would never have a chance to go through it.

"Most of it can be done online. You'll file a *Petition for Change of Name*. It will include a document where you must show cause for changing your name. It will probably take three months or so to get a court date. The judge will approve your request, handing down a court order called a decree, which allows for a legal name change. Then you'll be required to publish the cause for change in a newspaper for four weeks in a row."

McGreer glanced over his shoulder. "Why is it anyone's business what I change my name to? It negates the very thing I'm trying to do—avoid publicity."

Jackson shrugged. "That's the just process, Gerard. The court will give you a list of approved newspapers for publishing legal notices. Then you'll be done."

They entered the courtroom, his heart now racing. He felt awful that he hoped his client would be found guilty and sentenced to the maximum prison sentence.

Taking a seat at the table, he rested his briefcase on the ground beside him. McGreer raised his hands, and one of the deputies uncuffed him.

Jackson looked over his shoulder, seeing the room quickly filled with spectators. Most were reporters, but a handful were what he thought of as mayhem murder fans, retired people or those who worked night jobs and enjoyed attending murder trials, gravitating toward the gruesome details.

Lisa Fennel, the prosecutor, came in and headed straight for her table, nodding curtly at him. They had worked together on a few cases during his time at the DA's office. Jackson rose and crossed the aisle to speak to her.

"You put on a helluva case, Lisa," he complimented.

She gave him a tight smile. "You put on a better one," she admitted. "I'm worried, Jackson. Afraid of that man being out on the street again."

"Same," he said softly, not wanting anyone to overhear him.

He offered her his hand and she took it, saying, "I hope I don't have to go up against you again."

He smiled, keeping his news to himself. He had yet to tell anyone other than Willow that he was planning to return to the Cove. Not even Bill, his law partner, knew of Jackson's plans to leave the state after this trial. Originally, he had planned to stay until Clancy's planned retirement date of July fourth. The McGreer case, though, had left such a sour taste in his mouth that he had decided to pack up early. If Clancy weren't ready to hand over his practice, it would give Jackson time to himself to heal from the ugliness of this murder trial.

Returning to the table, he sat.

"Fraternizing with the enemy?" McGreer asked.

"We worked together several years ago," he said to his client. "She was a formidable opponent."

The bailiff called out, "All rise!"

Jackson came to his feet as the judge entered the courtroom, robes swishing as he climbed the steps and sat.

"You may be seated," the judge commanded. "Bring in the jury."

He watched as they filed in. None looked his or McGreer's way, which usually indicated a guilty verdict. What he found odd, though, was that several of them looked angry. The bad feelings churned within him again.

The judge asked if the jury had reached a verdict, and the foreman said they had. The rest was like a dream unfolding, as if Jackson swam underwater. He listened to the words being spoken. Heard the eruption behind him. Turned to scan the jury. Glanced to his opponent's table.

Then he turned to face a beaming Gerard Mc-Greer, a smug smile on his face. He pushed his glasses up on his nose. Jackson noticed the sweat beaded along his receding hairline.

"Told you," his client said. "Piece of cake."

The judge was hammering away, calling for order, but it was a done deal. Gerard McGreer was going to walk out of this building a free man. The judge dismissed the jury. People began racing from the courtroom.

Jackson stole a quick look at the victim's family. Her parents sat, stunned expressions on their faces. Her sister had angry tears streaming down her face. She glared at McGreer.

And Jackson.

He wanted to go offer them a word of comfort but knew to stay far away. Next to Gerard McGreer, he was the last person they might wish to speak with.

Turning to his client, he briefly told him what to expect. How McGreer would be processed out. Once again, he advised McGreer not to speak to the press, telling him how easy it was to turn words against him and how statements could be taken out of context.

He ended by saying, "You'll receive our final bill soon. Be glad you've been set free, Gerard."

His client smiled. "Oh, I am, Jackson. You were worth every penny. And I hope I never need to engage your services again. But if I do? You better be there for me."

The threat hung in the air.

By now, the deputies had come to escort McGreer

from the courtroom. Usually, he would go with his client, being alongside him every step of the way, even offering a ride to wherever he wished to go. Jackson couldn't do that. He sat, mute, watching Gerard McGreer being led away.

His eyes drifted across the aisle. The prosecutor's table had already been vacated. Jackson waited until everyone had left the courtroom, savoring the quiet, knowing it would be a circus outside.

He removed his cell phone from his briefcase and texted Bill, who had been his second chair through the trial but had chosen to remain at the office instead of appearing for the verdict since he'd just agreed to represent a new client in an aggravated robbery case.

Client got off on all charges.

Bill's congratulatory text came back through, praising Jackson's efforts, promising champagne would be waiting for him back at the office.

Finally, he stood, picking up his briefcase and leaving the courtroom. He stopped in the men's room, killing time, and then the vending machines. He hadn't eaten all day and it was almost four o'clock. Sweets weren't his thing, so he went for the peanut butter crackers, pocketing them, thinking he would eat them in the car on the way back to his office. He intended to tell Bill about his decision today. Suggest a couple of names of attorneys who might want to join the two-man practice, knowing how unhappy Bill would be. They had been acquaintances in law school, Bill being a year ahead of Jackson. It was Bill who had contacted Jackson when he put out feelers about leaving the DA's office and giving private practice a whirl. His partner would be incredibly disappointed in Jackson's decision.

He headed to the bank of elevators, the halls almost deserted on this late Friday afternoon. The elevator arrived and he got in. Two others followed. Both got out at lower floors, while he took the elevator to the ground floor. Heading to a little-used back entrance, he waved at the lone security guard and left the building, avoiding the reporters who would be gathered outside the front of the courthouse and the few who would gather in the rear of the building, looking for him. Again, Bill would be disappointed that Jackson didn't grab some of the limelight and help raise the profile of Watterscheim & Martin.

He reached the garage and headed to his car, weariness overcoming him. It didn't matter how tired he was. He owed it to Bill to go in and smile for the staff, drink a glass of bubbly, and then have a private word with his partner regarding his future plans. They would need to hash out a separation agreement. He wouldn't ask for Bill to buy out his half of the partnership, feeling that would be the decent thing to do. The new, incoming partner could buy in, helping Bill— and the firm—financially.

Suddenly, someone stepped in front of him. It was Juror Number Four, Sarah Peterson. Thirty-six. Married. A high school biology teacher. Catholic. When jury selection had started at the beginning of December, he hadn't known she was pregnant. As the weeks went by, however, her belly began to grow. Now, at the beginning of February, he could visibly see her bulging belly, figuring she might be about six months along.

"Mrs. Peterson, are you lost? Do you need help finding your car?"

She visibly trembled, the color drained from her face. "I have to tell someone," she said, her voice breaking.

"The DA often will call and speak with jurors about the verdict," he said gently. "Whatever you have to say about the case, you should share it with her."

"I can't," she hissed, glancing around. "He would know."

Jackson didn't have to ask who *he* was.

"I think you need to go home, Mrs. Peterson."

She reached into her purse, fumbling a moment, then bringing out her cell phone. She tapped in her passcode and took a moment bringing something up.

Turning the phone so it faced him, she said, "Here. See?"

He looked at the picture on the screen. A decapitated cat hung from a porch rail. His stomach twisted violently as he met her gaze.

"That was Pudding. My cat," she whispered, returning the phone to her purse.

Jackson already knew what would come next.

"*He* texted me. After closing arguments." She cradled her belly protectively with both hands. "Told me that I better vote *not guilty*—and that I would know why. When I got home, I found Pudding." She shuddered. "Then another text came in. It said that would happen to my baby if I didn't vote the right way. *My baby!* That monster threated to cut open my belly and pull out my baby and behead it, Mr. Martin. How sick is he?"

"You should have gone to the judge," he said neutrally, disgust filling him.

"I couldn't!" she said, her voice rising with hysteria. "The text messages had disappeared. I know he's some IT guy. Somehow, he made that happen. And he must have some accomplice. Someone... who would do... that. To my cat."

By now, tears streamed down her cheeks. "I had no

proof. I was terrified. For me. For my baby. I was the lone holdout on that jury, Mr. Martin." She wiped at her tears. "They berated me. Bullied me. But I wouldn't change my mind. I can't tell that to the DA Or the judge. But I had to tell you."

She paused, her body now shaking violently. "In case you didn't understand just how violent and crazy your client is. Be careful, Mr. Martin."

Sarah Peterson turned and walked away.

Jackson watched her go, bile rising in his throat. McGreer was clever enough to get text messages to disappear. After all, he was a computer whiz. Something like that would be child's play for him. But the dead, decapitated cat meant he had someone on the outside, someone just as depraved as he was, that had helped send Juror Number Four that physical threat. That someone might have been an accomplice to the rape and murder Gerard McGreer had been tried for.

Cold fear pooled in Jackson's belly. Quickly, he ran to his car and unlocked it, climbing in and locking it. Blood pounded in his ears.

If he had any doubts before now, hearing Sarah Peterson's confession cemented his decision.

Jackson was leaving L.A. tomorrow.

For good.

CHAPTER 2

APRIL—MAPLE COVE

Jackson cracked his window as he drew closer to Maple Cove, wanting to smell the hint of sea breeze in the air. He inhaled deeply and caught it. Slight—but still there, and so very familiar. He rolled up the window, though, wanting to keep the cold air out for now. Once he reached Boo's house, the first thing he wanted to do was go for a long walk along the beach.

It was now April, two months since the conclusion of the McGreer trial. Though Jackson's goal had been to get out of L.A. quickly, it had taken almost ten days before he actually left. First had come a lengthy talk with a disgruntled Bill Watterscheim, who couldn't understand why Jackson wanted to dissolve their partnership and return to his hometown to practice-of-all-trades law. Bill had been raised in San Francisco and liked all the advantages of a big city, including the large clientele to draw from.

Fortunately, one of the attorneys Jackson had suggested to replace him in the two-man firm had been thrilled to come on board. Bill had insisted Jackson take the buyout, telling him it would help him purchase Clancy's practice and hopefully have something left over to help him with housing. Jackson had said his goodbyes to the staff and spent a final, private few minutes with Bill, passing along what Sarah Peterson had shared regarding Gerard McGreer. Bill had been just as appalled as Jackson with what the juror shared. His partner had pushed for them to go to the judge in the case or even Lisa Fennel, the prosecutor.

He had shut down that idea, knowing no good could come from it. Because of double jeopardy, Gerard McGreer couldn't be tried for the same crimes again. New charges of jury tampering weren't feasible, especially with no proof. Jackson also believed it would imperil Sarah and her baby if they came forward, and he shared that with Bill, asking his partner if he would be willing to be responsible for that woman and her baby being murdered. Jackson had no doubt McGreer would carry through with his previous threat, despite Sarah voting as she had been blackmailed to do.

Finally, Bill had agreed, saying he appreciate the warning about McGreer, and would never represent him again if he came to the office.

After that, Jackson cleaned out his desk and took a few days to pack. He placed his furniture in storage and packed up his clothes. He rented his condo on a monthly basis, having sunk the majority of his money into the practice and not having enough left over for a down payment on a home despite his healthy income. His lease ran out at the end of each month, and he informed his landlord he would not be renewing, eating the final two weeks as he headed out of L.A. for a much-needed road trip to clear his head.

Jackson had visited Arizona, New Mexico, Colorado, Wyoming, and Idaho over the past several weeks, stopping when the spirit moved him, staying at out of the way inns and motels. He had spent time hiking in Rocky Mountain National Park and the Grand Tetons before crossing into southern Idaho and finally Oregon. The time spent alone had helped him to relax and ground himself. He hadn't picked up a newspaper or turned on a TV. He only sporadically checked his phone for e-mails and answered very few of them.

He had called Willow as he drove across the Arizona desert. They'd had a heart-to-heart talk about the McGreer trial and how it had tainted his soul. He refrained, however, from mentioning what Sarah had shared with him, merely telling his sister that he was ready to leave the big city behind and become Clancy 2.0.

They had spoken at least once a week during his time on the road and again last night, when he told her he would arrive in the Cove today. For now, he would stay with his sister and Dylan at Boo's. Their grandmother had left her house to both of them, but with Willow's marriage, Jackson had told his sister to take the house. Willow, like Boo, was an artist, and the house had a large studio on the top floor ideal for her to use. Willow mentioned to him in their last conversation that they would need to work out the details regarding the rest of Boo's estate once he arrived in the Cove, wishing for Jackson to take the bulk of what had been left in the bank and savings accounts.

He entered the Cove's limits, passing Fred Bell's gas station. Willow had kept Jackson apprised of the recent happenings in the Cove, including Fred's wife setting fire to the apartment located above Sid's Diner, where Willow's college roommate, Tenley Thompson, had been living. Tenley had recently married Dylan's best friend, Carter Clark, who came from a local family of firefighters. The Bells had been Carter's in-laws, and Wilma Bell had gone off the deep end when Carter became engaged to Tenley, feeling Carter was being disloyal to his wife, who had died five years ago. Wilma herself, in a twist of fate, had died of smoke inhalation from a fire in her own home.

Reaching the square, Jackson slowed to a crawl, passing by familiar restaurants and stores, along with new additions. He passed Buttercup Bakery, remembering the owner had catered food for Boo's memorial. He couldn't remember her name, only that Willow had become friendly with the woman.

He turned away from the square, promising himself he'd order a pizza from Crust 'n Stuff soon. Willow said the owners of the pizza parlor were from New York, and their pizza was New York style. Though he'd never been to New York, Jackson liked any kind of pizza and was eager to try it.

His focus turned to the small law office on one corner of the square, located next to the town barber. Clancy Nelson had occupied the space for as long as Jackson could remember.

This would become his office.

He had yet to speak with Clancy. As far as the other attorney knew, Jackson would contact him sometime close to the Fourth of July and provide Clancy with an answer as to whether or not he wished to take over Clancy's law practice. Willow was the only person who knew Jackson had left L.A. for good and would be moving to the Cove. Jackson had sworn her to secrecy.

Tonight, he would tell his new brother-in-law of his plans and contact Clancy. They could have a long chat tomorrow and discuss the transition. Jackson wasn't certain he wanted to leap into things immediately, but he didn't want to wait until July. Maybe they could reach a compromise in the middle regarding when Clancy would step away and Jackson would take up the reins.

Turning off the square, he made his way to Boo's house. How he missed his grandmother, the woman who had raised him. He vaguely remembered his parents. Their youth. Their vitality. Their constant air of good cheer. He did recall a book his mom had read him at bedtime—*Hop on Pop*—and his dad trying to teach him how to play catch. They had been snatched away in the prime of their lives. Boo had become mother and grandmother to Willow and him. His memories of growing up in the Cove were fond ones.

He hoped he now made the right decision of returning to practice law in Barton County.

Minutes later, he pulled into the long driveway and drove to its end. Tall trees were to his right, separating Boo's house from Gillian Roberts, the closest neighbor and a woman who had become like an aunt to the Martin orphans. In the other direction lay the ocean and a path going down to it, the private cove where he and Willow had spent so many afternoons playing.

As Jackson climbed from his car, the door opened. Shadow came bounding down the stairs, Willow not far behind the dog.

"Hello, boy," he said, petting the pup after it came to a stop, looking up at him. "Good dog."

"He is a good dog," his sister declared, throwing her arms around her brother. "It's so good to have you here. I can't believe you're finally home."

He returned her hug, suddenly feeling very sentimental.

"You really are going to stay? For good?" she asked anxiously.

"That's the plan."

She smiled broadly. "It's been so hard not to tell Dylan about this, but I've kept quiet. Just as you asked."

"I'll tell him at dinner tonight. I'll also need to set up an appointment with Clancy before he hears from someone else that I'm back in town."

Jackson popped his trunk and claimed the two suitcases which he hadn't opened since he'd been on the road. He'd lived with everything he'd placed in his duffel bag and backpack. Willow came and claimed both of those for him, and they went inside the house. He carried up his luggage, and she led him to his old bedroom.

Stepping inside, he chuckled. "Well, this has certainly changed since the last time I was here for Boo's funeral."

"All the renovations have been completed. After the rooms were freshly painted, I made some new curtains. Ordered new comforters. Collected all your old trophies and memorabilia. I left your books on the shelf, though."

She opened the closet and indicated a couple of boxes on the floor. "Everything is in there. You can go through and see what you want to keep and what can be thrown out."

He thought pretty much everything could go. He'd lived over a dozen years without needing to see Little League trophies or plaques from sports banquets. Still, it would be a fun walk down Memory Lane to go through everything a final time before he tossed it.

"I'll give you time to unpack, and then we can

talk," his sister said. "Anything I can put on to wash for you?"

He picked up the duffel bag she had placed on the ground next to the bed. "Everything in here. It's what I wore while I've been hiking the past few weeks."

Willow took the bag from him. "I'll throw on a load now. It may take more than one, though, as big as this bag is."

"I'll get everything out of my suitcases. The shirts are clean but will need ironing. I threw in some suits, as well. I'm not quite sure how I'll want to dress in the Cove while I'm at work."

"Most everyone is casual," she informed him. "Except Clancy. He still wears his bow ties to the office, along with a suit jacket."

"I'm hoping I can get away with a nice collared shirt and slacks most days," he admitted. "I'd love to think ties were a thing of the past. Unless I have to appear in court."

"I don't know how often Clancy had to do so," Willow said. "I'm sure he can fill you in on the kind of cases you'll be handling and the needs of Barton County's citizens." She hesitated. "I certainly hope you won't be representing any murderers anytime soon."

"Me, too."

Willow left and Jackson took the next half-hour sorting through things, placing items in drawers, hanging things in the closet. He would need to bring up the ironing board to get the wrinkles out of several shirts. He moved to the Jack-and-Jill bathroom, which he had shared with his sister growing up. They had liked being so close to one another and since it had dual sinks, they were often able to get ready at the same time. He noted the new tile in the shower and the marble countertops, as well as the mirror now being framed. After placing his toiletries in the medicine cabinet and in the top two drawers, he decided to shower and located towels in the linen closet.

He dressed in a golf shirt and pair of jeans and headed downstairs, finding Willow sipping tea in the kitchen.

"Wow. Now *this* is a kitchen."

Jackson admired the new appliances and painted cabinets, along with the large island. He took a seat on one of the stools, and Willow poured him a cup of tea from the teapot. He squirted a healthy amount of stevia into the cup and then took a sip.

"Ah, this hits the spot. As much as I love my coffee, there's always something comforting about a cup of tea," he said. "I recognize Boo's teapot."

"I know the kitchen looks new, but the cabinets are still full of her things," Willow told him. "The china and everyday plates. The pots and pans. Mixing bowls."

"How about her studio? Are you finding it meets your needs?"

She nodded. "The light is excellent. I didn't need any of the clay or molds she used, so I donated those our alma mater's art department. They were grateful to get it."

They talked for a while about what she was working on and then she caught him up on news in the Cove, sharing more about Tenley and Carter's wedding on Valentine's Day and the party afterward.

"I remember Carter pretty well. I spoke with him briefly at Boo's memorial," Jackson said.

"You'll get to meet Tenley and several others at Game Night tomorrow."

He had heard of their monthly gatherings and how competitive they became.

"Remind me who'll be there besides Carter and Tenley."

"Gage Nelson. He moved to the Cove last summer."

"Oh, the former Navy SEAL who does fitness training, right?"

"Yes, that's Gage. And two cousins, Ainsley and Rylie Robinson. Ainsley was two years behind me in school. Rylie didn't grow up in the Cove, but she did spend her summers here with Ainsley's family."

"Which one did you run into in Paris?"

"That would be Ainsley. She was attending some prestigious pastry school, and she now owns and runs Buttercup Bakery. I know you're not big on sweets, Jackson, but Ainsley may change your mind."

"We'll see. I'm more of a meat-and-potatoes kind of guy. I can take or leave desserts."

The door opened, and Dylan entered, carrying two large, brown-paper sacks with "Sid's Diner" stamped on the side. Dylan set the bags on the counter. Jackson stood and offered his new brother-in-law his hand.

"Thanks for having me," he said.

"Boo's house is plenty big," Dylan told him. "You're welcome to stay as long as you'd like."

He thought now was as good a time as any to break the news. "I'm staying for good, Dylan."

The town's sheriff grinned from ear to ear. "That's fantastic, Jackson. I'm sure Willow is over the moon."

"I am," his sister chimed in, smiling at him with a bit of the hero-worshipping little sister gaze he recalled so well.

"It looks as if I'm going to take Clancy Nelson's place," he continued.

"Clancy's retiring?" Dylan asked. "It'll be hard to

imagine him doing so. Will you take over his law practice?"

Jackson nodded. "That's the plan. I need to meet with him soon—hopefully, tomorrow—and work out the details."

"Why don't you call him now?" Willow suggested. "I asked Dylan to pick up dinner for us. Let me get everything plated and drinks poured. By then, you should be ready to eat. That can be your excuse to get off the phone, otherwise, Clancy will talk your ear off."

"Okay."

He left the kitchen and stepped into what Boo had always called the library because of the shelves lined with books that Murray Martin had brought home. By the time Jackson and Willow came to live with Boo, their grandfather had already passed, but they had spent hours going through his collection of books and reading them.

Closing the door, he brought up Clancy's name on his cell and touched the phone number, looking around at the improvements in the room as the phone rang.

"Jackson Martin," Clancy greeted. "I heard you were in town. Porter Williams glanced out his window and saw you driving by his office on the square. And Shayla Newton stopped by earlier. She'd also seen you."

He shook his head, recalling what small town life was life.

"I'd like to come visit with you tomorrow, Clancy, if you've got room in your schedule."

"Well, I don't work Fridays, Jackson. That's the beauty of being my own boss. I take Fridays off. Sleep late. Play a little golf. Drink a little beer."

"That must be the secret to your longevity," he quipped.

"Could be. But I'll make an exception for you. Want to stop in the office around ten-thirty? That way we can talk—and then you can take me to lunch."

"I'll see you then, Clancy," Jackson promised.

CHAPTER 3

Ainsley Robinson pulled her long hair back into a ponytail and left her small apartment, which was situated above her bakery. She moved quickly down the stairs, and reaching the bottom, unlocked the door separating her private space from the large kitchen area. Flicking on lights, she went immediately to the coffeemaker and set it to brew her first cup of the day. She limited herself to two cups—one when she first arrived and one more around nine o'clock. The morning rush was usually over by then, and she would take time to eat a little something and sip a second cup of coffee while she went over her To Do List for the day. Any more caffeine beyond that, and she would become certifiably crazy.

She removed the clipboard hanging from the wall and glanced over what she would be making this morning. The usual standards always appeared on the top of her list, including a variety of donuts and scones, bear claws, and cinnamon twists. Friday was also a good day for scones and muffins, especially blueberry. The bottom half of the list was devoted to orders that would be picked up that day. Since today was Friday, she had two birthday cakes to make and fifteen dozen cookies that a basketball mom had ordered for the local YMCA league, a standing Friday order.

Flipping the page, she looked over the second sheet on her clipboard. These would be the various items she would bake in addition to those on the first page. Different kinds of cookies. A few pies. Definitely cupcakes. She would also need to get ready for the weekend rush, which sometimes started on a Friday. That would include more homemade breads, brownies, and coffee cakes.

She put aside the clipboard and continued turning on lights throughout the bakery, unlocking the door so Gus could slip in. He was her Number Two and right-hand, having learned to bake in prison. While Ainsley had had qualms about hiring him, she had spoken to the names he listed on his resume, which included his probation officer, the head of the prison's kitchen, and even the warden himself. All three had given Gus a glowing report, and the warden said he believed Gus hadn't even committed a crime. That the car he was driving that smashed into a family of five had been driven by Gus' little brother and the two men had switched places.

Ainsley had hired Gus on a probationary basis and never regretted doing so. He was quiet and kept to himself, but he was also reliable and talented, assuming more responsibility as time went on.

She turned to head back to the kitchen when she saw a figure streaking across the square, which only had a few street lights dotting its perimeter.

Jackson Martin.

She had heard he was back in town. Two people

stopping in the bakery before it closed yesterday after-noon had mentioned it.

Ainsley had had a massive crush on Jackson when she was in seventh grade. He was a senior in high school and the quarterback of the championship football team. He also starred at guard for Salty Point High's basketball team and played outfield on the baseball team. Jackson was not only athletic but very, very smart. He had won an academic scholarship to college. As a twelve-year-old, Ainsley had thought Jackson Martin the ideal man, hoping to marry the handsome senior one day. Not that she had ever spoken a word to him.

But a little girl could dream.

He had left the Cove, and like many young people, hadn't come back. She heard through the gossip mill that he'd graduated from law school and gone to work in the district attorney's office in L.A., a world far away from the Oregon coast. She had run into Jackson's sister in Paris, where Willow was studying and painting and Ainsley was attending l'Ecole Lenôtre, one of the best-known pastry schools in the world.

Willow had recently returned to the Cove after the death of Boo, her grandmother. Ainsley had catered the memorial celebration at Boo's house and recon-nected with Willow, who was now one of her closest friends. Ainsley had seen Jackson at Boo's but hadn't spoken to him, her throat tightening just at the sight of the matured, even more handsome man he'd become.

Ainsley knew Jackson would be coming to visit the Cove, thanks to Willow sharing that information a few nights ago when they had dinner together, along with Rylie and Tenley.

She resolved this time if she ran into Jackson, she

would speak. And hoped that whatever came out of her mouth made sense.

Suddenly, he veered toward her. Startled, she retreated a few steps as he ran to the bakery's door and peered in. He caught sight of her and waved, his smile making her go weak in the knees, as if he were some leading man, stepping off the movie screen and into real life.

"Ainsley?" he asked, or rather mouthed, since she couldn't hear him through the thick glass.

She stepped to the door and opened it. "Hi," she managed to get out, feeling tongue-tied and much like that seventh grader who had crushed hard on Jackson Martin.

"Hi, I'm Willow's brother. Jackson. I saw your light on. You're certainly an early bird."

"I'm in the bakery by three every morning. There's lots to get done and put into the ovens in order to be ready to open at six-thirty." She swallowed. "You're also up extremely early."

"I'm a runner," he explained. "I usually would be up and run between four and five each morning before I got ready for a very long day. In L.A."

"I know. You're an attorney. I'm friends with Willow. She told me."

He smiled again, causing her heart to begin to pound rapidly. "And my sister told me you make the best sweets around. That you're a terrific baker. I'm not much into sweets, but Willow swears you can change my mind."

"I'd like to try." She almost cringed at how that came out. She didn't want to flirt with him.

Or did she?

"I won't keep you now. I will come back by the bakery later this morning. I've got a meeting with

Clancy Nelson. Thought I could bring him something sweet to put him in a good mood."

Ainsley laughed. "Sweets will definitely do the trick with Clancy. He's a sucker for fruit tarts. Cookies. And any kind of pie on the planet."

"Would you mind putting a little something together for me to take to him?"

She smiled. "I can do that. When is your meeting?"

"Ten-thirty."

"It will be ready by ten-fifteen," she promised, thinking what she might include.

"I appreciate it. And I guess I'll be seeing you tonight, as well. Willow said something about Game Night?"

She nodded, swallowing as she thought of a night in this man's company. "Yes. Tenley and Carter are hosting tonight. They bought the Garner place and have been doing all kinds of updates to it. The downstairs is ready, so the gang is heading there to see the work already completed. We usually have dinner and then play a few games. Have a few drinks and laughs."

"Sounds like exactly what I need." He raked a hand through his dark hair. "Well, I'll let you get back to your baking. See you later."

He gave a wave and took off again. Ainsley watched him jog away, his tall, athletic frame very appealing. He had runner's calves, muscled and well-developed, along with a natural grace.

She closed the door and went to get her coffee, doctoring it carefully, deciding what to include in a little gift basket to Clancy.

Gus appeared, startling her.

"Sorry. Didn't mean to upset you," he said quietly.

"You're fine. I was just woolgathering."

Immediately, Ainsley went into business mode,

breaking down what needed to be mixed, blended, and kneaded and put into the ovens or fryers. She was grateful to have something to do to keep her so busy.

Or else she'd melt into a puddle just thinking about Jackson Martin.

The next few hours passed quickly. Nine o'clock came and Sheila, who was learning how to bake and mostly worked the counter, brought Ainsley a cup of coffee. Gloria, her other baker who worked the counter during rush hour, joined them.

"Got our marching orders?" Gloria asked.

She put both women to work on the Little League cookie order and muffins. Gus was busy with baking bread and juggling several pies. Ainsley mixed the batter for both birthday cakes and placed the round tins into a different oven.

Then she thought over the goody package for Clancy, asking the two women to bake an extra dozen chocolate-chip cookies. She would put those in a tin, along with a personal chocolate pie for the elderly attorney.

She also needed to put together dessert for tonight's gathering. Others brought food and drink each time, but it was up to Ainsley to provide dessert, based upon the previous Game Night winner's choice. Dylan was the latest winner, and he had asked for cupcakes. She would bake a variety today since cupcakes were a big seller on Fridays and Saturdays. Many parents liked them for children's birthday parties, while others bought them because of their size. Where an entire cake might go stale after a few days, a customer could buy a few cupcakes and eat them in a day or two.

She finished her coffee and put in several tins of cupcakes, having Gloria and Sheila mix up even more varieties. She left them in charge, saying she would be back.

Not believing she did so, Ainsley stole upstairs just to see what she looked like. After being up for over six hours and around the heat in the kitchen, she looked a little bedraggled. Quickly, she brushed her teeth and applied a dab of perfume from a bottle that was almost empty, telling herself she was insane to be doing so. She slipped the plastic band from her hair and brushed it, again putting it back into her usual ponytail. If she showed up downstairs wearing her hair down, her staff would know something was up.

Blotting her face with a tissue, she returned downstairs, checking on one project and then another as tins came out of the ovens. She put together Clancy's treat basket and set it aside, not sharing with the others that Jackson Martin would be calling to claim it.

She wanted to be the one to give it to him.

Sure enough, she was moving from one thing to another when Sheila stuck her head in and shouted, "Ainsley. Some guy is here wanting a basket he ordered. I don't have a record of it."

"I'll take care of it," she said, retrieving the basket and moving to the front of the bakery, her heart beating so loudly she couldn't even hear.

Jackson awaited her, no longer the sexy, sweaty mess he had been hours ago. Instead, his hair, which had appeared dark this morning, gleamed with chestnut highlights in the light pouring into the bakery. He wore a crisp, button-down shirt and dark slacks. His sleeves were rolled up, revealing muscled forearms that made her mouth go dry.

"Hey, Ainsley," he greeted.

"I have your basket," she said, setting it on the counter. "Check over it."

"No need," he told her, his smile blinding. "I trust you."

She reached to lift it at the same time he did, their hands brushing against one another. Electricity rippled through her at the touch and she dropped hers, feeling scalded.

"Sorry," she mumbled, glancing down.

"Thank you for putting this together," Jackson said. "How much do I owe you?"

"Nothing," she replied quickly, not able to meet his gaze. "Consider it a welcome-home gift."

"Are you sure?"

"I'm sure," she said, forcing her eyes to meet his moss green ones, not quite certain of the look she saw in them. It was as if he mulled something over a moment—and then made a decision.

"Then let me return the favor," he said smoothly. "Let me take you to dinner tomorrow night."

"Oh!" she said, startled by his suggestion. "Um, okay. I guess."

He frowned. "I'm sorry. I should have asked first if you were seeing anyone. Boy, this is awkward." His gaze penetrated to her soul. "Are you seeing anyone, Ainsley?"

She shook her head. "No."

Again, that winning smile that stole her breath. "Good. Is the Old Coast Pub House still in business?"

He named the most expensive restaurant within twenty miles.

"Yes. It's still around. In Salty Point."

"Good. Boo used to take us there on special occasions. Our birthdays. To celebrate a great, end-of-the-year report card. I think we should celebrate there."

His words puzzled her. "Celebrate... what?"

His eyes shined at her. "Our new friendship. Dinner at eight?"

It took everything Ainsley had not to faint on the spot.

"Yes."

"Great." He removed his wallet and handed her a card. "My number's there. You can text me your address. I'll pick you up at seven-thirty."

"Okay," she agreed, her voice trembling.

Jackson raised the basket. "We'll see if this manages to put Clancy in a good mood. I'll see you tonight at the Clarks' house."

"Bye," she managed to get out as he left the bakery.

"Who *was* that?" Sheila asked, coming up behind Ainsley. "He's the best-looking man I've ever laid eyes on. "And he asked you out, Ainsley! What are you going to wear?"

She wasn't as worried about what she was going to wear.

Her biggest worry was staying awake until the end of their date.

CHAPTER 4

J ackson left Buttercup Bakery with the gift basket Ainsley had prepared for him. He had surprised himself by asking her out. He didn't date because he had never had the time to do so once he left law school. If he needed his itch scratched, he would text Erin Oakley. The petite redhead had started at the district attorney's office a year before Jackson arrived. Even after he left the DA's office and went to what Erin termed *the dark side*, they still got together on an infrequent basis. Both spent most of their waking hours devoted to their jobs and although they liked one another, Erin had told him she wasn't interested in anything long-term and had no plans to marry. She had aspirations to run for L.A.'s district attorney position one day and didn't want a family holding her back. Erin said it wouldn't be fair to have a husband or children because her heart, mind, and soul belonged to the law.

That had made her the perfect, occasional sexual partner. No strings attached. No commitment from either of them to the other. Just two busy, lonely people who made each other feel not quite as lonely every once in a while.

Now he was back in the Cove, however, he desired a more normal life, one not totally consumed by his work. He wanted a wife and children as he sank roots deeply into his childhood community. It was one of the most attractive reasons for returning to the Oregon coast.

The moment he had spoken with Ainsley Robinson this morning, Jackson knew he wanted to spend time with her. Willow had many favorable things to say about Ainsley, and he knew female companionship in the Cove would be limited. Most young adults left the Cove and small-town life, seeking big cities and new adventures. Because of that, he had known the dating pool would be slim. He might as well start with a friend Willow admired. It didn't hurt that Ainsley was easy on the eye. She must be about five-seven and was surprisingly slender for someone who owned a bakery. He wondered if she sampled many of her products. What had drawn him to her, though, were her large, periwinkle eyes. The unusual color had captivated him. She also seemed a bit shy. Women in L.A. were much more aggressive, wanting to take the bull by the horns and run a relationship. Ainsley had piqued his interest, which was why he had decided to pursue a date with her.

He cut across the square in a diagonal fashion, skirting the gazebo in the middle, and arriving at Clancy Nelson's law office. Opening the door, he saw the small waiting room. No receptionist was in sight. He figured Clancy did without in order to save money.

The man himself appeared, wearing his usual bow tie and jacket, and said, "Jackson Martin. I am glad you are finally here." His eyes lit with interest. "I see you are bearing gifts from Buttercup Bakery. Do you want to try and soften me up?"

Jackson handed the basket to the old man and smiled. "If you think it will help."

"Come on back," Clancy told him, leading them past a room on the right lined with law books. A large mahogany conference table surrounding by several chairs sat in the center.

Jackson assumed this was where most meetings occurred in the office. On the left, they passed a small kitchen and a closed door, which he assumed was the restroom. Clancy pointed out another closed door on the right, telling Jackson it was the file room, which held current case files and those that went back for five years.

They passed a final door, and the older man said, "Stairs lead up to the room above. It's large, the entirety of the bottom floor and all one space. I keep all my old case files there, organized by year and alphabetically by my client. The only furniture beyond the file cabinets is a large table. I use it to organize things before they go into the cabinets. On rare occasions when I'm up there looking at old files, I spread them across that table."

At the end of the hallway was an open door, and they entered the room.

"Welcome to my office," Clancy said. "Or I should say my sanctuary from the world. Have a seat, Jackson."

Clancy went and sat in the tall, leather chair behind the desk, while Jackson sat in one of two leather chairs in front of the oversized desk.

Opening the bakery basket, Clancy sighed. "You must have spoken directly to Ainsley because some of my favorite things are inside here." He closed it and met Jackson's gaze. "You couldn't do better than that girl. You're a nice-looking guy. I don't have to play Cupid for you, but Ainsley Robinson is a delightful young woman and would be quite the catch."

He grinned. "I figured that out for myself, Clancy. I have a date with her tomorrow night."

The old man beamed at him. "That's fast work, my boy. So, tell me what brings you to the Cove before my summer deadline? I suppose you're here to give me an answer to my very important question. Are you coming home for good?"

Jackson cleared his throat. "I am, Clancy. I'm thirty-three and have very little to show, other than my won/loss record as a prosecutor and then opposing counsel these past five years. I want a family. I need a sense of belonging to a community. I do want to take over your practice."

"I'm thrilled to hear this, Jackson. I have thought of you doing so ever since you told me that you wanted to attend law school."

He chuckled. "I was what—sixteen years old— when I mentioned that to you?"

"You were, indeed. I have been thinking about re-tiring for a good long while. I believe that you having sat on both sides of the table will be beneficial as you assume my practice. Besides that, you are empathetic and yet don't put up with nonsense. I think you will make a fine attorney for the citizens of Barton County."

"Tell me about what to expect from this practice, Clancy. I've spent years being a trial lawyer, either prosecuting or defending criminals. What is small town law all about?"

Clancy steepled his fingers. "It's being a jack-of-all-trades," he revealed. "You get to dabble in just about every branch of the law, and you're in close contact with individuals. You'll see results quickly and be able to be proud of what you've helped others accomplish.

"A lot of what you'll handle will be estate planning. People have to be educated that their estates include cars, homes, bank accounts, life insurance, and any investments, no matter how large or small. You'll help them come up with the best strategies for their current and future situations. Estate planning first and foremost is taking care of loved ones—by taking care of yourself."

"I know that will involve drawing up wills. Creating powers of attorney. That kind of thing."

"Estate planning goes far beyond that, Jackson. You have to consider the client. Is he married? Kids or no kids? Is it a blended family you're dealing with, or do you have a single parent? It might be a senior on her own. Setting up future care is paramount. Even providing for pets in case the client becomes incapacitated. I recently handled estate planning for a couple with a special-needs child. They wanted to make sure he was provided for long after they were gone."

Jackson rubbed his chin. "It is more complicated than I remember from my law school classes."

"You did take the Oregon bar, I believe."

"Yes. Boo and I talked about that. Although I was offered the job in L.A., where I attended law school, she and I thought it best to hedge my bets in case I ever did get a wild hair to return to the Cove. While I studied for the California bar exam, I did the same for the one in Oregon. Took them two days apart. Now, I'm glad I did so—and yes, my license to practice in Oregon is current. But dealing with nothing but criminal law since graduation? Just from our limited conversation, I'm going to need to study up on a good number of topics. I guess I'll be doing my homework before I can take over."

"Estate law is a good chunk of the practice, but there's more."

"Such as?"

"Family law is another moneymaker for a small-town lawyer. Divorce and alimony. Child custody and support. Adoption. Even emancipation of teenagers comes up on occasion, as do paternity cases and prenups."

Clancy picked up a pen and began rolling it between his fingers. "Then you have bankruptcy. Personal injuries and those suffered on the job. Immigrants wanting to get their green cards or apply for citizenship. I'm seeing more and more of that. A little regarding Social Security disability and SSI appeals."

"Anything criminal?" Jackson asked.

"The occasional DUI charge. Sometimes, felony criminal charges. Property crimes such as arson or vandalism. Drug offenses, from distributing and selling to trafficking. A few sexual assault cases. I haven't had to defend any white-collar crimes for several years. Embezzlement and securities fraud don't seem to be crimes often committed in Barton County."

Clancy set down the pen. "The good thing is that I was the only lawyer in the Cove and Crescent Cove for decades. I was the sole attorney for Salty Point until it went through its growth spurt twenty years ago. A couple of attorneys practice there now, mostly criminal. They're out of a big firm in Portland which has a few satellite offices around the region.

"My practice has served Barton County, as well as a few other small communities outside the county. You won't starve. The practice will keep you busy, but it won't dominate your life the way your recent murder trial did. I followed it in the news. That was an outstanding bit of defense work, Jackson. Are you certain you won't miss the bright lights of the big city and high-profile cases? I wouldn't feel good turning my practice over to you if, a few years from now, you up and shuttered it. I don't want to leave the people in Barton County high and dry."

"Defense work is tough," Jackson admitted. "A murder case, in particular, can steal your soul. I almost lost myself during this Gerard McGreer trial, Clancy. It's one thing to *think* your client is guilty and put on the best defense possible. It's another to *know* he is. I got off a man who had committed a heinous crime, the rape and murder of a young woman. And I don't think it's the only one he's committed. In fact, McGreer was trying to line up my services again in case he was in need of them in the future."

"That's troubling to hear, Jackson."

Briefly, he outlined Sarah Peterson's approaching him and what the juror had shared in confidence with him.

"As much as I wanted to go to the DA with this information, I thought it more important to protect Sarah, her husband, and her unborn child. It was a difficult decision. I believe I've put a murderer back on the streets—and it will only be a matter of time before he kills again. Yes, that case was my breaking point. It helped me to decide to leave L.A. and return to the Cove. Of course, I understand that there may be times when I need to defend someone against charges which have been filed against them, but I won't have to do it on a daily, soul-sucking basis."

"I know you had a partner," Clancy said. "Did you share with him what this juror revealed to you?"

Jackson nodded. "Bill is prepared in case Gerard McGreer comes calling again. I already had set it up with McGreer and told him if we were already busy with other cases, we couldn't drop those clients and cater to his needs alone."

"McGreer didn't know you were leaving California?"

"No, I didn't want him privy to that information. Bill Watterscheim knows not to defend McGreer again. But enough of that. What are your plans in retirement, Clancy?"

The lawyer grinned sheepishly. "I've been keeping company with a widow from Crescent Cove. A younger woman, in fact. Ten years my junior."

He laughed. "Robbing the cradle, I see."

"Myra is a wonderful woman. We're going to get married and move to Texas."

"What? Leave the Cove? You're a native, Clancy. Almost eighty-six years old. What's in Texas?"

"Myra has twin daughters who both live in the Houston area. They married brothers, as a matter of fact. The girls have five children between them. My lady is tired of the once-a-year visits to see her grandkids. She wants to attend Little League games and piano recitals." Clancy paused. "She told me she was going with or without me, Jackson. That's what spurred my wish to retire. In fact, she and I are flying down to Houston this weekend and will look for a place to live. She will be very happy to know you are in town, ready to take over my practice."

"We had discussed this summer. Do you want to move up that date? And what about a transition period?"

"You're a smart guy, Jackson. You don't need much of a transition. Yes, I'd like to spend some time with you, going through the files and updating you on a few matters. But I will be happy for you to take over as soon as we can sign the documents handing over the practice to you."

He thought about it for a moment. Thought he hadn't known Clancy would want to step away so quickly, it wasn't as if Jackson hadn't had any time off recently. He had reclaimed a bit of himself the past two months while driving through several states and hiking some of the most beautiful land in the country.

"I'm ready to take over whenever you wish, Clancy. Name the date. I'll make myself available."

"I'm going to be in Houston all next week. I've already informed my clients of this little vacation. I can leave you the keys to the office, and you can come in next week and familiarize yourself with things. Myra and I will be back next weekend, and I can take that Monday—and Tuesday, if needed—to go over any questions you might have. After that? I'd like to go on and head down to Houston with my girl."

"I can draw up the papers for the transfer while you're out of town," Jackson told him. "I suppose you'll also need to list your house for sale."

"I had planned on doing so soon. Myra sold hers back in October and moved in with me at that time. She put a few things in storage that she couldn't part with. Got rid of all the rest. I only have a few pieces of furniture myself that I'm wedded to, including my rolltop desk at home. I was going to ask Rylie Robinson to take on the rest of the furniture. She's Ainsley's cousin and runs Antiques and Mystiques. Besides selling antiques, she had a section in the store devoted to consignment furniture."

A gleam filled the older man's eyes. "Besides the law practice, would you be in the market for a home?

After all, Willow and Dylan will be starting their family soon. I assume you'll want to do the same. My house is perfect for that. Spacious. A huge backyard. You would need to get Pete Pulaski in to do some updating, though. Myra has complained that too much of my place is hopelessly out of date. She wants us to purchase something brand-new, or close to turnkey, when we buy in Houston."

Jackson had been to Clancy's home several times over the years and remembered the house was a large two-story, with mature trees in its front yard and a huge back yard perfect for hosting barbeques.

"I would be very interested." He chuckled. "Especially because of the short commute."

The attorney removed his key ring from his pocket and slipped off a key, pushing it across the desk to Jackson.

"Myra has her own house key, so we won't be locked out. While we're gone, go over and check out the house. See if you are interested in buying it. If you are, we can complete the paperwork. Shayla Newton won't be happy. She's our local realtor, and I was going to list the property with her. This way, though, neither of us will have to pay a commission if you do agree to buy it."

Clancy pushed himself to his feet. "Enough with business. I say we head over to Sid's Diner. And you're buying." He reached into his drawer and removed a set of keys.

Jackson laughed and followed Clancy out of the office. The older man locked the office door and handed over the key ring.

"Keys to the office. Front and back doors. Also my office and the file room, which has a copy machine and router. Make yourself at home while I'm gone.

Nose about a bit. I think you'll find that I keep a neat office. I've never used a secretary. Typed all letters on my own, first on a typewriter and then a computer. Printer's in my office. I keep my own calendar. Listen to my messages and make appointments accordingly. You'll have to decide if you'd like an assistant or if you wish to make do on your own."

They cut across the square and entered Sid's Diner. Nancy Mayfield, a former teacher and Sid's widow, greeted them.

"Hello, boys. I've got your usual booth waiting, Clancy. Good to see you, Jackson."

She led them to a booth in the corner, one which looked out over the square. Handing them each a menu, Nancy asked, "Will I need to reserve this same spot in case a new lawyer is coming to town to take over for an old dog?"

Jackson shook his head. "Not much gets by you, Nancy. We're working out the details now. Nothing's official. Yet."

She smiled. "It will be good to have you back in the Cove. Boo would be happy that both Willow and you have returned."

Tears stung his eyes for a moment, thinking of his beloved grandmother and how proud she had been of the two grandchildren she had raised.

"Boo knows," he confirmed. "She's watching over us."

Jackson knew that the citizens in the Cove would also be watching out for him.

It was good to finally be home.

CHAPTER 5

Ainsley changed clothes. Again. For the fourth time.

"This is getting ridiculous," she said aloud, glancing in the mirror and removing her blouse in favor of a plum tunic sweater that made her periwinkle eyes pop.

"Finally," she declared, telling herself to leave on this sweater. It looked fine with the black leggings she already wore.

She moved to her tiny bathroom. It had a small vanity barely wider than the sink, a toilet, and a shower stall that she doubted any male would fit into. The thought of a naked male in it brought to mind the very large Jackson Martin. She still remembered his stats listed in the weekly football program. Six-two. One hundred and ninety pounds. Friday nights in the fall meant attending games, and her father continually raving about Jackson and his throwing arm. He had also taken Ainsley to the high school basketball games, where Jackson's height had gone up an inch the last season he played before graduation. Having stood next to him twice this morning, she believed he had topped out at six-three, though he seemed even more muscular than his playing days. She recalled his calves and how they had made her grow faint.

"Even more ridiculous," she told herself.

Jackson was only visiting the Cove. Willow had told her he practiced criminal law in L.A. and that he had just wrapped up a huge murder case, getting his client off. Ainsley didn't keep up much with the news. She preferred spending her free time getting lost in old movies and books or biking and hiking outdoors. The news always seemed depressing to her, full of violence and heartbreak.

But Jackson was here this weekend. And he had asked her out. She wondered why he had done so. It had been a very spontaneous request, coming out of the blue. She wondered if Willow and Dylan might accompany them to the Old Coast Pub House since she doubted Jackson would be in town long and would want to spend as much time as he could with his sister.

Her heart began beating rapidly again as she thought of spending tonight in his company. Game Night was always a highlight for her. She enjoyed the group of friends. Their teasing and camaraderie. Their closeness. She would have to watch herself, though, and make sure her gaze didn't linger on Jackson too much. Though she'd never told anyone about her crush on him—not even Rylie—her friends were astute. They would pick up on anything out of the ordinary.

Besides, did she really have a crush this many years later? She had been twelve when she idolized Jackson Martin. She was twenty-eight now. An adult. A responsible adult who owned a bakery. She wasn't a gawky pre-teen any longer. She would behave in a mature, responsible fashion tonight. And tomorrow night, when Jackson picked her up. Their date was nothing special.

"Liar," she said under her breath as she freshened her lipstick and squirted the last bit of perfume on her wrists before rubbing them together and then dabbing them against her neck.

Ainsley ran a brush through her hair one more time. It fell into waves, striking just below her shoulders. She studied her image in the mirror with a critical eye. This was as good at it got. Time to leave and stop second-guessing herself.

She left the bathroom and slipped into her all-weather coat since rain was predicted for later this evening. Heading downstairs, she collected Dylan's cupcakes before she went out the back door of the bakery. Her SUV sat next to the door. She always parked it behind the bakery and requested that her employees do the same so that parking spaces were readily available in front for customers.

It was a short drive to Tenley and Carter's house. Normally, she would walk, but with the predicted rain, she thought it best to have her car available. She pulled up to the curb in front of their house, seeing Gage in front of her, getting out and locking his Jeep.

He waited for her and smiled. "If I remember, Dylan requested cupcakes for his win."

"You remember correctly," she told him.

"What kind?"

"Dylan left it up to me. It's a surprise."

His lopsided grin was endearing. "I wonder what Carter is making for dinner."

By now, they'd reached the porch and rang the bell. Tenley answered, glowing as she always seemed to nowadays. She had arrived in the Cove sad and unsure of herself. Falling in love with Carter had caused her to blossom, and Tenley now brimmed with confidence.

Ainsley inhaled. "Smells heavenly," she commented, handing over the two Tupperware containers of cupcakes and following Tenley to the kitchen. Gage trailed after them, placing two six-packs of beer in the refrigerator.

She glanced around. "I simply love everything you've done to the kitchen."

Tenley pointed out some of the highlights, and Carter chimed in, saying he liked the pot filler most of all.

The doorbell rang again. Soon Rylie entered the kitchen, followed by Willow, Dylan, and Jackson. Jackson greeted everyone and thanked Tenley and Carter for allowing him to crash Game Night.

"Another man is always welcomed," Carter proclaimed. "Sometimes we play in teams—and the girls wind up stomping us every single time. I remember you were smart. Weren't you the valedictorian of your graduating class?"

"High school and law school," Willow said proudly, grinning at her brother.

"What happened in college, Slacker?" Rylie teased.

"I did a program where I earned my bachelor's degree in three years. It was combined with my three years in law school. Since the first year of law school technically was the last of college, it wasn't factored into my bachelor's degree," Jackson explained.

"It doesn't matter," Willow said. "He's a member of Mensa. That means he's ultra-smart. With Jackson playing on their team, the guys are going to wipe the floor with us."

"But it's only for tonight, right?" Ainsley asked. "I

mean, it's not like you'll be here for future Game Nights."

His gaze pinned hers, causing her to hold her breath.

"About that," he said, looking at the others, his gaze finally returning to her. "I've moved to the Cove. I'm back. Permanently. I'll be taking over Clancy Nelson's practice."

Everyone began congratulating Jackson. Ainsley only swallowed, feeling her eyes had grown large. She glanced away, not wanting him to see what her face might reveal. She busied herself with opening the wine sitting on the counter.

Jackson Martin had returned to the Cove. Suddenly, she grew dizzy. She slipped onto a nearby stool and propped her elbows on the island for support.

Rylie came and sat on the stool beside her. "You okay?"

"I'm fine," she said quickly.

"Do you still have a thing for Jackson?" her cousin asked quietly.

She stiffened. "What?"

"You never said anything to me, but I knew you liked him. I mean, who didn't have the hots for Jackson Martin back in the day?" Rylie glanced over her shoulder. "He's still the fittest guy in the room."

"Don't say anything," she begged.

Rylie took her hand. "Of course not."

Tenley stopped near them. "Ready for some wine? Oh, it's already opened."

"I thought I'd let it breathe a little," Ainsley said, pulling herself together.

"Good idea." Tenley began pouring glasses for the women.

"Can I get one of those?" Jackson asked, sliding

into the open stool on Ainsley's free side. "I've found that as I've grown older, I'm more fond of wine than beer."

"I'm working on Carter," Tenley said. "He is beginning to use more wines in his cooking."

"So, he's the cook in the family?" Jackson asked.

Everyone laughed heartily, causing Jackson to say, "I guess there's a story in this."

"Everyone grab their drinks and take them to the dining room," Carter said. "I'll tell you what's up with me after I bring in our feast. Babe, would you get the salad from the fridge?"

Ainsley moved into the large dining room, one of the reasons the Clarks had fallen in love with this house. Tenley brought in the salad, followed by Carter bearing a large glass dish, oven mitts over his hands.

"Let me get everything on the table, and then I'll tell you what I'm serving tonight."

"Whatever it is, it smells terrific," Dylan piped up.

After they were all seated and began serving themselves, Carter detailed the meal as he placed small crocks of bubbling goodness beside everyone.

"You've got fresh, butterflied lobster tails in the center dish. The small dish of butter next to your plates is infused with lemon and chives. Use the brush to coat your lobster with it."

He finished distributing the crocks. "This contains my new take on mac and cheese. The pasta is mixed with crabmeat and Brie. And don't forget to pass around the Brussels sprouts. They've got bits of bacon in them to add a little extra flavor."

"I feel as if I'm dining at a Michelin star restaurant," Jackson said. "What's the story, Carter? The last I remember, you were a lean athlete who had a great swing in the batter's box."

"I became a fireman and learned how to cook the basics at the firehouse," their host explained. His features softened, and he smiled at his wife. "Then I met Tenley."

As they ate, Carter and Tenley recounted to Jackson how he had begun filming videos on how to cook everything from entrees to special-occasion dishes.

"Carter landed a cookbook contract with Sutton Press," Tenley said proudly, beaming at her new husband.

"I'd love to watch one of your videos," Jackson said. "I can barely boil water, but I'd love to learn how to cook a few things." He paused. "Not at tonight's level, though. This meal is outstanding and far beyond my skills set."

"You'd be surprised," Tenley said. "I couldn't cook much until I met Carter. He makes cooking easy for newbies."

They talked more about Carter's vlogging before talk turned back to Jackson's return to the Cove.

"What prompted you to leave California?" Gage asked.

Jackson discussed his recent murder case and how criminal law could be wearing on either side of the table.

"I was a prosecutor in the DA's office for three years and also served as the opposing counsel for five. Criminal law consumes every waking moment. I easily put in a hundred hours a week. Sometimes more. Sleep was non-existent. And the commute was killer." He smiled at his sister. "With Willow leaving Europe and settling in the Cove, it caused me to reexamine my life. Was I happy professionally? Personally? And the answer was

—neither. Yes, I had a high rate of winning cases, but every day felt like a beat-down. I had no personal life. I'm ready to find someone to share my life with. Hopefully, kids will follow soon. I want to coach Pop Warner ball and become involved in the community."

"Run for mayor," Rylie urged. "Eddie Wright is the current one and totally worthless. He wants the tourist dollars to pour in but doesn't want to invest any city funds in local businesses. Yes, I'm speaking as a business owner, but I think Eddie has done zip for the Cove."

"I'll take that under advisement," Jackson said seriously, though a smile tugged at the corners of his mouth.

"When will Clancy retire?"

Ainsley listened as Jackson told of Clancy retiring to Houston, along with his soon-to-be wife.

"They'll be in Texas looking for a home near Myra's daughters this next week. I'll use that time to go to his office—my future office—and look over the files. Become familiar with his set-up and current cases. Clancy will be back by a week from Monday. We'll formalize everything then, signing the paperwork. He'll also answer any questions I have. Then, I suppose, I'll be off and running."

Carter rose. "And that's a great segue into our evening. Let's clear the table. Dylan, you and Gage get Pictionary set up. Ainsley, grab your desserts and plates and bring them to the den."

Everyone leaped into action. She found the dessert plates. Rylie brought those and napkins along as Ainsley carried her cupcakes. The group settled onto the sofa, love seat, and chairs. It surprised her when Jackson took a seat next to her.

"Do you mind fraternizing with the enemy?" he teased.

"As long as you don't try to cheat. Or distract me," she told him.

He crossed his heart. "I was a Boy Scout. Eagle Scout, actually. I promise—no cheating."

That was all well and good, but the man smelled heavenly. The subtle spice of his cologne surrounded her. All Ainsley wanted to do was crawl into his lap and devour him.

"Ains?" Willow asked, her brow furrowed.

"What?" she asked, seeing everyone looked at her. She felt the heat come to her cheeks.

"I was asking what flavor of cupcakes you baked for me," Dylan said. Looking at Jackson, he explained, "The winner of the previous Game Night gets to name the dessert for the next session. I love a good cupcake. Ainsley can do wonders with them. In fact, you need to go to her bakery and study the shelves. You'll have a hard time picking just a few things."

Before Jackson could explain he had already visited Buttercup Bakery, she said, "I made two different cupcakes for you, Dylan. Tonight, we have a chocolate cupcake with peanut butter icing."

A murmur of approval sounded as she removed the lid from the first container.

"We also have a gingerbread cupcake with caramelized mango buttercream icing." Again, she removed the lid and heard the ahhs.

"Ainsley, I need to get you vlogging along with me," Carter said.

"No," she said quickly. "I could never be on camera. I would freeze up. You can be the star chef in our group. I'm happy to work behind the scenes in my kitchen."

"This is a talented group," Gage said. "Willow is gaining more fame with her paintings. Carter has his videos and cookbook coming up. Ainsley is a master baker. And Tenley is writing a fantasy trilogy. It's been sold to a big New York publishing house. Rylie is even head of the city's Chamber of Commerce, while Dylan is the youngest sheriff ever elected in the Cove."

"Gage doesn't like to toot his own horn," Willow added. "But he runs his own successful business, training others in both group and individual sessions."

Jackson raked a hand through his hair. The gesture made Ainsley's mouth grow dry. She could picture herself sitting on his lap, running her fingers through the silk of his hair.

"I see I'll have a lot to live up to. I suppose we should get started. Guys, we need to smoke the women tonight."

Good-natured grumbling sounded from the females. Carter flexed his muscles. Dylan suggested the girls spot the guys two rolls of the die to level the playing field since his wife was a professional artist and the females would have an advantage. Dylan was roundly booed by the women, though they did allow the guys to start play.

After rolling the die, Gage moved the men's playing piece. Then he stood and moved to the drawing board, rubbing his hands together. "Let's get this rolling." He drew the first card. Then a pained expression crossed his face.

"I would get this," he complained. "We are so screwed."

"Let the games begin," cried Rylie, a triumphant smile on her face as she began the timer.

CHAPTER 6

Jackson didn't know the last time he had had so much fun. Actually, he couldn't recall the last time he had any fun.

The group of friends Willow had assembled tonight was nothing short of remarkable. They were intelligent, quick-witted, and funny as hell.

And none interested him more than Ainsley Robinson.

He wouldn't call her shy, but she was a bit reserved compared to the others present. As the night progressed, however, her competitive spirit had come out, and she became just as boisterous as the others. Jackson couldn't remember when he had been so attracted to a woman.

Maybe never.

He could see the family resemblance between her and her cousin. Rylie possessed the same, unique periwinkle eye color and smile, but that's where the resemblance ended. While Rylie was brunette and curvy, Ainsley was blond and much more slender. When she did roll up her sleeves, however, the better to draw, he noticed the strength in her forearms and decided it must be from her baking. Maybe kneading bread.

He had eaten the gingerbread cupcake she had brought. Sweets had never appealed much to him, but the caramelized mango icing, as well as the moistness of the cupcake itself, made it a winner in his book. He was eager to visit her bakery again and peruse the shelves to see what she made and sold. Not only did she need to be creative in what she baked for the community, Ainsley also needed to be a businesswoman. If the cupcake he had devoured was any indication of her skills, she must be very successful. He liked that in a woman.

It was sexy as hell.

Surprisingly, the men had narrowed the gap after the women had surged to an early lead in Pictionary. They were both approaching the end of the game, and it was his turn to roll the die. He did so, landing one space short of the All Play square. Jackson moved to the whiteboard and uncapped the dry-erase marker as he turned over the card.

"Start that timer, Gage. These women are going *down.*"

Jackson was the best artist on his team, which wasn't saying much, but he knew exactly what to draw in this case. He felt that competitive wave surge through him, hoping he could pull off a victory for his team and new friends.

It was nothing but silence, and then Carter hollered the correct answer.

"Yes," he cried, throwing his arms in the air and then enthusiastically fist-bumping Carter for coming up with the correct response so quickly.

Jackson looked at the women, who had gravitated to one side of the room, and said, "I believe we are going to win this game, ladies. Should we start thinking about what dessert we want for the next Game Night?"

"Arrogance does not run in the family," Willow said, "despite my brother's comment." She stood. "And you are going down, Jackson Martin. You and the other guys."

Willow rolled, landing on the same space her brother had. She took a spot at the easel and drew a card. A smile lit her face. Quickly, she began drawing and within seconds, Tenley shouted out the right answer. The girls applauded themselves. Then the attention turned to Dylan. He didn't bother to roll the die since anything he threw would put him on the All Play space. He moved in his deliberate fashion to the drawing board and selected the top card but didn't view it. They had decided previously to let whichever team reached the All Play space first draw only for their team, a subtle change in the rules that Tenley now lamented.

"Pressure's on, Dylan," Rylie called out, trying to rattle him.

"We have a better chance with you up there than me," Gage declared. "I don't even draw a decent stick person."

"Come on, Dylan," Carter encouraged. "We need to wipe the floor."

Pausing dramatically, Dylan surveyed his audience. "This is for the win." He lifted the card, studying it a moment. His poker face revealed nothing. Then he set the card aside as Gage started the timer.

Dylan began to draw. The men threw out several answers as Dylan continued adding to his drawing, his mouth tight as he concentrated.

Time ran out, and the girls cheered.

"Was it arachnophobia?" Ainsley asked.

Dylan nodded, and the men groaned as Ainsley took a card and then met Dylan, claiming the marker from him.

"No pressure, Ains," Gage called out, a huge grin on his face.

"This is nothing compared to what I went through at l'Ecole Lenôtre. *That* was pressure."

Jackson had heard that name before but couldn't remember where. He assumed it was the cooking school she had attended in Paris. Maybe Willow had mentioned it to him when she had run into Ainsley in Paris.

Ainsley removed the next card for play from the box. She turned the card over and nodded to herself.

"Start the timer," she told Gage as she began drawing furiously.

Her teammates called out a few suggestions as she drew. Then Tenley bounded to her feet, and shouted out, "Panama Canal!"

Jackson watched the smile light Ainsley's face. "Yes!" she cried. "We win!"

The women leaped to their feet, dancing joyfully, hugging one another. Competitive as Jackson was, he didn't mind this loss in the least.

"What should we ask for as winners?" Willow asked her teammates.

"Leave it to me," Ainsley said, brimming with confidence. "I'll come up with something fantastic."

"Maybe something with chocolate in it?" Gage asked hopefully.

Ainsley shook her head. "No, because that would be like a victory for you, chocoholic that you are. And it certainly won't be cannolis." She glanced to Jackson. "Those are Carter's favorites."

Tenley said, "Time to get this cleaned up."

Everyone swung into action, clearing plates and bringing them to the kitchen. Jackson glanced at his watch and saw it was only ten till nine. Surprised filled him. In L.A., a night out would just be getting started. Still, they had enjoyed an amazingly good dinner, filled with wonderful conversation, and had played an entire game of Pictionary.

He took his wine glass and plate into the kitchen, where he overheard the women once more complimenting Tenley on how the remodel of her kitchen had turned out.

"Oh, I didn't even show you everything else downstairs," their hostess said.

"It's late," Gage said. "I'll look at the new stuff next time."

Jackson was interested in hiring Gage to train him and said, "Let me walk out with you."

They stepped into the cool Oregon night, and as he inhaled deeply, Jackson could smell the sea, something he had missed in the smog of L.A.

As they moved toward Gage's truck, Jackson said, "I run to keep in shape, but I may want to add something to that now that I'll have more time for exercise. Willow said you do one-on-one sessions, as well as group classes."

"I would need to spend a little time with you," Gage said. "Talk over what you've done in the past. What your fitness level is like now. Learn what goals you might have for yourself now and in the future." He paused. "Saturdays are my busiest day in my business. A lot of weekend warriors. In fact, I get up and run at four myself."

"That's usually the time I run, as well," Jackson told the former Navy SEAL.

"Then let's run together tomorrow morning," Gage suggested. "I'll meet you at Boo's. We can run along the beach."

"I'll be waiting outside on the porch." Jackson offered his hand. "It was good meeting you, Gage. And thanks for your service to our country."

Gage's smile faded. His mouth tightened. "Thank you," he said brusquely. "See you in the morning."

Jackson headed toward the house again as everyone else spilled out the front door.

"I see Dylan is in charge of the leftover cupcakes," he noted.

"Winner take all," his brother-in-law said with a laugh. "Although with you living with us now, I might be willing to share. Emphasis on *might*."

Everyone laughed and started heading toward their cars. Jackson fell into step beside Ainsley.

"I confirmed our reservation for eight," he told her. "You haven't texted me yet as to your address."

She smiled shyly. "You know where to find me. I live above my bakery. If you will come around the back, text me when you get there, and I'll come down. Still seven-thirty?"

"I will text you when I get there, but Boo raised me to be a gentleman. I will come to your door."

She laughed. "That will prove to be difficult because the outside door is always locked. I would have to leave my apartment and come down to let you in, then allow you to climb the stairs to my apartment— only to come back down. Let's save time and not worry about all the up and down, all right?'

"All right," he agreed. "I'm looking forward to our date, Ainsley."

She bit her lip, and a surge of desire flared through him. He wanted to sink his teeth into that full bottom lip. He also wanted to do more than that with this woman and told himself he needed to take things slowly for both their sakes. The Cove was a very small town. If the date fell flat, they hopefully could remain friends, chalking romance up as a lost cause.

But if he pushed for too much too fast and they became involved, only to split—it would be awkward to be around one another, especially since Ainsley was such good friends with Willow and a part of this tight-knit group that he was eager to belong to.

She pulled her key card from her purse and unlocked her SUV. Jackson stepped forward and opened the door for her.

"Boo's training," he said with a smile as she slipped behind the wheel. "See you tomorrow night."

He closed the door and moved back a few steps as she started the car and pulled away from the curb. Then he went to Dylan's truck, where his brother-in-law and sister waited for him. Rylie drove away, and Jackson waved to her and then Carter and Tenley, who stood on the porch, their arms wrapped around each other's waists.

Climbing into the truck, he sprawled in the back seat as Dylan started it.

"How did you like Game Night?" Willow asked. "Even though you were on Team Loser," she teased.

"I had so much fun that I can actually let go of the loss. You have some terrific friends."

"You seemed to be interested in Ainsley," his sister said.

"I'm taking her to dinner tomorrow night," he informed the couple.

"That was fast work between the house and her car," Dylan said.

"Oh, I just confirmed our date during that brief walk. Actually, I asked her out this morning."

"What?" Willow said excitedly. "When did you run into her?"

"You had said some good things not only about her but her baked goods. I decided to stop and take something to Clancy since I remembered what a sweet tooth he had and how he and Boo used to bond over cakes and cookies. Ainsley put together a nice little gift basket for me." He shrugged. "I asked her out."

"Ainsley would be good for you, Jackson," his sister said, her face growing serious. "She's had a little bit of a tough life. She's a hard worker, though, and could use a bit of fun."

"How so?" he asked.

"Her dad died of a sudden heart attack when she was sixteen. Her mom had breast cancer during Ainsley's middle school years. She beat it—only to have it recur. Mrs. Robinson passed away just as Ainsley graduated from community college."

"That is rough," he agreed. "Wait, was she the little girl who always sold desserts before games? I have a vague recollection of hearing about that, but I was always on the field."

"Yes, that was Ainsley," Dylan said. "She was hustling when she was a preteen. She sold mostly cookies before the high school football, basketball, and baseball games."

Willow added, "Along with Rylie, she also had a table set up at summer league baseball games. Rylie spent summers here in the Cove because her dad traveled so much and her mom died when she was young."

Jackson was even more impressed with Ainsley

now. Beautiful and a great work ethic. No wonder she already owned her own bakery.

They arrived back to Boo's and entered the house. It was just a little after nine and he was a bit restless. Dylan handed the Tupperware containers to Jackson and took Willow's hand, telling her it was time for bed. By the look in Dylan's eyes, Jackson knew sleep would be delayed for a while in favor of something else.

He retreated to the kitchen, opening one of the Tupperware containers and removing a chocolate peanut butter cupcake from it. Sealing it again, he poured himself a tall glass of milk and sat at the table, thinking about his new life in the Cove and how it was shaping up. He would soon take over Clancy's law practice and possibly buy the attorney's house, as well. Suddenly, it seemed important to him to take Ainsley with him to view the house for the first time, wanting her opinion.

Rinsing his glass, he placed it in the dishwasher and then headed upstairs to bed. Though he rarely went to sleep before midnight, he climbed under the covers just shy of ten.

And fell asleep thinking of Ainsley Robinson.

CHAPTER 7

A insley stepped from the shower, wound a towel around her long hair, and then slathered body lotion on her dampened skin. She usually used it instead of perfume, which was far too pricey for a business owner with limited means. She couldn't remember the last time she had gotten ready for a date. She hadn't dated much over the years because of family obligations and then school and work. Her focus was on her career goals, and that left little room for seeing men. Not that there were that many single men in the Cove. The few in her acquaintance had recently dropped like flies. Dylan. Carter. Of course, both of them—along with Gage—were like big brothers to her, friends whom she had never had a romantic thought about.

Jackson Martin was an entirely different barrel of fish, as her mom used to say. She still had trouble understanding why he had asked her out. He didn't seem the type to feel obligated to do something. He wouldn't do so merely because she had prepared the gift basket for Clancy. It was still hard for her to believe that her childhood crush had asked her out.

Quickly, she applied her makeup and then went to her closet, trying to decide what to wear. She knew women who could artlessly throw outfits together without even thinking about it. Ainsley, however, usually wore jeans with a T-shirt, her chef's pastry coat over them. Most of her wardrobe beyond that was extremely casual. She did own two dresses, though, that might be suitable for a nice dinner at the Old Coast Pub House. She removed one from the closet and held it up to her. It was a maroon sweater dress, which looked more expensive than its sale price had been. She would pair it with her black pumps and the gold hoop earrings which had belonged to her mom, the only piece of jewelry her mother had ever worn. Neither of her parents had bothered with wedding rings. Her dad, being a mechanic, refused to wear any kind of ring on his hands, saying it was too dangerous in his line of work. Her mom had told Ainsley that money was tight when they married, and she had said she didn't want an engagement or wedding ring. Ainsley knew her mother would have liked to have had something, even a simple gold band, but she rarely spoke up, always deferring to her husband in matters both large and small.

Ainsley had learned how to be an advocate for herself and her mom, thanks to her mother's lengthy illness, coupled with her father's early death.

She dressed and then removed the blow dryer from the hook on the wall, finger-combing her hair as she dried it. It fell about her in soft waves after she finished. She didn't own a nice evening purse, but Willow had appeared at the bakery today with a small, black clutch that she said she had picked up at a flea market in Paris. Ainsley thanked her friend for the use of the bag this evening and now transferred the few items she would need into it.

The loan of the purse let Ainsley know that Jackson had shared with his sister that he had a date coming up. She hoped that was a good thing.

Glancing at the clock, she saw she had ten minutes before Jackson would arrive. Sitting on the dilapidated sofa which had come with the apartment, Ainsley wondered how this date would go. What they would talk about.

And if Jackson would kiss her at the end of the evening.

She had dreamed of kissing the star quarterback her entire seventh-grade year. Everyone in town knew Jackson Martin. He had dated a girl who was head cheerleader, and the two of them had been elected King and Queen of the high school's homecoming court that fall. Ainsley had yearned for Jackson that entire year.

Then he graduated from high school and left the Cove for college in California, and her crush died with his absence. She had only seen him twice when he came home from college during the Christmas holidays. She hadn't spoken to him either time, knowing he would have no idea who she was.

She straightened, tossing back her shoulders. Well, he knew who she was now. She would make the most of this date. If they got along, hopefully there would be more of them in the future. If there was no spark between them, she hoped she would be able to count him among her friends.

Her cell sounded, and she glanced down, seeing his text.

I'm here. Eager to see you.

Just reading his words brought a thrill to her, and her heart began beating faster. She stood, smoothing her skirt, slipping into her coat, and then claiming the clutch as she made her way downstairs.

When she unlocked and opened the door, Jackson appeared before her. Butterflies exploded in her stomach. He wore a suit of deep navy, along with a crisp, white dress shirt. The shirt was open at his throat, no tie in sight.

"Hi," he greeted. "I hope you're hungry. I'm starving."

Ainsley locked the bakery's rear door, and he escorted her to his car, a sleek, sporty sedan. He even opened the passenger door for her, unlike so many other men. Then again, he was Boo's grandson. He *would* have impeccable manners. As he came around and climbed into the driver's seat, she thought this was the first time a man had ever opened a car door for her. Her other dates had texted from their car and sat behind the wheel, waiting for her to come out and get in before they took off. Already, Jackson Martin was a cut above the few men she had gone out with over the last dozen years.

"Hope you don't mind that I didn't bother with a tie," he began as he pulled from the parking space. "I've had my share of wearing ties in the courtroom. Although I know Clancy is always seen in his bow tie —and I'm betting he probably sleeps in one—I'm hoping I can be a little more casual as I practice law in the Cove."

"It is a relaxed place," she agreed. "I think other than infrequent court appearances, you can easily get by without wearing one. Actually, you probably can just wear a nice shirt and slacks to the office each day. Citizens of the Cove and beyond won't judge you on what you wear. They'll be eager to be represented by the area's most famous athlete."

"Think so?" He chuckled. "My playing days are far behind me. I am hoping to get in better shape, though. I met with Gage early this morning for a run. He quizzed me about what I've done to stay in shape since high school and what I plan to do in the future. We decided to schedule several one-on-one sessions to get me started on the right path."

"Gage is the best. He's quiet, but still waters do run deep. I'm glad you're here and can offer your friendship to him, as well as becoming a paying client. He's done a fantastic job building his business from scratch."

"He told me that at this point he has no overhead. That all his sessions take place outdoors, rain or shine."

"A little rain never hurt an Oregonian," she teased. "Especially former all-state quarterbacks."

He glanced to her and then turned his eyes back to the road. "You remember that?"

"How could I not?" she asked. "You always were the talk of the town. Leading Salty Point High to the state football championship your junior year and the semi-finals the next year. Named to the second team state in basketball. District MVP two years in a row in baseball."

"Wow, I feel like I'm walking down Memory Lane with you. I'm surprised you remember all of that. I barely do."

"Well, you were a big deal in the Cove when I was in middle school. Middle school girls are very impressionable. Besides, everyone was shocked when you turned down those athletic scholarships and accepted an academic one instead. Speculation went on regarding your decision long after you left the Cove."

"Is that so? I never knew. Boo wasn't one for gossip,

either starting or spreading it." He paused. "I loved playing sports. It was my life. At one point, I thought it would be my only ticket out of the Cove. Then Boo had me tested in Portland. It was a long test. Several hours' worth. I had to score within the upper two percent of the general population in order to qualify and did so."

"Was it Mensa?"

"The very one. I learned that they have all kinds of opportunities for members. They host lectures and have special-interest groups. Assist researchers in intelligence projects. Arrange regional, national, and international gatherings. I didn't have time for any of that then. Or even after I finished law school.

"What *was* important was they told me they could help find me a scholarship to whatever university I wished to attend, in or out of state. Having already been an athlete on winning high school teams, I knew how much time would be necessary to devote to athletics on the college level. I worried my studies would suffer. There was also the possibility of an injury lingering in the back of my mind. I decided I would rather have an academic scholarship and focus on my studies—and my future—instead of spending the bulk of college in practice and on the playing field, missing class because of game commitments."

"That was an awfully mature decision for a teenager," she pointed out.

"I had input from others. Boo, of course. Clancy. My coaches and a few favorite teachers, Mrs. Clark, in particular."

She chuckled. "I think everyone in the Cove goes to Carter's mom for advice."

By now they had arrived at the restaurant. Jackson eased into an open parking spot and then quickly got out, coming around to assist her from the car. He escorted her inside, his hand on the small of her back, causing heat to ripple through her. She got a whiff of his cologne, the same scent he wore last night, and blinked rapidly several times, trying to pull herself together.

They approached the hostess' stand, and Jackson smiled at the woman manning it. Ainsley saw the effect of that smile on the hostess.

"How might I help you?" the woman asked huskily, giving Jackson a look that told him she would be available—all he had to do was ask.

"A reservation for two. Under Jackson Martin," he said, his hand remaining on Ainsley's back.

"Ah, yes, Mr. Martin. Right this way."

Jackson continued guiding her as they followed the hostess to a circular booth in the corner. Ainsley slid into it, and he followed after her, sitting close. The hostess handed them their menus and with a saucy smile said, "Enjoy your dinner, Mr. Martin. Let me know if there's *anything* I can do to make it a more pleasant dining experience for you."

Ainsley wanted to remind the hostess of her presence. Instead, she smiled up at her, a smile that told this woman to back off.

"Thank you so much," Jackson said, and the hostess turned away.

She wondered if this would be what might lie in her future if Jackson continued to ask her out. Would she be looking at every woman with jealousy? She pushed the thought aside, determined to enjoy this date and live in the moment.

Their server appeared and asked what they'd like to drink. Jackson ordered a bottle of merlot from one of the local vineyards, one of her favorite wines. She wondered if Willow had told him to do so. He also asked for a carafe of water and then turned to her.

"Anything else for you, Ainsley? Iced tea?"

"No, water and wine will hit the spot."

The server said, "I'll be right back with your drinks, Mr. Martin."

She perused the menu and was startled at the prices listed. She had known the Old Coast Pub House was the nicest restaurant in the area because she had grown up nearby. She had never dined at it before, though, and doubted she ever would again, especially on her own dime. She worried for a moment that she might be on the hook for half of their bill and decided to find out now before the server returned and they'd placed their orders.

"Jackson?"

"Hmm?" he said, as he looked over the menu. "What looks good to you?"

"I'm going to be blunt. I can't afford the prices here."

He frowned. "This is a date, Ainsley. I'll be paying the bill."

She felt heat rush to her cheeks. "I didn't know if this might be friends going out for dinner together or not."

"I hope we're friends, Ainsley." He gazed deeply into her eyes, causing her to shiver. "I'm hoping we can be much more, though."

Butterflies exploded again in her stomach as Jackson reached for her hand. He wrapped his fingers around hers.

"Dinner is on me tonight. Order whatever you wish."

"All right," she said quietly, going back to the menu.

But he kept holding her hand.

It was hard to concentrate as warmth from him flooded her. She blinked again several times, focusing on the writing in front of her.

"If you haven't been here before, would you mind if I order for us?"

Ainsley set down her menu. "That would be lovely."

The server returned and uncorked the wine, pouring a small amount into a glass and offering it to Jackson.

He passed the glass to her. "It's waiting for your approval. Willow said it's your favorite."

It touched her that he had taken the time to find out her favorite wine and that he was allowing her the final say. She took a small sip and nodded at the server, who then filled both their wine glasses and placed the bottle in the center of their table. He also filled glasses with water and placed the carafe next to the wine.

"Are you ready to order?" the server asked.

"Yes," Jackson replied. "We'll share the salmon cakes as our appetizer. Entrees will be the bacon-wrapped filets with the pan-seared scallops. Make my steak medium rare. Ainsley?"

"Same for me."

"I'll put in your order now, Mr. Martin. The salmon cakes will be out shortly." The server left.

Jackson turned to her. "You remember me, but I don't really know much about you, beyond the fact that you own your own business at a very young age and make the best damn cupcakes I've ever eaten. So, what's the Ainsley Robinson story?"

She wanted this man to really know the true her.

"I might be a business owner, but I came from

lower middle-class stock. Dad was a mechanic at a body shop in Salty Point. We lost him to a heart attack when I was sixteen."

"That's a young age to lose a parent. I know because I lost both of mine when I was six. I'm grateful that Boo had pictures of them because, as I grew older, I only had bits and pieces of a few treasured memories. I guess losing him made things tough for you and your mom."

"Mom had her own troubles," Ainsley revealed. "She battled breast cancer when I was in middle school. That's when I started my fundraising activities. I told people it was to put me though college someday. In reality, it was to help pay Mom's doctor bills. I would bake cookies and brownies and sell them before all the athletic events because they were so well attended. Fortunately, the people of the Cove—and even our opponents—would stop at my table and buy something from me."

She paused. "Boo was one of my best customers."

Jackson chuckled. "My grandmother had a sweet tooth. If she could have had sweets three times a day, she would have been in heaven."

"Boo would always ask how much something cost —and then give me double the price, telling me I was an artist in my own right and my sweets were edible art. She told me to never stop believing in myself."

He squeezed her fingers. "That's my Boo. And based upon the cupcakes you brought to Game Night, I do believe you are an artist. I saw the shelves of pastries and desserts when I was in your bakery yesterday. They were works of art. You are incredibly talented, Ainsley." Jackson grinned. "Besides, if you can convert a non-dessert eater like me, you deserve a gold medal."

He took a sip of wine. "You also showed a lot of maturity, starting your own business as a preteen, helping your family with your mom's medical bills. I'll bet your mom is proud of you. I'd love to meet her."

She swallowed painfully. "Mom's cancer recurred after I graduated from high school. I was attending Central Oregon Community College in Bend, where the Cascade Culinary Institute is housed. I was a week shy of earning my AAS in Baking and Pastry Arts when I got a call from Sheriff Willingham telling me Mom had passed away."

"That must've been hard, being so far away at school while she battled cancer again."

A tear rolled down her cheek. "I didn't know," she whispered.

His hand tightened on hers. Concern filled his face. "She kept it from you."

Ainsley nodded. "She left a letter for me. It told me how much she loved me—and how she hadn't been willing to ruin my life with her illness. I was staying in Bend year-round, not coming home, because not only did students have opportunities to study in the state-of-the-art kitchen facilities and take part in cooking labs, but we also cooked and served in the school's Elevation Restaurant."

She closed her eyes, the painful memory of hearing about her mother's death sweeping over her. "I also was finishing up an internship, which was part of my degree program." She opened them again. "When the cancer returned, Mom still didn't have insurance. She cleaned houses for a living. Though her doctor told her she would regret her decision, Mom chose not to undergo chemo and radiation again. Her letter told me she wanted to go quietly, without causing a fuss, and encouraged me to follow my dreams."

The sympathy she saw on Jackson's face almost did her in.

"I am so sorry," he said quietly. "I can't imagine how rough that was on you, hearing about her death. Reading that letter."

"Oh, I was angry for a while. Angry that she had taken away any chance for her to survive. Angry that I hadn't had a say-so in her decision. It took a few years to get over those feelings. I understand more now, though. I know she loved me, and that love caused her to act in what she thought was my best interest."

Their appetizer arrived and they fell silent, waiting until the server left. Jackson placed two of the salmon cakes on her plate and took the other two for himself.

"Do you have any brothers or sisters?"

"Rylie is it. We're cousins, but closer than sisters. Her family life was no picnic either. She spent summers with us. We shared a bed. Clothes. All our secrets. I'll always be close with her. She's the one that convinced me to seek the help of a therapist. By then, I had left a job working in Portland, where I was a line cook, and had moved to Seattle. They have an amazing restaurant community. I became a sous chef and eventually went to work for a well-known catering company, which gave me free rein on creating desserts.

"I got the therapy I needed. I forgave Mom. And myself. By then, I had saved enough to study abroad in Paris at l'Ecole Lenôtre."

"Last night you mentioned it being high pressure."

"It's considered to be in the top three best pastry schools in the world. Students from over one hundred countries come to study there each year. It's mostly a traditional French cuisine. Gaston Lenôtre, its founder, was one of the best-known names in pastry. Ever. It's a tough place. Extremely competitive. But I learned from the best and came away confident in my skills and creative process."

Ainsley took a bite of the salmon cake and moaned. "Oh, this is to die for. I'm glad you ordered for me."

"You came home from Paris and started Buttercup Bakery?" he asked, attacking his own portion of the appetizer.

"I did. I became close with one of the instructors at the Cascade Culinary Institute. She really served as my instructor, mentor, and friend. Just before I returned from Paris, I received word from her attorney that she had died from a sudden stroke. She had no children or relatives. Her students had always been her family."

Ainsley sighed. "She left me thirty thousand dollars. I used it to lease the space on the square. Put in the best commercial ovens money could buy. I invested in the kitchen equipment I needed. Hired one person to help with the baking. Nothing was left after that. I have done well enough to hire on two more employees, but I really have to watch expenses."

"You're happy, though, aren't you?" Jackson asked.

"I am," she freely admitted. "Unlike so many others who are desperate to leave the Cove, all I wanted to do was come back to my hometown and fill a need in the community."

They finished their appetizer, which was soon replaced by their entrees. Jackson poured her another glass of wine. Ainsley didn't want it but didn't want to sound churlish by refusing it, especially because he had gone to the trouble of finding out what she preferred.

As they finished the meal, he talked some about his caseload and what it was like to be a trial lawyer.

"My last criminal case, though, was the straw that broke the camel's back. My client was accused of raping and murdering a young woman in her early twenties. I got him off and only hope I don't live to regret that."

Their server appeared. "Any dessert tonight?"

Jackson looked to her. Ainsley shook her head. "Much as I would like to try something, I am too full."

"Just the check, please," he said as Ainsley turned her head away, stifling a yawn.

They paid the bill and went to his car. Once more, he opened her door for her. She slid into the leather seat, yawning again. She never stayed up this late, and the two glasses of wine and her full belly didn't help matters.

He got inside the car, rubbing his hands. "It's a little cold out. Want your seat warmer on?"

"Sure."

She couldn't imagine having a car this nice. Hers was functional, but luxuries such as seat warmers or Sirius XM radio weren't a part of her world.

As Jackson drove, she felt the warmth envelope her and yawned again. Her eyes began to droop. She closed them a moment, wanting to rest them just a bit, but she slipped into the darkness.

CHAPTER 8

Jackson asked Ainsley a question. When she didn't reply, he glanced over.

She was fast asleep.

He didn't realize he had become so boring that he would put a woman to sleep on their first date. Up until now, he had thoroughly enjoyed the time he'd spent with Ainsley. She was easy to talk to. He appreciated how she had opened up and shared a part of her past that must have been a painful time in her life, one that still haunted her today. He appreciated how smart she was. How she'd worked from the time she was young, wanting to support her family. How she hadn't let the past get in the way of building her present and future.

Then it hit him. She was exhausted. That's why she had fallen asleep.

As he and Gage had run this morning, Jackson had teased about how early Game Night had broken up. Gage explained that it always did because he, Ainsley, and Rylie had businesses to run, ones which saw their busiest times on the weekends. In the past, Carter would have been included in that group, with his twelve-hour firehouse shift starting at seven the next morning. Willow and Dylan consistently got up well before the sun because they were runners. Dylan often had Saturday events to work, making his presence known at the farmers' market or youth sports games. Willow was all about capturing the light and began painting soon after the sun came up, wrapping up her day in the late afternoon.

Guilt flooded Jackson, having kept Ainsley out so late. The clock on the dashboard read ten-twenty. While he was used to running on very little sleep, he now realized Ainsley had already been hard at work yesterday morning when he ran through the town square. She probably rose at three or so and went downstairs, getting a head start on baking donuts, croissants, and other pastries customers bought for their breakfasts. Then she would also spend a good portion of her day in the kitchens, baking the many items in her display cases. Even though she had told him she had hired additional help, Ainsley would be a hands-on owner, working from well before the bakery opened until after hours.

That didn't even take into consideration the books she would have to keep. Supplies that needed to be ordered. Deliveries that had to be made. She had probably gone straight home from Game Night and fallen into bed, up early for the Saturday rush this morning. Sundays would be much the same, with people wanting donuts and pastries for their weekend breakfasts and churches placing orders for donuts for Sunday school classes.

Why hadn't she mentioned this when he set the time for their date? He would have easily adjusted it to a couple of hours earlier. He had to remember he was in a small town now. People rose early and went to bed early. They worked hard for their livings.

Jackson reached over and slipped his hand around hers. He had taken it earlier in the restaurant. When he had told her he wanted to be more than friends. He also had wanted to let her know he found her attractive, especially after the hostess ignored Ainsley and flirted shamelessly with him.

He liked this woman. Very much. While he wasn't ready to start planning a future with her, he could see that becoming a real possibility. No, a probability. Something had attracted him to Ainsley from the moment they had first spoken. The idea of love at first sight seemed improbable. At the same time, he wanted to get to know her better. Find out what she liked to do. What her favorite foods were. What kind of books she read. He was at a point in his life when the idea of settling into a marriage and having children appealed to him greatly.

Doing so with this sleeping beauty was worth pursuing.

He pulled into the alley behind the square and turned into the spot behind Buttercup Bakery's rear door before cutting the engine. His hand still covered hers. He leaned closer and caught the scent of vanilla. More than anything, Jackson wanted to kiss her awake —but he had never taken advantage of a woman and wouldn't start now, especially with one he was interested in building a relationship with.

Instead, he said softly, "Ainsley? Ainsley, wake up."

She stirred. His eyes went to her mouth and that full bottom lip that was so sensual.

"Ainsley?" he repeated, a little louder.

She smiled sleepily and stretched, the sweater dress she wore clinging to her breasts. Then she blinked a few times. Suddenly, a look of horror crossed her face.

"Oh, no," she muttered, shaking her head. "Tell me I did not fall asleep on you. Please, no." Even in the dark, he could see the blush rising on her cheeks.

Jackson chuckled. "I won't tell you."

She pulled her hand from his, covering her face with both hands. "This is so embarrassing. I apologize, Jackson. It's not you. Nothing to do with you. It's all me. I should have been more upfront with you."

"What time do you usually go to bed?"

Ainsley bit her lip. "Eight-thirty. Maybe nine. Game Night is the exception. We try to wrap it up a little before nine. I hurry home. Wash my face. Brush my teeth. Fall into bed."

"And how early do you get up?"

She shook her head. "You don't want to know. Early enough to get all the breakfast goodies into the cases, although on the weekends, I continue to make donuts until almost ten o'clock. Donuts are a weakness of people living in the Cove."

"When do you make everything else?"

"I get help with that. Gus, my first hire, really bakes most of the breads these days, and a lot of the cakes and pies. Gloria is on cookies and brownies and works the counter. Sheila, my newest employee, was strictly hired for counter service, but she's shown an interest in baking. We've all taken her under our wings. She works the most with Gloria, though, on basic cookies."

"What's left for you?"

"I do all the specialty items. Eclairs. Cupcakes. Cannolis. I also handle any order that comes in, other than the church groups which order donuts by the dozens. I bake cakes for birthdays, anniversaries, and graduations. Engagement parties and weddings."

"I suppose at some point, you have to keep your books."

Ainsley tucked a lock of hair behind her ear. "I have to keep up with supplies and do all my own ordering. Fortunately, Gillian Roberts keeps my books."

"I haven't seen Gillian since I got back to the Cove. I need to stop by and have a long visit with her. She was like an aunt to Willow and me. Coming to games. Attending Willow's dance recitals. She even would go with Boo to Willow's art exhibits."

"I couldn't make things work without Gillian," Ainsley admitted. "She's trained me to keep up with my receipts. Plan ahead. Keep track of all tax information." She began yawning again. "Sorry."

"You need to get in bed." He only regretted that he wouldn't be in it with her.

"I do." She hesitated. "I want to thank you for a lovely evening. I was able to eat at a place I've always wanted to go. You were terrific company. I'm only mortified I fell asleep on the way home."

"Well, you did have a couple of glasses of wine in you," he pointed out. "And with the seat warmer on, I'm sure that contributed to your drowsiness."

"I appreciate you understanding. I also know that while I had a great time, you're probably looking for someone very different from me."

Her words perturbed him. "Why do you say that?"

Ainsley snorted. "Because you're Jackson Martin. *The* Jackson Martin. You can go out with anyone you want. I'm surprised our hostess didn't slip you her cell number. Or if she did, she was really subtle about that. She sure wasn't about anything else."

Jackson cupped her cheek. "But I'm not interested in her—or anyone else, Ainsley. I'm interested in *you*."

He leaned in and kissed her softly. Just one sweet, simple kiss. Then he broke it, his thumb stroking the smooth satin of her cheek.

"I hope you'll want to try this again. Soon."

He saw doubt in her eyes.

"Let's play it by ear, Jackson," she said softly, and then opened her door.

He hurriedly opened his own and met her at the hood of his car. "I walk a lady to her door. Even if it's an industrial-sized one."

She smiled and opened the clutch she carried, removing her keys and slipping one into the lock, turning it.

"Thank you for a nice evening, Jackson."

He placed his hands on her shoulders and brushed his lips slowly against hers once more.

"Thank you, Ainsley. You'll be hearing from me soon."

She pushed open the door and turned on a light, squinting a moment at its harshness. "I hope so."

"Do you ever have any free time?"

"The bakery is closed on Mondays and Tuesdays during the off-season."

"Then plan on doing something with me Monday. *And* Tuesday."

A slow smile spread across her face. "Okay."

"Okay," he repeated. "I'll call you."

Ainsley closed the door, and Jackson heard her throw the lock. He returned to his car and sat in it a moment.

He was more than interested in Ainsley Robinson.

～

Her alarm clock went off, which was very unusual. Ainsley couldn't remember the last time that had occurred. She set it every night, of course, and turned it off before it buzzed with daily regularity. Then again, she hadn't been awake after ten o'clock in a long, long time.

She jumped into the shower, hoping it would help wake her up. By the time she got out, the coffee she'd put on to brew was ready and she sipped on it as she dressed. She may not have gotten much sleep, but she was on an adrenaline high now.

When Ainsley arrived downstairs, she was surprised to see Gus already there, hard at work. He nodded to her and went back to placing donuts into the numerous cardboard boxes set out for pickup.

Ainsley had hesitated to hire Gus when he originally applied for a job with her. He had been up-front with her, explaining he had learned how to cook in prison and that he was currently on probation. Gus had laid his cards on the table, telling her that he'd had a lifelong drinking problem which had caught up to him. He had collected several DUIs before crashing his car into another one. One person died and one was injured in the wreck, and Gus had served several years in prison after pleading guilty to a felony DUI charge.

He assured her that he hadn't had a drop to drink before his sentencing or while in prison. He had lived in a halfway house in Portland for a year, finding work at a diner before his cousin in Salty Point took him in. Gus assured Ainsley he had learned his lesson and that his drinking days were behind him, and if he ever did fall off the wagon, he would quit Buttercup Bakery immediately.

It was a combination of the sadness in Gus' eyes and the sincerity in his voice that had led her to give the ex-con a chance. It was one of the best decisions she had ever made. Gus had proven to be a hard worker. He kept his head down and was quiet and pleasant. They did talk some in the early morning hours when it was just the two of them in the bakery. She learned he had two children, both whom had cut him from their lives because of the many disappointments they had suffered, thanks to his drinking. Gus knew he had let them down, as well as the wife who had divorced him years ago. Still, he sent both his son and daughter a birthday card each year with a message saying he knew he didn't deserve their forgiveness, but asked for it all the same.

So far, neither had contacted him.

Ainsley slipped into her chef's coat and went to work on two birthday cakes. The bakery closed at noon on Sundays no matter what the season. She had learned off-season there was always a good rush in the early hours when Buttercup Bakery opened, and during tourist season, they would get walk-ins all the way up until noon. She usually used Sunday afternoons to assess how the week had gone, making lists of supplies to order come Monday morning, and collecting receipts to file for Gillian.

Today, however, she was more in need of a brief nap at closing time and would put off the paperwork until later this afternoon or even this evening.

As her cakes baked, Ainsley made the icing for each, one buttercream and one cream cheese.

She greeted Gloria and Sheila when they arrived. Sheila stocked the cash register, while Gloria helped Gus with the donuts and croissants. The bakery opened, and she let the two cakes cool before icing them. The morning went by in a blur, as weekend mornings usually did. She was conscious, though, when her phone buzzed in her pocket. Normally, she wouldn't take the time to look at incoming texts until after the bakery closed. This time, she slipped inside the employee restroom and washed her hands before pulling her cell from her pocket.

Her heart raced when she saw the message was from Jackson.

Hope you got a little sleep. Still feel guilty for keeping you out so late. Have a few ideas for Monday & Tuesday but would also like your input.

Ainsley decided not to answer the text right away. She placed the phone back into her pocket and returned to the kitchen.

Sheila appeared in the doorway. "Someone to see you, Ainsley."

For a moment, she hoped it might be Jackson. That he had texted her from just outside the bakery.

She tamped down her excitement and stepped into the bakery front, seeing the long line—and Rylie. Her cousin waved, and Ainsley went over to her, giving her a quick hug.

"The girls are getting together this afternoon at my place," Rylie informed her. "Tenley has offered to bring lunch, and I'm banking that Carter will have prepared it for us. We haven't been together in a few weeks. It's time." She paused. "Especially since we have quite a bit to talk about."

Though tired, Ainsley knew being around her friends would energize her. "I'm in."

Rylie's brows rose. "Aren't you interested in what we have to talk about?"

She shrugged. "I'm always up for whatever we talk about when we get together. Why?"

Her cousin's mischievous grin tipped off Ainsley. "Why, we need to discuss a certain gentleman who has returned to the Cove recently. One who couldn't keep his eyes off you last night. One who has already called both Tenley and me this morning, pumping us for things you like to do."

Her cheeks burned. "Is that so?" Her heart thumped in her chest.

"Definitely so. I can't believe you had a date with Jackson last night, and you didn't even share that with me."

"I was going to," she quickly said.

"Well, we'll definitely do a postmortem because all three of us are dying to hear how your date went. We're meeting at my house at twelve-thirty. That gives you time to close the bakery and head on over."

"I'll be there," Ainsley promised. "After all, I know it's *be there—or be talked about.*"

Rylie laughed. "You've got that right, Cuz. See you soon."

As Rylie left the bakery, Ainsley saw none other than Jackson holding the door open for her. Her cousin glanced over her shoulder, giving Ainsley a wicked grin before she left.

Jackson spotted her and smiled. Lord, his smile should be outlawed. It was inviting and drew a person in.

He joined the end of the line as if he were any other customer. She waved him over and turned abruptly, heading back into the kitchen area, hoping he would follow her.

She turned and found him standing in the doorway, and she motioned him closer.

"I thought I would stop by for a little treat," he told her, bending and brushing his lips against her cheek, causing goosebumps to blossom along her arms.

"I thought you might like to see behind the scenes," she said. "The nickel tour."

"Lead the way," he told her.

Ainsley showed him the industrial ovens that she had poured so much money into, knowing they would be the heart of her bakery and determine the quality of her baked goods. She pointed out the racks where dozens of trays stood, waiting to be brought out to the display cases, as well as the various work stations used to knead bread dough and ice cakes and cupcakes.

She stopped and said, "Gus, I'd like you to meet my friend Jackson Martin."

The baker wiped his hands on his apron and offered a clean one. "I saw you play in the state championship years ago," Gus said. "You were a helluva ballplayer."

"My glory days are pretty far behind me. I practice law now."

Ainsley noticed Gus stiffen slightly. Quickly, she said, "Jackson has been practicing criminal law down in L.A. He's moving back to the Cove and will be taking over Clancy Nelson's practice."

Gus nodded abruptly. "Gotta get back to work."

She led Jackson away and then asked, "What can I box up for you? It's on the house."

"Did I say something wrong?" he asked quietly. "I saw Gus' reaction."

"Gus is a former inmate," she revealed. "He learned to cook in prison. He's paid his debt to society and is very remorseful for what he did." She saw the crease form between his eyes and added, "He's a wonderful employee. Punctual. Hardworking."

He nodded. "I think I'd like a cinnamon cake donut for myself, and you better make it three cannolis. Carter bragged about them so last night that I thought I better try one."

"So, you're ordering three?"

"If I come home with one, I won't feel like splitting it with Dylan. Or Willow. I think it's best each of us have one of our own."

"Willow is coming to lunch at Rylie's today. The girls are having a little impromptu gathering. I'll make sure she has dessert there."

"Keep it at three cannolis. That means Dylan and I can split that third one." He grinned wickedly. "And my sister will be none the wiser."

Ainsley laughed. "I can do that." She picked up a box and claimed a fresh donut from the waiting tray and then went to the front. Jackson followed and went to the customer side of the counter, while Ainsley placed three cannolis alongside the lone donut. She handed the box to Jackson, and he thanked her.

"Hey," said Ed Ferguson, who was known as the chief complainer in the Cove. "Why doesn't he have to pay?"

Before she could reply, Jackson said, "Because I'm the owner's boyfriend."

Every head in the bakery swung to look at Ainsley, who felt her cheeks catch fire.

Jackson grinned shamelessly at her. "Call me after you're through with the girls. Remember, we have plans to make." He sauntered out the door.

As the buzz began, Ainsley retreated to the kitchen, knowing she and Jackson would be the topic of conversation over the next several days.

Sheila followed and said, "Quick work, Ainsley." Then she winked. "He looks like a keeper."

Ainsley's head—and heart—agreed.

CHAPTER 9

Gloria helped Ainsley carry out the two birthday cakes since both customers had arrived to pick them up at the same time. Ainsley opened the box of the first one, a cake with Disney princesses covering it.

She watched the five-year-old birthday girl's face light up with pleasure as she said, "It's too pretty to eat."

"Then have your mommy take a picture of it before you and your friends eat it. Because, as a baker, I can tell you that cakes are meant to be eaten. And enjoyed."

The little girl giggled. "I like cake. It's my favorite food. I like Disney. Belle is my favorite. I was Belle for Halloween. I'm always going to be Belle."

"Belle is my favorite, too," she told the child. "Because she's smart and resourceful—and she likes to read books. I'll bet you like to read books, too."

The girl nodded. "I can read a little. I get to go to school next year. Mommy says I'll learn to read lots there."

The mother thanked Ainsley and moved to the side to pay for the cake.

While Sheila rang them up, Ainsley opened the box for the second customer. It was for a husband who loved the Dodgers, and so Ainsley had decorated it with baseball insignia all in Dodger blue.

The man's wife smiled approvingly. "You always do such great work, Ainsley. Bob is going to be over the moon with this. We're actually going down to L.A. in June for a week. The Dodgers have a four-game homestand, and we'll be at every game."

"I hope you'll enjoy your trip to California—and the cake today." She glanced to Gloria, who said, "I'll ring you up, ma'am."

Ainsley returned to the back, where Gus was tidying up. The bakery would close in fifteen minutes.

"You like him," Gus said, the first words he had spoken since she had introduced him to Jackson hours ago.

"Yes, I do. I didn't know him when he lived in the Cove years ago. I knew of him, but I was too young to be friendly with him."

"You're not too young now," Gus proclaimed. "He seems like a good man, Ainsley. I hope something will come of this for you."

She did as well but told herself to temper her hopes. One date did not make a relationship, but it had been a fun date—and a good start.

She pitched in with the cleaning, and soon, Sheila brought the cash till to the back, quickly counting everything out for Ainsley, a task she had taken upon herself recently and one Ainsley appreciated.

Gloria leaned around the corner. "The front is cleared of customers and clean. I'll see everyone Wednesday."

Sheila also said goodbye, following Gloria out, leaving Ainsley with Gus. He took the trash out the back to the alley and returned. She thanked him and followed him to the front, changing the sign to *Closed* and locking the door behind him after he exited.

As Ainsley climbed the stairs to her apartment, she unbuttoned and removed her chef's coat. She changed from the short-sleeved T-shirt she wore underneath it to a long-sleeved sweater in blue, leaving on her jeans. Tossing on a light jacket, she came back downstairs and claimed the box of cannolis she had put aside for today's gathering and went out the back door, locking it. She had decided to walk the four blocks to Rylie's house. Her cousin had bought the small cottage when she decided to move to the Cove after her father's death. Rylie had had a bit of a strained relationship with her father. Once he was gone, she sold his Portland antiques store and used the profits to open a new one in the Cove. She had told Ainsley that she always felt most comfortable here, having spent every summer in the Cove with Ainsley and her parents. The coastal town drew a lot of tourists, some of them interested in antiques. Rylie had already established her reputation, though, in the world of antiques, and many people made sure Antiques and Mystiques was a regular stop on their list of stores to peruse.

As she approached Rylie's house, Tenley pulled up to the curb, parking next to Willow's SUV. Ainsley paused, waiting for her friend to get out of the car.

"Hey, Ainsley," Tenley called, exiting the vehicle and opening the rear door to pull out two large canvas bags.

"I see you're providing dessert," her friend said, as they moved up the sidewalk.

"Yes, it's cannolis today."

Tenley groaned. "I can't let Carter know that. Unless there are any left over and you let me take them home with me."

"With Carter providing us lunch, I knew to stick a couple of extras in for him."

They came up the porch stairs, and Willow opened the door before they even knocked. They entered, taking everything straight to the kitchen.

Rylie greeted them, stirring a pitcher of lemonade. "What did your lovely husband make for us today?"

Tenley set the two bags on the counter and began pulling out sealed containers. "We've got a cold pasta salad, along with some fabulous lobster rolls. We just shot the video this morning where he put them together."

"I watched last week's video where he made chicken parm," Willow said. "He inspired me to try it, and Dylan said it was the best meal I've made since we've been married. Be sure and tell him that."

"I will," Tenley promised. "He'll be tickled to hear it."

Rylie pulled plates from the cupboard, and the four women filled their plates. They took their food into the cozy dining room for four, taking seats.

"Everything looks wonderful," Ainsley said, before biting into one of the lobster rolls. "Mmm. Carter did a wonderful job on these."

"Enough talk about food," her cousin said. "We want to hear about what's really important. You and Jackson."

She could feel the flush spreading across her cheeks. "We went to the Old Coast Pub House last night for dinner."

"Nice," Tenley said. "How was it?"

"The food—or our conversation?" she teased.

"The food is always good," Willow said. "We need

to know how the date went. All I know is that Jackson came in from his run this morning humming. Humming! I don't recall him ever doing that."

"We had a really nice time," Ainsley said. "It was a lot of getting to know one another. You have to remember, Jackson was a senior in high school when I was a seventh grader. Back then, five years was a huge gap. I knew all about him because he was the town hero in several sports, but I wasn't on his radar. Well, that's not exactly true," she amended. "He did remember some little girl who sold baked goods before games, which he never got to sample because he was always taking the field or court."

"Obviously, you had to tell him a little about yourself," Rylie said. "Was it surface conversation, or did you go a bit deeper?"

"Deeper. We got along really well. That is, until I fell asleep on him," she added sheepishly.

"Oh, no!" cried Willow. "At dinner?"

"No, thank goodness. It was on the ride home. Jackson made the reservation for eight."

"*Big* mistake," her cousin declared. "You should have told him that would be way past your bedtime."

"I should have spoken up, and I know now to do so in the future," Ainsley said. "But I was so surprised that he even asked me out, that I just nodded my head and smiled at him. We didn't finish dinner until a little after ten, and I had drunk two glasses of wine. When we got in the car, he put the seat warmers on." She shook her head. "I was a lost cause."

"A full belly and seat warmers will do it every time," Tenley declared.

"It was a little embarrassing to have him wake me up. I apologized and explained how early I get up to begin baking. He was very understanding and even asked when I had time off from the bakery."

"Well, we know you have Mondays and Tuesdays off. And I already know my brother mentioned seeing you both days."

She nodded. "We don't have any firm plans yet, but he asked if we could do something together during my time off." She hesitated and then added, "He also asked if I would call him when we finished up here."

"I thought it was cute, bumping into him when I left the bakery this morning," Rylie said. "He had already called and pumped me for information about you. I told him that you like to watch old movies and enjoyed biking and hiking."

"I told him the same thing," Tenley added. "It surprised me when he called. But that let me know just how interested he is in you, Ainsley."

"It's a good thing that Jackson has decided to take over Clancy Nelson's law practice," Willow stated. "That way, he'll be in the Cove fulltime, and you can see if anything develops between the two of you. He certainly couldn't keep his eyes off you during Game Night."

"Enough about Jackson and me," she protested. "The inquisition is closed. For now. Let me hear what else is going on for all of you. Tenley, how is your book coming along?"

"I'm working on the second of my trilogy now. It's nice to already be familiar with the world I created in the previous book. It's flowing so well, thanks to having an outline this time and not flying by the seat of my pants from the beginning. Carter has taught me the value of being organized and prepared. He is attacking his cookbook project very methodically."

Tenley told them about some of the recipes her

husband had tried and which ones had, so far, made the final version, which would release in November, the same time the first book in her fantasy trilogy would come out. Their PR firm had coordinated the effort with both publishing houses, and Tenley and Carter had agreed to a series of book signings they would do together.

Willow shared a little about a series of paintings that she was beginning and how her agent had already arranged a showing of them at The Runyon Gallery in New York next fall. The Soho art gallery had also hosted a showing of Willow's paintings last fall, and she was working exclusively with the gallery now.

"The series is set entirely along the Oregon coast," Willow told them. "I'm drawing inspiration from not only my childhood but places Dylan and I have gone to on the weekends with Shadow. This area has always spoken to my soul, and I have high hopes for when the series is launched."

Rylie took the floor next, discussing an estate sale she was going to tomorrow morning. The deceased had a fascination with Queen Anne furniture. Rylie had studied the catalog and was hoping to pick up several pieces for Antiques and Mystiques.

After that, they talked about happenings in the Cove and Salty Point, the next town over. Willow said Jackson had mentioned that Clancy would be out of town for a week and that her brother would be spending time in Clancy's office, combing through the files and familiarizing himself with the practice and its clients.

"I'm sure, though, Jackson will be able to make plenty of time for you, Ainsley."

She returned to the kitchen and brought back the

cannolis. Willow ate one, and Rylie gobbled down two. Tenley took a pass, saying she was too full and would take her portion home to Carter. Ainsley boxed up what was left, saying she needed to go and work on her order for the coming week.

Hugs were exchanged and goodbyes said, and the three guests left Rylie's house.

"Want me to drop you off?" Willow asked, seeing that Ainsley hadn't driven.

"No, I think I'll walk. Thanks, though."

As she headed down the street, she took out her phone and called Jackson, who answered on the first ring.

"Girls gossip group over?"

"Yes, I'm walking home now. I hear you pumped my friends and your sister on what I like to do."

"Guilty as charged," he freely admitted. "I know you've got to be tired and need to get your sleep, but you have to eat. I'd really like to bring dinner over for you. I don't have to stay."

"I usually work on what I'm going to order come Monday morning each Sunday afternoon," she revealed. "I'm going to take care of that now as soon as I get home. Once I finish, I'd love to have dinner with you."

"How about I bring dinner by at six? Or is that too late?"

"Six will be fine because of my late lunch," she told him.

"Then I'll see you at six."

Ainsley arrived at the bakery and went upstairs to her apartment. She decided a quick nap wouldn't throw her off her sleep schedule too much—and it would keep her from falling asleep on Jackson two nights in a row. She set her alarm for an hour ahead.

She hoped it would refresh her, and it would still give her time to shower and touch up her makeup before Jackson arrived.

As she closed her eyes, she thought how happy her parents' marriage had been and how she had hoped to one day have one just as strong and loving as theirs. With her laser focus on school and work, she hadn't devoted much time to her personal life.

As she drifted off, Ainsley hoped things might be changing soon.

CHAPTER 10

Although Jackson had hoped to spend the entire day with Ainsley, she had told him she would not be available until at least one that afternoon, explaining that she placed specialty orders every other Monday and went to Portland to pick them up. She also stopped at Costco every week for general supplies for the bakery. When he had offered to go with her, she had seemed surprised but agreed to him accompanying her. He now drove into town and would meet up with her at the bakery.

Last night's dinner had been relaxing with just the two of them. He had brought sandwiches and soup from Eats 'n Treats Café. The sandwiches were tasty and the soup hit the spot on a cool, rainy evening. He'd made certain to leave by eight. Even though he had learned she did no baking on Mondays, she tried to keep to the same sleep schedule so her body wouldn't go haywire. She did say she sometimes went in on Tuesdays if she had a big order coming up, such as designing and creating a wedding cake. This week, she didn't have one.

He planned to spend all day with her tomorrow.

For now, he was going to take what he could get this Monday morning. When he arrived and parked, he saw Ainsley was already sitting behind the wheel of her SUV. He locked his vehicle and slid into the passenger's seat of her car.

"Thanks for offering to go along with me," she told him. "Don't think I won't put you to work."

"If it involves lifting sacks of flour, Gage will be pleased," he replied. "We are embarking upon a few weeks of training together, three times a week, and we started this morning. He had me doing some lifting, which he wants me to add to my workout regimen. He had all kinds of equipment in the back of his truck for me to use, from kettle balls to dumbbells to medicine balls. I haven't touched any weights since my high school playing days, so I'll probably be more than a little sore tomorrow. It's a good thing you're catching me today before the soreness sets in."

They left the Cove as a misty rain began, taking the highway that would lead them into Portland. Conversation between them was easy once again, and he had a good feeling about this day.

And this woman.

They stopped at Costco first, arriving just as the doors opened. Ainsley knew exactly what she wanted and where it was located, directing Jackson to stack sacks of flour and sugar on the flatbed cart she pushed. She pitched in, as well, and they also went to an aisle with various spices. Ainsley explained which ones she used in baking different sweets. She also added two large bottles of vanilla and boxes of confectioner's sugar before they proceeded to the checkout stand. By the time they paid and unloaded her purchases and got in the car, it was ten-thirty.

"That went pretty quickly," he told her.

"I've got a routine and know now how much to buy during each season. Costco is a weekly stop for me because they stock the basics I need. The next place we're heading to has more specialty flours and caters to business owners of bakeries."

They arrived twenty minutes later, and Ainsley took him inside. Not only did this store have edible items, it also had ones to aid in baking, such as large cookie sheets and baking tins. She walked him around the store briefly, pointing out various things she used. She then led them to the register and gave her name to the clerk manning it.

After consulting the computer, the clerk said, "Your online order is almost ready, Ainsley. You can go ahead and drive around back to the loading dock."

She thanked the clerk, and they returned to the car, driving to the back side of the warehouse.

"I suppose you do a lot of business here."

"I do. I tried one other distribution place on the far side of Portland, and I found their prices to be a little higher and their customer service to be nonexistent. A fellow baker recommended this place, and I've been using them ever since."

She got out of the car, so he did the same. Ainsley opened her tailgate and one of the rear passenger doors. A worker appeared and greeted her by name, rolling a dolly to her car. Jackson helped the man place some of the boxes in the rear. When they ran out of room, they loaded the rest into the back seat.

"One more trip and we'll be done, Ainsley," the worker said, disappearing.

"You buy this much each week?" Jackson asked, wondering about the volume of business Buttercup Bakery did.

"Actually, more at each place once the tourists hit the coast. Today, I'm buying a little more than I usually do. They have some new muffin and cupcake tins I want to try out. If I like them, I'll eventually replace all the ones in my bakery."

The worker appeared again, and Jackson helped him load the last three boxes into the back seat. Ainsley thanked the man, slipping him some cash. Jackson thought about teasing her as to what kind of tip he could expect but decided to wait. He still was aware that he might be rushing things, having seen her three nights in a row, as well as asking her to spend part of today and tomorrow with him.

It was now almost eleven-thirty, and they were ready to head back to the Cove.

He said, "We're going to need to eat lunch at some point. Why don't we grab a bite here in Portland for something different?"

"That's fine with me. I have just the place. It's nearby and the food is fantastic."

Ten minutes later, they arrived at a strip shopping center and parked. He knew from L.A. that some of the best places to eat were the small, out-of-the-way ones, the mom-and-pop restaurants that had a fiercely loyal clientele.

"I hope you like Italian," she said, as they headed toward the door.

"One of my favorites."

They entered and although it wasn't even noon yet, the place was already three-quarters full on a Monday.

"Ainsley, dear. How good to see you," a large woman with dark hair greeted. She enveloped Ainsley in a hug. "How is your bakery coming along?"

"It's doing really well, Marta. I was in Portland stocking up on supplies, and I thought I'd bring my friend here to eat. This is Jackson."

He noticed she hadn't called him her boyfriend, even though he had applied the label of girlfriend to her in her bakery yesterday morning. Knowing how gossip spread in a small town, he figured most of the Cove by now knew of their budding relationship. It didn't upset him that she didn't say anything now. Ainsley seemed to be a person who valued her privacy. Not knowing who this Marta was, Jackson decided to keep quiet. For now.

But the day would come when he wanted to clarify —and solidify—their relationship.

The woman took his hand and squeezed it, giving him a warm smile. "Hello, Jackson. It is so good to meet you. I'm sure you have eaten some of Ainsley's fabulous desserts."

"I've had a few and plan on many more, Marta."

The woman led them to a table for two, and Ainsley waved away the menus.

Looking at Jackson, she said, "Let me return the favor and order for you today."

Quickly, she reeled off an order that included a toasted ravioli appetizer, pasta fagioli soup, and lasagna.

Marta smiled. "The appetizer will be out soon, Ainsley. I hope you'll have time to say hello to the kitchen staff."

"I will after we eat," she promised.

"Did you eat here a lot, or did you work here?" he asked after Marta departed.

"Both. After I graduated from the culinary institute in Bend, I started working as a pastry chef at a Japanese steakhouse a few blocks from here. Many people don't know it, but some of the top pastry chefs in the world are located in Japan, especially Tokyo and Osaka. Most of them train in Paris. One of the line cooks at the steakhouse recommended this place to me. Eventually, I put in my notice and came to work here fulltime. I liked the family atmosphere and total freedom Marta gave me over the dessert menu."

"How long did you work in Portland?"

She thought a moment. "Close to two years, then I made my way up to Seattle. I worked in a variety of restaurants there, saving every dime I could for my tuition at l'Ecole Lenôtre."

They chatted amiably as they worked their way through the ravioli appetizer and hearty soup, which was accompanied by the most delicious bread Jackson had ever tasted. After he bragged on it, Ainsley told him she made something very similar at her bakery.

"Or at least Gus does the honors now. I still bake the occasional loaf to keep my muscle memory in shape, but Gus has a wonderful touch with breads. Kneading is a fine art. I'm lucky to have him."

"Did you have any reservations in hiring an ex-con?"

"I know you have probably worked with plenty of clients who have already been to prison. Your experience is mostly likely very different from mine. Yes, I did have a few qualms, but Gus had glowing recs from several people, including the warden."

"Might I ask what he did to be sent away?"

Ainsley explained the car wreck Gus' drinking had caused. "The saddest thing is that it cost him any kind of relationship with his son and daughter. His drinking over the years had led to his divorce and had already put up a barrier between him and his kids. Being sent to prison was the final blow. He sends them a birthday card each year, but neither has ever responded."

They finished their meal, and Ainsley brought him back to the kitchen with her. She knew almost every worker there and was greeted warmly by all.

As they paid their bill, Marta said, "If you ever tire of the bakery, Ainsley, you know you always have a place here."

"Thank you for the kind offer, but I've come to enjoy owning my own business. Yes, the hours are long, as you know, and the responsibility is heavy, but I'm able to devote myself to my sweets. I hope I'll remain in the Cove, providing baked goods for decades to come."

They returned to her SUV, and he asked several questions about the bakery. Why she had chosen the location she had. How she planned out what to bake each day. Ainsley explained the difference between weekdays and weekends and the various seasons.

"Off-season is easy to predict because my clientele is mostly those in and around the Cove, and they buy on a fairly regular basis. Once May arrives, that means tourists begin pouring into the Oregon coast, mostly on weekends. I have to step up ordering supplies and make adjustments as to what to bake. That increases once students get out of school, and traffic in the Cove picks up even more, with families on vacation. The crowds grow throughout the summer and then taper off after Labor Day, though I still get some of that tourist trade on the weekends throughout September."

"I'm sure it's a fine line between baking enough

and not running out of popular items, balanced with having too much left over at the end of a day."

"It happens. I can't always predict the whims of customers. There is a small food bank in Salty Point now. They established it a few months ago. If I have anything left with a short shelf life, Gus takes it with him and delivers it to the food bank after his shift."

"That's nice. People in need rarely get treats such as sweets, I'll bet. They must look forward to finding your desserts on the shelves."

"It is for a good cause, and I don't often have too much left over. I do allow Gloria, Sheila, and Gus to take whatever they want when they leave, free of charge. Certain items just aren't good the next day. Things like cookies can roll over for a day, so I don't have much waste in that department."

They arrived back in the Cove and she drove directly to the bakery. The rain had ended, and Jackson helped unload the many boxes and sacks, as Ainsley instructed him where to place things. Her kitchen was very well organized, and he knew that was part of her success.

"Just leave everything for now. I'll unpack it later. Thank you for helping me so much today. It takes me a long time to bring things in by myself."

"Just text me any Monday when you arrive from Portland. I can walk across the square and help you unload your SUV."

"No, you'll be dressed for work. Besides, you might even be with a client. When are you going to look over Clancy's case files? I don't want you spending too much time with me and neglecting that."

He took her hand and pulled her toward him, again smelling the tempting vanilla scent on her skin.

"I don't want to miss out on time with you," he admitted freely. "I can bury myself in files starting Wednesday morning. Right now? "He smiled down at her. "All I want to do is be with you."

He searched her periwinkle eyes and saw welcome there. Slowly, Jackson lowered his head, placing his lips against hers.

Magic...

CHAPTER 11

Ainsley's heart beat in triple time as Jackson's lips touched hers. A moment she had dreamed of. *And it was better than she ever could have imagined.*

He brushed his lips against hers tenderly, one hand cradling her nape, the other going to the small of her back, his fingers spreading against it, drawing her closer to him.

Jackson was different from every man who had kissed her. They rushed things, all about immediate access, where he took his time, savoring her, making her feel cherished. His kiss eventually became more demanding, firing her blood. He brought her flush against him, and she could feel the hard muscles of his chest. Slowly, he teased open her mouth, and she granted him access willingly. His tongue began a sensual exploration, which caused the blood to pound loudly in her ears, almost deafening her.

Her hands went to his broad shoulders, and she gripped them tightly, still not quite believing her girlhood fantasy now sprang to life.

Suddenly, his hands moved to her waist and lifted her, placing her on one of the large work tables where she and Gus kneaded their dough. Jackson stepped between her legs and framed her face with his long fingers, never breaking the kiss. Instead, he tilted her head back slightly for better access and continued his barrage of her mouth and senses.

Time stood still as the kiss went on, her body begin to hum with need. Jackson's hands returned to her back, slowly gliding up and down as his tongue explored every crevice in her mouth. Timidly, Ainsley finally stepped up and instead of being a receiver, became an active participant in the kiss. Her arms went about his neck, and her fingers locked behind his nape as her tongue began stroking his. Jackson let out a low groan, full of need, and their tongues went to war with one another, battling for domination. But no matter what, they were both winners with this kiss.

Jackson finally broke it, his lips gliding across her cheek and to her ear. His teeth tugged on her earlobe, causing a wild sensation to spread through her. She had never felt it before, but she immediately put a name to it.

Desire...

He teased her lobe with his teeth and then outlined the shell of her ear with his tongue, causing a tremor to run through her. Who knew an ear could be an erogenous zone? He eventually left it, his lips trailing back to her cheek and down to her throat. He located her pulse point and nipped at it with his teeth, then soothing the place with his tongue. Ainsley began trembling almost violently with need.

She wanted this man. All of him.

Now.

His mouth returned to hers, and he bit softly into her bottom lip, pinning it. A frisson of desire rippled through her as he tasted her. Slowly, he eased her back until she was flat against the work table's surface. His hands slid beneath the sweater she wore, grazing her belly, moving higher, their warmth causing her breath to catch. He hesitated a moment.

"Touch me," she urged, seeing the heat in his eyes.

His hands moved up, finding the front clasp of her bra, undoing and parting it. Her nipples ached as they brushed against the wool of her sweater. His hands glided over them, his gaze pinning her as he kneaded each breast, much as the dough which was kneaded on this very table. He playfully tweaked her nipples, causing her to gasp.

"May I lift your sweater?" he asked huskily.

She merely nodded, not trusting that any sound would come from her.

He pushed the sweater up, her breasts now exposed to him. She watched his face, a slow smile appearing on it.

"Perfect," he murmured, lowering his head.

When his mouth touched her breast, she cried out, sheer pleasure running through her. His tongue circled her nipple, even as he kneaded her other breast. A blaze shot through her, acute and almost painful. His teeth grazed her nipple, and her back arched. Jackson took and took and took.

And she reveled in it.

He sucked and laved until a yearning deep within her was ready to explode. She realized it was an orgasm—and it was about to occur. Something she had never experienced before. Her limited sexual partners had never taken this kind of time making love to her. Ainsley only knew she was in the hands of a master lover. He continued worshiping her breast, sucking hard on it, as he lovingly touched the other one.

Suddenly, the pressure building within her exploded, causing her to buck against him. Jackson kept on stroking her with his tongue, teasing her nipple as she rode out the orgasm. It went on and on, and then finally drew to a close. She felt so limp that she didn't think she could raise even the smallest finger on her hand.

He lifted his mouth and smiled at her boyishly. "I didn't know a woman could come so easily. You must be a tigress in bed, Ainsley Robinson."

She didn't reply. She didn't want him to know that she had never experienced an orgasm before. Then she changed her mind, waiting no secrets between them.

"That's never happened to me before," she admitted. "I've never had an orgasm. Period."

"You mean with someone touching your breasts," he said.

"No," she corrected. "I mean *ever*."

His eyes widened and then the slow smile spread across his face. "Shall we try again?" he asked, a wicked gleam in his eyes.

Jackson didn't bother to wait for her reply. His mouth immediately went to her other breast, and he began working his magic on it. Soon, she writhed beneath him, small, mewling sounds coming from her as he brought her to the heights of ecstasy again.

When she came back to earth, he kissed each breast reverently and fastened the clasp on her bra. He kissed his way down her belly, bringing her sweater with him, until once more she was fully covered. He captured her hands in his and pulled her to a sitting position. He touched his lips to hers gently and then took a step back, pulling her from the table, back to her feet. Her knees buckled, and he caught her by the waist, lifting her again and placing her back on the table once more. They were on eye level.

"Thank you," he said softly, before leaning in and brushing his lips against hers. "I didn't mean to go as far as I did, but I'm glad I did. I hope you're not too upset with me."

"Upset? Not with the man who gave me my first two orgasms," she teased.

"I meant what I said before, Ainsley," his features growing serious. "I do want to be your friend—but I want much more from you than friendship. I came back to the Cove not only to change the trajectory of my professional career, but there are things I want in my personal life, as well. I want a wife and children. I want to explore that possibility with you. I know our relationship is in the earliest stages, but I feel a deep connection with you. Are you willing at this point to commit to being exclusive? That we only see each other and see where this might lead?"

Ainsley had never been more certain in her life about something.

"I could see a future with you, Jackson. I don't want to rush things, but I do want to explore that possibility."

He gave her that winning smile, the one that stole her breath away. The one that made her think she could have it all.

A loud pounding sounded at the rear door, just feet away from them.

"Jimmy!" she gasped. "Jimmy."

She nudged Jackson back and hopped from the table, rushing to unlock the rear door of the bakery.

"Hi, Jimmy," she greeted cheerfully.

"I texted when I got here, Ainsley, but you didn't

reply." He glanced over her shoulder, and she knew he was looking at Jackson.

Through her blush, she said, "Have you met Jackson Martin, Jimmy?"

Jackson stepped forward, and the two men shook hands.

"This is Jimmy Simpson. He's a local farmer and provides my milk, eggs, and cream," she explained.

"Nice to meet you, Jimmy," Jackson said easily. "I was helping Ainsley unload supplies from her trip into Portland." His swept a hand, indicating the many boxes stacked around them.

"Uh-huh," Jimmy said, his tone leading Ainsley to believe that he wasn't buying the story.

"Can I help you bring in what you brought for Ainsley?" Jackson asked.

"Sure," Jimmy said, and the two men left the kitchen.

Ainsley touched her fingertips to her lips once they went out the door, believing they must be swollen. She was grateful that she was fully clothed and able to quickly answer Jimmy's knock. Already, there would be gossip about her and Jackson in the Cove, thanks to his proclamation in her bakery yesterday of being her boyfriend. Jimmy would probably add more than a little fuel to that fire with his observations.

They brought in crates of eggs and the other dairy products. Ainsley opened the walk-in refrigerator and began organizing items as they did.

Jimmy brought in the last bit of butter and then told Ainsley, "That's it for this week. I e-mailed you the list." He named the price for today's delivery.

"I'll transfer the funds electronically now. Thanks again, Jimmy."

The farmer said goodbye and turned, telling Jackson, "Let me get with my wife about Friday night. I'll text you."

Jackson waved as Jimmy exited the building.

"What was that about?" Ainsley asked.

He grinned shamelessly. "It seems we may be double dating with Jimmy and his missus come Friday night. That is, if you're free."

She went and wrapped her arms about his waist. "Nice save, Mr. Martin."

He shrugged. "I figured he was going to be spreading a little gossip. One look at you and those kiss-swollen lips, and Jimmy knew why you weren't answering his texts. He seems nice enough, though, and I invited him and his wife to have dinner with us. He suggested Friday and is going to check with her. I told him I would check with my girlfriend."

"So, I'm really your girlfriend, Jackson?"

His eyes softened. "That—and a whole lot more."

He gave her a lingering kiss, and Ainsley wanted to pinch herself to see if this was truly real.

Jackson broke the kiss and glanced at his watch. "It's too late for the walk on the beach I had planned for us. Besides, it was misting again as I helped Jimmy bring everything inside. How about we take the time to put away all the supplies sitting in theses boxes and then watch a movie? I hear you're a fan of old ones."

"I love black-and-white ones from the thirties, forties, and fifties. Dramas. Film noirs. And I also have a thing for the seventies."

He smiled. "That's a decade of films I'm familiar with. I took an elective film class at USC for my undergraduate degree. We studied all the greats. Coppola. Scorsese. Lumet. Altman. Kubrick."

She placed a palm against his chest. "Ah, I see you aren't a beginner, after all."

He clasped her shoulders. "But I am about old black-and-white films. I'm ready to learn, Ainsley. Whatever you want to teach me."

"I love the classics. *Casablanca. Sunset Boulevard. Rebecca. All About Eve. On the Waterfront. Inherit the Wind.* Don't get me started because I could go on all night."

Jackson kissed her. "I could do this all night. How about we watch one of you favorites—and then make out like high schoolers?"

She laughed. "You are a man with a plan. I like that idea. A lot. Especially the kissing part."

They opened the boxes they had brought home from Portland. Ainsley told him about some of her favorite films and why she liked them. As they put away all the new supplies and equipment, she thought how happy she was, having Jackson here. Talking to him. Kissing him. Spending time with him.

Once everything had been put away, he told her he would run down to Crust 'n Stuff and pick up a pizza for them to nibble on as they watched her choice of movie. He left and she went upstairs, cuing up *Casablanca*, which she considered the best film ever made. Most critics went with *Citizen Kane*. While she liked that film, she thought it fell flat in its last few minutes. Nothing about Bogart and Bergman was boring, though. She only hoped Jackson would enjoy the movie as much as she did.

Making a decision, she went to a drawer in the kitchen and removed a key ring, placing it in her pocket. She went and freshened up a bit, removing her hair from its habitual ponytail, which she had worn to keep it out of her face as she carried in her purchases.

She brushed it until it gleamed and smoothed lotion along her hands and arms. Maybe she would splurge and buy some new perfume since she had used the last of hers for her date at the Old Coast Pub House.

Jackson returned with the pizza, and Ainsley pulled cans of sparkling water from her refrigerator as he collected plates and napkins. They took the pizza to her small living room, and she started the movie. He asked her to stop it several times, and they talked about a scene and its characters. She was amazed at how he picked up on small details that many people missed until their third, fourth, or fifth viewing of the film. She supposed he was used to drilling down and finding the small stuff in the cases he tried.

Once the movie ended, she turned off the TV. His arm was around her shoulders, and he took her chin in hand and pressed his lips to hers. For an hour, they made out like horny teenagers. Ainsley was giddy—and breathless—when they finally stopped.

"Let's clean this up," Jackson said. "I need to go. We both need to get some sleep. Tomorrow, I want us to go for a bike ride and a picnic on the beach."

"Will there be any time set aside for kissing?" she teased.

He kissed her hard. "Definitely. Not on our bikes. I'm not that skilled. But I think a picnic lends itself to kissing. Lots and lots of kissing."

Jackson kissed her again. She was sad when he broke the kiss, knowing he would be leaving now.

Walking him to the door, he wrapped his arms around her, hugging her tightly.

"I'll miss you," he said, kissing the top of her head. "Text me before you go to sleep. And when you wake up tomorrow morning."

"I won't text you that early. But I will before I ride my bike over to Boo's. What time do you want me?"

"As early as you like. I'm not meeting with Gage tomorrow. And I'll get in a quick run and shower before you do show up."

"Okay, I'll be there at nine."

"Nine?" he protested. "That's late."

"Eight then," she compromised.

He kissed her. "Eight is way better than nine."

Ainsley pulled the key ring from her pocket and handed it to him. "The gold one is the key to my apartment. The silver is to the back door of the bakery. I want you to have them." She smiled. "After all, you are my boyfriend. We are seeing each other exclusively."

Jackson glanced from the keys to her. "This means a lot. You've put your faith in me. In us." He kissed her softly. "I'm not even gone and I already miss you, Ainsley."

"Same."

He pocketed the keys and pulled out his cell, tapping it. Suddenly, hers began to ring.

"Better get that," he advised. "It could be an important call."

She went to her phone. "Hello?"

"Hi. I thought we could talk on my way home."

Ainsley beamed at him. "I like that. Let me walk you out."

"No, I'm going to use my new keys and lock up downstairs. I'm afraid if I let you go with me, I might not leave." He kissed her a final time. "See you tomorrow."

Jackson left her apartment. Ainsley listened as he talked about where they might ride their bikes tomorrow. Where he wanted to take her for their picnic.

They talked until he told her he was pulling into Boo's driveway.

"Now I'll say goodnight. Goodnight, Ainsley."

"Goodnight, Jackson."

She disconnected the call and placed her phone on the coffee table—and then did an impromptu dance around the apartment.

Without a doubt, Ainsley knew she was in love with Jackson Martin.

CHAPTER 12

Jackson knew he was already in love with Ainsley Robinson. He wasn't a man who had ever believed in love at first sight. He'd never even had a crush on a woman. In high school, he had dated several girls, none of the relationships serious. His senior year he had spent most of his time with a pretty, vivacious cheerleader who was fun to be around, but Jackson had never been in love with her. They merely had a few things in common and ran in the same crowd. Once high school ended, so had the romance.

In college, his studies had taken priority, knowing he had to maintain a certain GPA in order to keep his academic scholarship, as well as have the grades to get into USC's Gould School of Law. Yes, he dated a variety of women, wanting to balance studying with a social life. Yes, he had plenty of sex with many attractive coeds, both during undergrad and law school. None of them had claimed his heart, though.

Not like Ainsley Robinson had.

He wanted her in the worst way. Wanted to touch every part of her. Bury himself deep inside her. Stake his claim so that others would be warned off.

But as powerful as his feelings were, he needed to give Ainsley time to catch up to his. Yes, they certainly had physical chemistry. He could have kissed her into next year without stopping. Jackson knew sex with her would be off the charts. No, not just sex. Ainsley would be the first woman he had ever *made love* with. That realization almost knocked him for a loop.

He turned into Boo's driveway, jogging half its length and then slowing, walking the last half before bounding up the steps and collapsing into the porch swing. He pulled out his cell on the off-chance Ainsley might have texted him while he had been on his run.

No, no texts. She had told him she would let him know when she was on her way over.

He couldn't wait that long and tapped out a quick message.

Morning, Beautiful. Thinking about you.

Jackson waited. Then the three little bubbles appeared, indicating she was replying.

Hi, Handsome. Can't wait to see you.

Good enough.

He went inside, making his way straight to the kitchen. Willow leaned against the counter, sipping a cup of coffee from the smell hanging in the kitchen. Shadow was nearby, eating from his bowl.

"You have a good run?" she asked.

"Yeah." He filled a glass with water and downed it, then filled it again, slowing this time.

"How is Ainsley?" his sister asked.

"Ainsley is... pretty incredible."

"I didn't see you at all yesterday."

"We drove into Portland. She makes a run each Monday to stock up on bakery supplies. We ate lunch at a restaurant she used to work at." He paused to drink the rest of the water. "Then we came back to the

Cove. Unpacked. Some farmer named Jimmy dropped off dairy supplies."

"Boring," Willow proclaimed. "Get to the good stuff."

He gave her an innocent look. "Do I seem like someone who would kiss and tell?"

"You're my only brother. She's my good friend. I need a status report."

"We also had dinner and watched *Casablanca* together. Before dinner and after the movie? I would say there was a whole lot of kissing going on."

She grinned at him. "Now, that's more like it. I don't need details. I can tell by that silly grin on your face that you've connected."

Jackson grew serious. "It's more than that, Willow. I... I really like her. She's different from any woman I've ever spent time with."

"She is unique," Willow agreed. "Ainsley is smart. Dedicated to her bakery. Always fiddling with new creations. She volunteers her time to different organizations. She's one of the kindest people I've ever known. I think you would be good for each other."

"I think I love her," he blurted out, embarrassed at his outburst.

But his sister only smiled. She put down her mug and came to him, wrapping her arms around him.

"It hits hard, doesn't it?" she asked.

"Like a sledgehammer," he admitted. "I've never been in love, Willow. I'm not bragging, but I'm a good-looking guy. I've always had my pick of women at any age, wherever I was. But I never gave my heart away. It's not as if I were guarding it. I was always open to the idea of love. Someday. Well, someday has arrived."

"When are you going to tell her?"

"Not now. I'm afraid she'd freak out if I told her. We've only known each other for a few days."

"But she's always known you," Willow pointed out.

"That worries me. That she thinks I'm the guy from fifteen years ago. I'm not."

"No, but he's still a part of you. Yes, Ainsley knew of that teenager, but she'll also come to know the man you've become." She cupped his cheek. "For some of us, it happens fast. Once I kissed Dylan after I came back from Europe, I knew I would never look at another man again. Tenley and Carter were the same way. I know people dis the whole insta-love thing, but I believe we're all mature adults who know our minds —and our hearts. If yours is telling you Ainsley is The One, then you need to be honest with her and tell her so. If it scares her, you back off some.

"But if she's feeling the same way? Don't waste time, Jackson."

He nodded slowly. "It's a lot to think about."

Dylan came into the kitchen wearing sweats, and Shadow went to greet his master. "Hey, Jackson. Ready for a run, Bear?" He came to his wife and wrapped his arms around her, kissing her soundly.

Jackson instinctively knew he wanted that for himself and Ainsley. That enduring love. That connection. That ability to be comfortable—even around others— as he expressed his feelings for her.

"Let's stretch," Willow said. To her brother, she said, "See you later."

He went upstairs and showered and shaved, wanting to be ready when Ainsley arrived. Once he finished dressing, he headed outside and to the garage to get his bicycle. When he had first learned that Ainsley enjoyed biking, he had asked Willow if his old bike might still be around. If it hadn't been, he wasn't worried. The Cove was a coastal town, and you could rent everything from bikes to paddleboats nearby.

Willow told him that Boo had kept both their bikes. Once she and Dylan married, her new husband had taken the two bicycles in to a shop and had new tires put on both since all four were flat after so much time. Jackson had told her Dylan was welcome to keep the bike, but he wanted to borrow it for his outing with Ainsley. Since she enjoyed biking, he would seek her advice on what to buy for their future bike rides.

He retrieved it from the garage and walked it to the front porch, leaning it against the steps before he went to sit in the porch swing to wait for Ainsley.

He felt good about his conversation with his sister just now. Willow, though not quite as deliberate as Dylan, was always thoughtful in her actions and words. If she encouraged him to express his feelings to Ainsley, then that is what he would do. Today. He hoped the words wouldn't burst from him the moment he saw her, though.

Jackson didn't have long to wait. Ainsley texted him she was on her way, and he knew it was a short ride from the center of town to Boo's.

Minutes later, she appeared, riding down the driveway and stopping just short of the porch. His throat swelled with emotion just seeing her, and he hurried down the steps and went to her. She stood with both legs on either side of the bike's frame, and he took her face into his hands, giving her a sweet kiss.

Breaking it, he said, "Good morning."

She glowed as she answered him. "What a nice way to start my day. I checked the weather and believe it or not, no rain in sight today. It's the perfect day to spend outdoors."

He claimed his bike and swung a leg over it, settling into the seat. "Where are we headed?"

"Since you've been gone, the county has built several new bike trails. I thought we would check those out."

"Lead the way," he told her, as she got back on her bike and peddled down the long driveway.

Jackson followed and soon they reached the trails Ainsley had mentioned. For two hours they explored them. He enjoyed the view ahead of him even more than the scenery around him.

They finally made their way back to Boo's. Ainsley parked her bike in front of the porch, while Jackson returned his to the detached garage. They went inside, and she excused herself, heading to the restroom. He did the same, and they rendezvoused in the kitchen. He took glasses from the cupboard and filled them with water. They both drank greedily after their long ride.

"We need to make a picnic lunch. I would have done so earlier, but I didn't want our sandwiches to get soggy. We have a ton of stuff to choose from."

"Oh, I forgot. Be right back," Ainsley said.

When she returned, he saw the large Ziplock bag full of cookies in her hand and she said, "I baked these fresh this morning while I was working on a wedding cake design for a couple who just announced their engagement. They are chocolate chip with macadamia nuts."

"That was thoughtful of you."

She smiled at him. "I wanted to do this for you. After all, you say you're not much for sweets, so it could possibly mean more for me."

He laughed. "Not if Dylan sniffs this out."

"There are two dozen in here. I fully intended to leave some for Dylan and Willow."

"Let's make some sandwiches."

He began pulling items from the refrigerator, and they tag-teamed on creating two sandwiches full of meats, cheeses, and veggies. Jackson also packed grapes and chips to add to the sandwiches and cookies and claimed bottled waters from the refrigerator.

"This is plenty," she told him. "More than enough."

"You can eat your fill, and I'll finish whatever's left. I've already been for a run this morning, as well as our bike ride. I'll be ready to eat."

He retrieved a blanket he had gotten from the linen closet that morning and then placed the food and drink into his backpack. Slinging it over one shoulder, he grabbed the blanket and with his free hand, took Ainsley's hand, threading his fingers through hers.

"Where are we going?" she asked. "I know we're close to the beach because I can smell the ocean from here."

As he led her out the door, he explained, "There's a path to the beach over here. It's a little steep, so you'll need to watch your step. I can't tell you how many times Willow and I used it to go down to the water and play. It's an area far away from the tourists and was like having our own private area growing up. There's even a small cave close by. We'll go there first and leave our things inside it."

They descended the stairs his grandfather had built and finally reach the sand. He stood a moment, taking in the view as the water rolled into shore.

"This is breathtaking," Ainsley said. "You are so lucky to have this right outside your door."

"It was great growing up here. Boo's house was large, and she always welcomed our friends. Starting in middle school, I had a group of buddies who would come and camp down here. Willow and I also took solace from being near the water. She's painted this view before."

"You should hang a few of her paintings in Clancy's office. I mean, your office," she amended.

"That's a great idea. It was pretty bare bones when I went to visit him the other day. Clancy wasn't much on frills. I may want to replace a few pieces of his furniture. Art on the walls would be a nice touch."

"Rylie could help you with that. My cousin has a great eye for how to arrange things and what looks good where."

"I may call upon her for something else, as well," he revealed. "But I would like you to see it first."

He led her toward the protective shelter of the cave, where they left the blanket and backpack full of food. They moved to the beach and strolled leisurely as he began telling her about Clancy's second offer.

"I knew I wouldn't be able to stay with Willow and Dylan forever. Yes, Boo's house is large, but they need their privacy. Besides, I figure they'll be starting a family sooner rather than later. So I decided to find a place to live. I had thought about the apartment above Sid's diner, where Dylan had lived, but when I met with Clancy the other day, he pitched the idea of me buying his house."

He carefully watched for her reaction.

"Really?" she said enthusiasm filling her voice. "That would be incredible. Clancy's house is located close to the square, so you would easily be able to walk to and from work each day. It's also one of the largest and nicest homes in the Cove. I've never been inside before, but I've driven by it many times. Those old maples in his front yard are breathtaking in the fall."

"I haven't been by to see it yet. Clancy did give me the keys, though. He will be moving to Houston, as I mentioned on Game Night. Since he's leaving a good deal of the furniture behind, I need to see what shape the house is in, as well as the furniture. I also have some furniture of my own still in storage back in L.A., along with lamps, my TV, and more clothes and shoes."

"If your taste doesn't run to what Clancy has, you could always place it with Rylie. Antiques and Mystiques has a section devoted to consignments. She also can help you furnish the house with new things if you wish. She has some kind of business discount she can use. I've wanted to take advantage of it to get a new sofa myself, but I keep pouring my money back into the bakery."

"As you should. It's your livelihood. As long as the sofa is sittable—and it is because I've sat on it—it doesn't matter if it's a little dilapidated."

In his mind, he thought she wouldn't even need that sofa in the future.

If she moved in with him.

"I'd like to go see the house today. Clancy said it might need several updates. Myra, his fiancée, did complain about several things being old and needing to be replaced."

"Pete Pulaski would be your man then," Ainsley said. "He has his own construction business. Carter used to work for Pete on his off-days, as do several firemen in the area. Pete did all the work at Boo's and also fixed up the Garner place for Tenley and Carter."

"If you don't mind then, we'll go over after lunch and see it."

"I'd like that," she told him.

They strolled the beach for another hour, Ainsley collecting a few shells along the way, telling him she had a jar of them by her bedside. Eventually, they turned and went back to the cove itself, claiming the blanket and backpack. They had yet to see a soul, which didn't surprise Jackson. It was a weekday, and children were still in school. The beach near Boo's was as private as it would ever be. His heart told him it was the place to tell Ainsley how he felt about her.

She opened the blanket and let the slight breeze catch it, spreading it on the sand and anchoring it with a few nearby rocks. Jackson removed the food from the backpack and soon their feast was before them. They ate slowly, watching the waves go in and out. Conversation had ceased between them, and a companionable silence blanketed them. He had never been more relaxed in anyone's company.

Ainsley reached for the bag of cookies she had baked and handed one to him. "I won't get my feelings hurt if you don't like them. I know you're not big on sweets."

"It's not that. I enjoyed both flavors of cupcakes you brought to Game Night. I ate one there and even came home and had the other with a large glass of milk. I would be hard-pressed to tell you which was my favorite."

He bit into the cookie, savoring the rich chocolate and crunch of the macadamia nut.

"This is delicious," he told her. "It's not that I'm against sweets. I just didn't eat many growing up. While Boo had a tremendous sweet tooth, she never kept many sweets in the house. My coaches always stressed eating clean and lean, so I filled up on proteins and vegetables, with a little fruit mixed in for sweetness. Old habits die hard, I guess. When I left the Cove, I still never ate many sweets."

Jackson took her hand. "But I think that's going to change now, with my girlfriend being a world-class baker and pastry chef. It's a good thing I've hired Gage to help train me, so I don't put on any weight or if I do, I can work it off."

"I'm glad you like the cookies. But don't ever feel obligated to eat anything I make." She turned her gaze back to the ocean, and for a few minutes, he ate cookies and watched the waves roll in.

He reached for his water, taking a long swallow, finding his mouth dry as nerves filled him. He needed to tell her now.

Placing the empty water bottle down, he took her other hand in his, facing her.

"I have something to say, Ainsley. I thought long and hard if I should say this to you or wait a while, but Willow encouraged me to tell you what was in my heart. I don't expect you to feel the same way after so short a time, but I want us to always be open with each other."

He took a deep breath and blew it out. "I've fallen in love with you, Ainsley. I... I just needed you to know that. I don't expect you to share the same depth of feelings toward me, but I hope you will grow to love me." He squeezed her hands. "I also need you to know that I've never said those words to anyone. Ever."

She burst into tears.

CHAPTER 13

Ainsley felt like a fool as she blubbered away, hard sobs shaking her body violently. Blinded by her tears, she felt Jackson scoop her up and place her in his lap, his strong arms going about her. He held her protectively, rocking her, brushing kisses against her temple.

"I'm sorry, babe. I'm sorry," he finally said, as her sobs subsided. "I knew it was too soon. I should've kept my mouth shut and my feelings to myself."

She gazed up with him. "No," she said through watery eyes, knowing her mascara ran down her cheeks and that she must look a fright. "You were right to tell me. Jackson—I love you, too. So much, it scares me to death."

She buried her face against his shoulder, her arms going about him, gripping him tightly. He was her lifeline. Her reason for being. Her everything.

And then he began... laughing.

His body shook with contained laughter. It finally bubbled up from within him. She raised her head and met his gaze.

"Oh, babe, I'm so relieved. I thought when you began crying a river of tears that I'd totally blown it." He kissed her, swift and hard. "I love you. I love you, Ainsley Robinson."

Jackson kissed her again, this time slow and thorough, causing her bones to melt away into nothingness. She clung to him, kissing him with a desperation that she couldn't explain.

When he broke the kiss, she took his face in her hands and brought her lips back to his, believing she could never get enough of this man.

She felt his smile against her mouth, and then he erupted in laughter again, causing the kiss to end. This time, though, she was okay with that.

"I love you, Jackson," she said. "I did have a case of hero worship back in seventh grade. At first, I was afraid that my feelings for you were left over from that wild crush. But you are so much more than a star athlete from years ago. You are smart. Kind. Funny."

She paused as he used his thumbs to wipe the tears from her cheeks.

"I've never been in love," she admitted. "To be honest, I haven't even dated that much. I was always focused on making enough to money to help with Mom's medical treatments and then paying for community college. I worked double shifts at the restaurants that employed me so that I could bank enough for the tuition at l'Ecole Lenŏtre. Yes, I've seen a few men over the years—but no one compares to you."

Ainsley touched her lips to his.

He smoothed her hair. "I'm the opposite and am man enough to admit it. I've gone out with a lot of women over the years. I was only turned down twice, and I let those slide off me. I worked hard, studying my ass off in college and law school. I've worked even harder ever since I became an attorney. But no one —*no one*—has touched my soul as you have, Ainsley. All my relationships were short-term, with no investment of myself in them. Yes, I've treated the women I've dated well. I've been respectful. But I've never given my heart to anyone.

"Until you."

Jackson kissed her again, a long, drugging kiss that made her forget everything but him.

When he broke it, he framed her face in his hands. "You are the woman I love. Wolves and coyotes mate for life. Swans, too." He smiled. "I want you to be my swan, Ainsley Robinson."

She blinked rapidly. "What are you saying, Jackson?"

"That I want to marry you. I want to be by your side through the good and the bad. I want to have babies with you. I want to be your best friend and lover forever."

A fresh wave of tears blinded her. "It's too soon," she protested, bringing her sleeve to her eyes and wiping it against them.

"Will most people think it's too soon? I'd venture that's a given. But it won't lessen my feelings for you. I believe they will continue to grow over time. That I will love you more tomorrow than today. More next year than this year. More fifty years from now than on our wedding day."

Ainsley buried her face against his chest, hot tears continue to spill from her eyes. She gripped his shoulders tightly.

Raising her head, she whispered, "Is this really happening, Jackson? Tell me I'm not dreaming and that I'll wake up alone in my bed."

He brushed a soft kiss against her lips. "It's real,

love. As real as it gets. Yes, I think everyone in L.A. that I know would think that I'm certifiably crazy at this moment. A good deal of the Cove will, too. But I know my mind and heart." His hand swept back a stray curl from her cheek. "You'll always be the one that I want. The one that I need. The one that I yearn to come home to after a long day at the office."

Jackson kissed her. "We don't have to rush anything, though. We can get married next month. Next year. Five years down the road. I'll leave that up to you."

She laughed, hiccupping as she did so. "I'd marry you tomorrow, Jackson. That's how certain I am." Ainsley paused. "On second thought, tomorrow is a work day for me. Better make it next Monday or Tuesday," she teased.

He roared with laughter, hugging her tightly, kissing her again and again until she was breathless.

"Are you serious about next week?" he asked.

"Are you?" she countered.

He pulled out his phone. "I'm Googling it," he explained. "Give me a minute."

After a quick search, he said, "We need to apply together at a county clerk's office and pay the fees. The license is good state-wide. Can only be used in Oregon." He continued skimming. "We'd need to use it within sixty days."

"How expensive is it?" she asked.

He grinned. "I'm good for it." Then he frowned. "There's a three-day waiting period. No, wait, we can pay another ten or twenty bucks, and they'll waive that." His thumb scrolled down the page. "No blood test needed. They do ask for a government ID."

"Like a driver's license?"

"That'll do the trick. Oh, good. The county clerk

can perform the ceremony for a little over a hundred bucks." He met her gaze. "So, what do you say, Miss Robinson? Are you free next Monday? Oh, damn. I forgot. I'm supposed to meet with Clancy that day. He'll be back from Houston. I need to prepare the documents to take over his law practice."

"Do those have to be filed with the county clerk?" she asked. "If so, we could kill two birds with one stone. If we need a witness, Clancy could be one of them. Willow could be another." She paused. "Of course, if Willow comes, I'll need Rylie there. And Tenley. I don't want her to feel left out."

"Then I better check with the men of Game Night. See if they can come, as well. I'll go by the Barton County clerk's office this week and smooth the way for us. See when he or she has an opening next Monday. Then we can invite our family and friends." He thought a moment. "I'd also like Gillian Roberts there. She's as close to family as Willow and I have now."

"I'd be happy to have Gillian there," Ainsley said. She shook her head. "I still can't believe we're doing this so fast. My head is spinning."

"If you think it's too fast, I can put the brakes on, Ainsley," Jackson said, sincerity shining in his eyes. "I don't want to push you into something."

"You're not," she assured him. "If anything, I'm the one doing the galloping."

"We'll gallop together. Right now, though, I think we need to go see if Clancy's place appeals to us as a place to raise our kids."

He stood, pulling her up with him. His arms went around her. "I'm on a natural high right now. I'm with the woman I love, and she loves me back. We're going to get married. Married!" he shouted, causing a nearby flock of seagulls standing in the sand to scatter, taking flight.

"Let's pack up and head over to Clancy's place," he said.

They gathered their trash and placed it in the backpack, shaking the sand from the blanket and folding it. Jackson took her hand, and Ainsley felt on top of the world, as if she were the heroine in some crazy romance novel. Well, she'd found her own, real-life hero in Jackson Martin.

"Ainsley Martin," she said aloud as they began climbing the steps. "Just practicing."

His eyes gleamed at her. "I like the sound of that." Jackson lifted their joined hands and brush a kiss across her knuckles. "I like it a lot."

They reached the top and returned to Boo's, leaving the blanket in the laundry room and clearing the trash from the backpack. There were still cookies left, and Ainsley set the bag on the kitchen island, where they would be easily spotted, leaving a quick note telling Willow and Dylan to help themselves.

They drove into the Cove, passing where his law office would be on the square, and continuing the few blocks until they reached Clancy Nelson's home. As Jackson got out of the car, it seemed mindboggling that he would be able to walk to work in less than ten minutes, compared to the tortuous commute he'd experienced in L.A.

He removed the keyring from his pocket which Clancy had given him as he and Ainsley started toward the house.

"I like that it's a corner lot," she said. "And I already had mentioned the beautiful maple trees in the yard. Have you been here before?"

"Several times over the years. Boo and Clancy were

tight. Clancy and my grandfather were fishing buddies, and Clancy's wife was a great cook. One thing I really liked about this house was the back yard. It's large and level and would be great for our kids to run around." He hesitated and then said, "I've mentioned kids without even asking if you want any."

"Would it be a dealbreaker if I didn't?" she asked, and his heart sank.

"I would be disappointed because I've always wanted a family of my own, but I could find other outlets. Coaching Little League. That kind of thing."

"It wasn't a test, Jackson, though it may have seemed like one," Ainsley said. "I really want children. I always regretted being an only child, and I was blessed enough to have Rylie act as my sister." She paused and then added, "I guess I wanted to see if you still wanted me without children in the picture."

He reached for her, pulling her into his arms, giving her a reassuring kiss. "I'll always want you, Ainsley. Even when your hair has turned white—or even fallen out. I am happy, though, that you do want to have children. I suppose we can negotiate how many down the line. For now, let's go inside."

They mounted the steps, and she looked at the large porch, thinking about sitting in the swing after dinner with Jackson and talking over their day.

He unlocked the door, and they went inside.

"Let's walk through without making any comments," he suggested. "Then we can discuss what we think of the house."

"All right. I'm going to head upstairs and check it out first."

Ainsley climbed the stairs and went through each room, noting its size and condition. The bathrooms definitely needed updates, but the paint seemed fairly fresh and the carpet, though slightly worn, had no stains.

She passed Jackson on the stairs as he went up and she went down. She explored the first level and then took a seat at the kitchen table to wait for him.

He turned up a few minutes later and joined her, asking, "What do you think?"

"For the most part, it seems to be in good condition. As my dad would have said, it has good bones. On the other hand, the kitchen appliances are ancient, and it's way too small for my taste. All of the bathrooms are so out of date, I would be embarrassed for anyone to see them, much less use them. I do wonder what's underneath this carpet, though."

They began discussing the layout and what it might take to update it to their style. Then they went into the back yard, where Ainsley could see their future children playing and hosting friends for a barbeque. Returning to the house, they sat at the kitchen table again.

"Is this where you can see us?" Jackson asked, his face neutral. "I don't mind putting the money into this place if you do, but I don't want to spend too much, only to find you really didn't like it."

"I love it," she said. "I love the size of the lot. The number of rooms. The location. It would need quite a bit of work, though, and that could get expensive. I suppose we should get Pete Pulaski over here so he could give us an estimate."

"Let's call and see if he's available now. Do you have his number?"

"No, but let me text Willow for it."

Within two minutes, her friend had texted back, providing the contractor's number. Jackson called Pete, speaking directly to him, explaining that he was taking over Clancy's law practice and also might be purchasing Clancy's home.

"I was wanting to get an estimate to see what it would take to put it in the condition I want," Jackson told Pete.

Once he hung up, he told her that Pete was coming over. "He'd been out checking on a job as we spoke, and he's only a few minutes away."

The contractor arrived and walked through the house with them, pointing out things he would do if he himself were moving into the house. He also made a few suggestions, notably knocking down a few walls to open up the floorplan more and to combine the primary bedroom with a smaller secondary one in order to enlarge the bedroom and allow for a larger en suite bathroom.

Jackson asked, "What do you think the house is worth in its current condition?"

"I'm not a realtor, but I could give you a ballpark idea." Pete named a figure and then added, "You can decide what renovations you'd like completed, based upon a list I can provide you tomorrow morning. I'll break it down by job so that you can mix and match, putting together what you might like done if you do buy the place."

"I'm not fond of carpet," Ainsley said. "Is there any way we could pull up a small section and see what the flooring looks like underneath it?"

"I can do that," Pete said, leading them from the kitchen. He pulled a pen knife from his pocket and knelt, slicing away a small portion of carpet and pulling it up. He grinned up at them. "Looks like you have some pretty sweet hardwoods here. I'd have to have more of the carpet pulled, but the boards look in fantastic shape. After a good polish, these floors would gleam like new again."

Pete rose and shook both their hands. "I'll have that estimate for you tomorrow morning, Jackson." He asked for an e-mail address and then wished them a good afternoon.

Once Pete left, Jackson turned to Ainsley, pulling her into his arms. "What do you think, my lovely fiancée? Is this where you want to make a life together?"

"I do. I really do."

"What are your must-haves on the list Pete's providing?" he asked.

"Gutting the kitchen would be my top priority. Then again, I like to cook and spend a lot of time in the kitchen. Pulling up the carpets and restoring the hardwoods would be next. After that? I would leave it up to you."

"I got a decent buyout for my half of the partnership. I'm hoping what I received would cover the cost of buying the house. If we're lucky, even some of the changes we wish to make."

"I feel bad because I don't really have anything to contribute financially," she told him.

"No, your funds are tied up in your business. I get that. We're a team now, though. Our own partnership. What's mine is yours and vice versa. Whatever I can't cover, we can take out a loan. Together."

"What about how much it will cause to purchase Clancy's practice?"

"No need to worry there. Clancy really low-balled that. He has wanted me to take over for him for a long time. I'm hoping he will give us a good price on the house as well, seeing how much needs to be done to the place to make it ours."

He gave her a slow, very thorough kiss, her favorite

one so far because it was in the home they would share. She thought of the many kisses in the years to come and the family they would raise here. It caused tears to spring to her eyes.

Concerned, Jackson asked, "Is there something wrong. Are you having any regrets? I still worry that I pushed you too far and too fast. I never really asked if you wanted a typical wedding. The white dress. Walking down the aisle. Reception after."

"I've never been that kind of girl. My parents also went to a courthouse to get married. They were so poor, Mom didn't even get an engagement or wedding ring. So no, a fancy wedding has never been on my bucket list. Frankly, I think they're a waste of money— money which could be put to better use."

She cupped his cheek. "Now, finding a man I love and deciding to spend the rest of my life with him, definitely on the list."

"I'm afraid we won't be able to take a traditional honeymoon. Your busy season is about to arrive, while I don't want to walk off the job I've just accepted."

"I don't need a honeymoon. I only need you, Jackson."

Ainsley pulled him down so that his lips met hers. Yes, this was all she would ever need.

Jackson broke the kiss. "I think we need to have an impromptu gathering of the Game Night crowd ASAP. The way Pete eyed us, I know he was putting two and two together. I'd hate for gossip to spread about us moving in together without our friends and family knowing first."

"You're right," she agreed. "I'll call Rylie and Tenley. You take care of Gage and Willow."

"Let's plan for pizza at six at Boo's," he said. "Then we can share our good news."

It wasn't just good news. Ainsley knew it was life-altering news.

And that change was possible because of this man. Her man. Her love.

Her future.

CHAPTER 14

Everyone had gathered at Boo's by six o'clock that evening, Gage being the lone exception. He finished with his last client at six and had said he would head over as soon as the training session finished.

Ainsley got out plates from the cupboard as Tenley asked, "What is going on?"

"Don't even bother," Willow said. "I tried to get it out of her when Jackson left to pick up the pizzas. She's not budging."

"Hmm." Tenley studied her, and Ainsley felt a blush creeping up her neck. "I guess we'll have to wait for Jackson to return."

"And for Gage to get here. He should arrive any minute," Willow reminded.

Jackson entered the kitchen with pizza boxes in hand and set them on the island. Dylan and Carter followed him in, and everyone grabbed a plate, going through the makeshift buffet line, claiming slices of pie.

Gage joined them, curiosity written across his face. "Tell me I didn't miss anything," he said.

"Ainsley has been a fortress of steel," Tenley kidded. "We weren't able to get anything out of her. And Jackson just got here with the pizzas."

"Let's everyone get situated, and then we'll talk about this impromptu meeting," Jackson said, placing a slice of sausage and mushroom on his plate.

They headed into the dining room, taking their seats. Jackson sat to Ainsley's right and took her hand beneath the table, squeezing it encouragingly. He looked to her, and she nodded for him to be the one to break their news.

He cleared his throat and said, "Everyone knows I came back to the Cove to take over Clancy's law practice," he began. "I was burned out on criminal law, and the weeks I hiked after my last trial ended helped me to realize a few things. One, I had missed the Cove deeply. L.A. is a sprawling mess of millions of strangers. The Cove is a community, where people look out for one another. I missed being a part of such a group, having that sense of belonging."

He paused, taking a sip of his iced tea. "But more than wanting to live in the Cove again, I had a more personal purpose in mind than professional. I'm thirty-three and more than anything, I wanted to find someone to share my life with and start a family."

Jackson squeezed her hand. "I found the perfect house—and the perfect woman. I know others will think this was lightning fast, but Ainsley and I are on the same page. We want the same things in life." He turned and looked at her, tenderness in his eyes. "And I have found love for the first time in my life."

He raised their joint hands and kissed hers.

Their friends broke out in raucous cheers, everyone standing and wanting to give them congratulatory hugs. All three women had tears in their eyes, and Rylie's began spilling down her cheeks.

"I knew Jackson was the one for you," her cousin said, hugging Ainsley tightly. "I think we all saw the connection between the two of you. It was instantaneous."

By now, Ainsley, too, was crying tears of joy. Jackson put an arm around her, holding her close against his side.

"I know tongues will wag in the Cove about the speed with which we're doing this, but I'm old enough —and confident in us—so I don't care," he told them. "Ainsley and I are adults, and we know our minds. Neither of us has been in love, until now. I think we'll try this for forty or fifty years, and if it doesn't work out, then people can say *I told you so*."

The group laughed, and Gage said, "I think it's great you both know what you want out of life and aren't afraid to go after it. I've never been in love myself, but if I ever find that special someone, I wouldn't waste a single minute apart."

Ainsley marveled at the short speech Gage had made. He rarely said anything personal or took the attention of the group.

"Thanks for your support, Gage," she said, looking directly at him before gazing at the others gathered around. "Thanks to you all. You are both family and friends to us, and your support means the world."

"When is the wedding?" Willow eagerly asked. "I assume you'll want to have a quick ceremony as Dylan and I did, but we'd be happy to host a reception for you at Boo's."

"We were thinking about next Monday," Jackson revealed. "We'd like all of you there, if possible."

"Don't hold off on my account," Dylan said, "but I have a state law enforcement conference that starts this Friday and runs through Monday. I'm sorry to miss the ceremony."

Carter cleared his throat. "I'm afraid Tenley and I are out, too. I'm filming a pilot on Monday. It's taken a lot to get it scheduled, and I would hate to have to throw a monkey wrench into all the planning. We weren't even going to say anything to you until the shoot was over and we learned whether or not the network would pick it up, but I want to be up front about why we can't attend."

She glanced at her fiancé. "It doesn't have to be this coming Monday. Are you willing to wait another week or longer?"

Love shone in his eyes as Jackson said, "I would wait a lifetime for you, love." He turned and faced the group. "How does the next Monday look for everyone?"

"Good for us," Willow said enthusiastically, and Tenley echoed the same.

Rylie said, "You know Antiques and Mystiques is closed on Mondays. I'll be there."

Ainsley turned to Gage. "What about you?"

"I do have clients on Mondays. If you could narrow down a timeframe for me, though, I would like to be there. I could give my clients a week's notice and schedule a makeup session that way."

"Then it's settled," Jackson said. "Not this coming Monday, but the next one. That will also give Ainsley time to talk to her staff at Buttercup Bakery and make arrangements. Someone will have to fill the Monday order for her. Ainsley and I will go to the county clerk's office next Monday while she's off and pick up our wedding license. I'll even run by there tomorrow and arrange a time for the ceremony so I can let you know. Gage, what would work best for you?"

She thought it incredibly sweet that Jackson would ask Gage, who was such a new friend, what might be convenient for him. It let her know what a thoughtful man she was marrying.

"Monday mornings are really booked for me until noon," Gage replied. "I only have two individual clients on Monday afternoons, and they would be easy to reschedule."

"Good to know," Jackson said. "I'll arrange with the county clerk for an afternoon wedding. I'll aim for two. That will give everyone time to tend to whatever business they need to that morning and still make it over to the courthouse."

"It will also give me more time to pull together a reception to celebrate," Willow said. She looked to Tenley and Rylie. "I'm expecting the two of you to help." She looked back at Ainsley. "Would it be all right to have a party that night? About six?"

"That would be perfect," Ainsley told her friend and soon to be sister-in-law. "Thank you for doing this for us."

Willow smiled. "Well, I only have one brother. I do feel rather fond of him. I would like the two of you to be able to celebrate in casual style."

As they ate, they talked about the wedding celebration, with Jackson saying he would like it to be similar to the one they held in Boo's honor after her passing.

"Ainsley, work on a list of guests you want there," Tenley suggested. "And we need to find someone else to bake the wedding cake."

"No," Jackson protested. "I want my future wife to bake it. I know wedding cakes are a lot of work, but it would be special if she made it for us. I know I'll be able to taste the love baked into it."

"You do know a small groom's cake should also be baked," Gage said. "Hopefully, chocolate."

Everyone laughed, knowing what a chocoholic Gage was.

"I will take care of our wedding cake, but I think I'll let Gus do the groom's cake. He has a nice touch when it comes to smaller cakes."

The women made plans to meet at five the next day for an early dinner at Eats 'n Treats. Ainsley suggested inviting Gillian, saying she was someone Jackson wanted at both the wedding ceremony and reception.

"I'll call Gillian tonight," Rylie volunteered. "We'll nail down everything needed to be done at tomorrow's dinner." She hugged Ainsley once more. "I couldn't be happier for you, Cuz. Jackson is an amazing man and will make an excellent husband and father."

They all started toward the door, with Jackson claiming Dylan's truck keys so he could put Ainsley's bicycle in the back and take her home.

As they walked out, he said, "We forgot to tell you about buying Clancy's house."

"That's wonderful," Tenley exclaimed. "I know Willow and I were pleased with the work Pete Pulaski did on our houses, in case you think anything needs to be done to it."

"We're a step ahead of you, Tenley," Jackson informed her. "We met with Pete today. Some of the furniture we like, and some we'll want to get rid of. If you have room for those pieces in your consignment section, we'd like to place them there. I have a few pieces in storage down in L.A., but we'll also need to order some new items for the house. Ainsley says you have a great eye. We'd appreciate your help in getting our home furnished."

Rylie rubbed her hands together in glee. "This is right up my alley. I'd be happy to help out in any way I can."

Ainsley went to Dylan's truck, while Jackson placed her bike in the truck's bed.

As they drove into town, he laced his fingers through hers. "That went well," he said. "I hope you don't mind waiting that extra week. I also thought it was important to make Gage part of this celebration. I know I've just met him, but he's a friend of yours and everyone else's. I like him quite a bit."

"Waiting two weeks will certainly give us more time to plan. I like that we won't be rushed. That way, you can get everything settled with Clancy regarding assuming his practice and hopefully handle the sale of the house, too. It'll also give Pete a chance to start working his magic once we decide what projects to move forward with."

"I would hate to have us try and move in while construction is going on. Do you think we could stay at your apartment until the house is ready?" he asked.

"Well, since I am the landlord, I can easily arrange that," she said with a laugh.

"Once we do move into the house, are you going to try and let the apartment?"

"No, I could actually use it for storage. It could also serve as my office. It would be convenient to have office space on site and not clutter up our home with business stuff."

"That's a terrific idea." He pulled into a spot directly behind the bakery. "And I have an even better idea now."

Jackson leaned in for a slow, sweet kiss, flooding her with warmth.

Breaking it, he said, "Ainsley, more than anything, I would like to make love to you. Tonight."

CHAPTER 15

Jackson watched carefully as Ainsley blinked several times, taking in his request. He knew from their previous encounter that either her experience with sex was limited or her sexual partners had been selfish jackasses.

Probably both.

But more than anything, he wanted to be one with this woman. He had pulled Dylan aside and asked his brother-in-law if he had any condoms handy. When Dylan handed over his keys, he also passed Jackson three condoms, telling him he hoped that would be enough, a roguish smile on his face.

He tucked her hair behind her ear. "But only if you want to make love. There's no rush. I know it's been a long day."

"It's not that," Ainsley began. "I do want to be with you in the worst way." She glanced down. "But... well, you're Jackson Martin. You've had a string of women falling at your feet since kindergarten. I remember how girls used to throw themselves at you. I'm sure college was no different. And you've lived in L.A. for years now." She raised her eyes, meeting his gaze. "I'm not sophisticated. I'm definitely not very experienced. I mean, I'm not a virgin, but I am pretty limited in what I know and how to do it."

He framed her face between his hands. "Babe, you practically exploded when I touched your breasts. You came with very little effort. I think all you've needed is the right lover to come along. A man who cares about making *you* the priority." He kissed her lightly. "I'm that man, Ainsley. I love you."

Still, doubt flickered in her lovely periwinkle eyes. "But you've made love to dozens of women, Jackson."

"No," he said firmly, his thumbs caressing her cheeks. "I've had sex with more than my share of females. But you'll be the first woman I've ever *made love* with. And I know this experience will be sensual and meaningful—because you're the only one I've ever loved."

He gave her a soft kiss, hoping he had talked her off the ledge. She was a beautiful woman, confident in business. Like him, though, she had never been in love. He wanted time with her to show her how good they would be together.

"Would you like to come up?" she asked.

"Definitely."

Jackson claimed her bike from the bed of the truck and escorted her inside the bakery and up to her apartment, which he was seeing for the first time. It was incredibly small, and he hoped after reading over Pete Pulaski's bid tomorrow and okaying it, that the contractor could start work immediately. Jackson liked having space and hoped he and Ainsley wouldn't have to live here for too long. On second thought, he might actually prefer living at Boo's with Willow and Dylan. But that could wait. Tonight was all about Ainsley and introducing her to what physical lovemaking was all about.

With someone you loved...

"It's not much," she apologized, removing her jacket and taking his, setting both down on the couch. "But it's home."

He wrapped his arms around her, pulling her to him. "Home is where you are. It always will be."

Jackson bent and pressed a soft kiss on her lips, lips he wanted to devour. But he wanted tonight to be special. The first time between them. The first in what would be the beginning of their life together.

Ainsley was the one eager to kick it up a notch. She teased his mouth open, lighting him on fire as her tongue swept into his mouth, stroking his tongue. As the kiss progressed, he realized it was the best kiss of his life—because it was instigated by the woman who had claimed his heart. Who had made him realize he could build a life in his childhood hometown with her. A woman who was smart and resourceful and kind. One who was a balm to his soul.

His arms tightened around her, and Jackson relished the feel of her warm, lean frame against his. Everything about this moment felt right. Real. Wonderful.

She broke the kiss, breathless, staring up at him. "I love you," she declared. "I hope I don't disappoint you."

"Never."

"I want you to teach me, Jackson. I want to learn how to please you. I don't want you to think you've made a mistake in proposing to me."

His hands slid to her ass, squeezing it. "No mistakes on my part. You feel amazing."

"No, seriously," she said. "I know I'm lacking as far

as sexual experience goes—but I've never backed down from a challenge in my life. I've worked hard to get everything I have. I will work hard to make you so happy, you'll never regret—"

He cut her off with a hard, demanding kiss, his hands kneading her buttocks, his nostrils inhaling the vanilla scent rising from her skin.

When Jackson finally broke the kiss, he said, "No regrets. Ever. *You're* the one that I want, Ainsley. We'll learn together what pleases each other." He smiled. "And have a whole lot of fun while we do so. It won't all happen the first time. In one night. But we've got a lifetime to discover everything about one another."

He swept her into his arms. "I also know if I don't get these clothes off you soon, I might explode."

A teasing light came into her eyes. "Well, we can't have that. I am getting rather warm. I could stand to shed a few layers. And I am eager to see what's under your clothes, too."

Her words caused him to rush into the bedroom. Fumbling with the light switch, he turned it on. She frowned.

"We are not doing this in the dark," he told her. "I want to see the beautiful package I'm unwrapping. Not just feel and smell it. I want to watch you come and hear you cry out my name."

Ainsley's eyes widened. She swallowed visibly. "I want to see you, too," she said softly.

He set her on her feet, kissing her again, his fingers pushing into the silky tresses as he devoured her mouth. She moaned low, clinging to him, making him smile.

He broke the kiss and proceeded to remove her sweater, his fingers skimming her skin once it was removed. They danced up her arms and across her shoulders. Down her back, unclasping her bra and discarding it. Bare to the waist now, she blushed.

"I've told you before—and I'll say it every day of our lives together. You are beautiful. So very, very beautiful."

He nuzzled her neck, finding her pulse, sensing her jump at the touch of his lips against it. Her scent drove him wild, and he kissed her throat, finally nipping at it, hearing her whimper.

"I could gobble you up," he declared, his eyes dropping to her breasts.

"I see where you're looking, Mr. Martin," she said primly. "And I have a request. I'd like to feel your bare skin against mine."

"That's an easy fix." He grabbed the hem of his shirt and quickly pulled it over his head, tossing it aside, then reached for her again, his arms enveloping her. "Mmm. Good idea," he murmured, his lips returning to her throat.

He kissed his way downward, his hands moving to cup her breasts, his thumbs finding her erect nipples and moving in slow circles around them. Her sigh was music to his ears.

"You're still wearing too much," he told her as he unbuttoned her jeans, backing her to the bed.

She bumped into the mattress and sat as he knelt and removed her shoes and thick socks, setting them directly under the bed. Standing, he took her hands and pulled her to her feet again. This time, he slid down her zipper and peeled the skintight jeans from her. She lifted each foot, helping him remove them totally.

Now, she stood in a pair of black panties, dark

against her pale skin, his heart beginning to pound, the blood rushing to his ears. He cupped her, feeling how damp she already was, and pushed aside the material, sliding a finger into her. Ainsley groaned, her hands grasping his waist.

"Oh, you're definitely wet for me," he purred into her ear, his teeth tugging on her earlobe, her shiver a true turn-on.

Jackson removed his finger and slipped both hands inside her panties, kneading her ass again, thinking it was perfect. Then he slowly pulled them down, letting them drop to the floor. He captured her waist and lifted her, leaving them behind as he placed her on the edge of the bed. She looked up at him, her eyes hooded. He nudged her back onto the bed, her legs dangling from it.

Exactly where he needed her.

He knelt and placed his hands on her knees, pushing them apart. Feeling her stiffen, he glanced up. Her head had risen from the bed, a worried look on her face.

"Do you trust me?" he asked huskily.

"Yes," she whispered, her eyes large.

"This is me loving you. Only you, Ainsley."

He squeezed her knees, his thumb stroking her lightly as they continued to gaze at one another. Then he opened her legs wider, his fingers lightly dancing up her thighs. He placed one palm flat against her belly, and she lowered her head again. He could still feel the tension within her, though.

"I'm nervous," she said quietly. "I think I know what you're going to do. I've... no one... I haven't done this before."

"Then we'll see if you like it," he said in a nonthreatening way. "If you don't, we won't do it again. But if you do, we'll see what you like about it."

"Okay," she said, so softly he almost missed it.

Jackson traced the seam of her sex with a finger, and she whimpered. He continued to do so slowly, letting her get used to him. Then he slid a finger inside her, stroking her deeply. She mewled like a kitten. He added a second one, going deeper, holding her steady with his other hand against her belly as her hips started to rise. He knew from before that it wouldn't take much. She had come easily when he feasted on her breasts, and it was the rare woman who did so. He figured Ainsley was a powder keg ready to explode.

He kept up the motion, caressing her, and she began moaning. Writhing beneath him. The little noises gave way to his name.

"Jackson? Jackson. This is... incredible. I feel like... I'm out of control."

"Hush," he told her. "Don't try to talk. Just feel. Go with it. Ride it, Ainsley. Let go."

"I'm scared," she admitted.

"Look at me," he commanded.

She lifted her head.

"You're with me. You'll always be safe with me."

"I know."

"Then all you have to do is enjoy."

His fingers found her G-spot and he applied a little more pressure. Suddenly, she gasped, her hips thrusting, her breathing shallow and quick.

"Let go, baby," he urged.

And she did.

Jackson felt her tremors, and her juices flowed as she exploded. She cried out his name, and he couldn't help but smile. Love for Ainsley flooded him. Happiness filled him.

She stopped moving, but he didn't want her to stop feeling these new sensations. He slipped his hands beneath her buttocks and slowly licked her, tasting her sweet juices.

"Jackson!"

He glanced up. "Yes?"

"What are you doing?"

"Making love to you, babe. Let's see how this goes."

"Goes? Goes? What... ah... oh! Oh, yes!"

He smiled against her, his tongue plunging into her, the sweetness surrounding him. He proceeded to feast upon her, hearing her cries of pleasure as another orgasm rocked her body. When she stilled, he kissed his way up her belly to her throat and finally her mouth. He dragged his tongue along the seam of her mouth, parting it, and then plunging inside. The kiss was full of heat and desire, and Ainsley moved underneath him.

She whipped her head, breaking the kiss. "Get those damn jeans off," she demanded. "I don't think I can wait."

Jackson pushed off the bed and quickly unbuckled his belt as he slipped out of his shoes. He made quick work of the jeans and slipped off his socks, returning to the bed, hovering over her.

Her hands went to his chest, exploring its planes. "Ooh, a six-pack. I like it." She leaned up and kissed along his ribs and then flicked her tongue across his nipple, causing him to growl.

"Wait," he said, remembering the condom.

He scurried off the bed, retrieving it from his pocket and tearing open the foil packet, slipping it over his aroused penis.

"Ready now," he told her, returning to the bed.

He kissed her deeply, his hands roaming her body, hers doing the same to his.

"I can't wait," he murmured against her mouth. "I want you now."

"I need you now," she urged.

He brushed his finger along her, seeing she was more than ready for him. He pushed inside her, reveling in the feel of her.

"Wrap your legs around me."

She did—and he went even deeper, hearing her moan.

They found their rhythm quickly, so quickly it startled him. It was if they had always done this together. His mouth sought hers and his tongue mimicked his penis, thrusting into her, dominating her, giving, taking, giving, taking more and more until his climax slammed into him. He pumped away, pure joy spreading through him.

Jackson collapsed atop Ainsley, quickly rolling to his side in order not to crush her. He enveloped her in his arms, holding her close, feeling her heart as it thumped wildly in her chest, knowing she could feel the same from him. He kissed her slowly, still inside her, reveling in the feel and smell of her.

"That was unreal," she said when he broke the kiss. "I'm not sure if I even know what just happened."

He kissed her brow. "That was us coming together. Two people who are in love. Who want to make the other perfectly happy."

"You did all the work."

He kissed the tip of her nose. "It wasn't work at all, babe. It was pure pleasure."

"Well, I liked everything you did," she said saucily. "And I plan to do some of the same to you the next time." She paused, turning shy. "You'll have to guide me, Jackson. Help me understand what you like."

"I will," he promised. "For now, go to sleep."

"I don't want to," she pouted. "I don't want to miss a moment with you."

"You, young lady, have a bakery to run." He glanced at the clock on her bedside. "And it's your bedtime. Besides, I need to get home. I've got a training session early tomorrow morning with Gage." He grinned. "Although this was quite the workout. I may turn all my training over to you."

Ainsley giggled, a sound of pure joy that tugged at Jackson's heart.

"Do you really have to leave?"

"I think I should," he told her. "But I'm happy to come back whenever you like."

"I'm meeting the girls at five tomorrow for dinner. Remember, we're going to talk about the wedding."

"Then I should be here around seven," he promised. "I'm going to go to the courthouse tomorrow and arrange a time for our wedding. And then I've got to make it to the office and start looking over Clancy's files."

He kissed her soundly and then left the bed, dressing as she watched him, an approving look in her eyes.

"We didn't talk about what updates we would have Pete do," she said.

"You told me your priorities. I'll forward the estimate to you, but I plan on talking to Pete tomorrow. The sooner he can get started on things, the better. I also will call Clancy and tell him we're buying the house and that I'm drawing up the paperwork."

Jackson bent and kissed her. "I'll see you tomorrow. Goodnight, sweetheart."

He left her in the bedroom, the hardest thing he'd ever had to do, and drove Dylan's truck back to Boo's. The entire way, it was as if his blood sang out her name.

He couldn't wait to be married to Ainsley—and start their lives together.

CHAPTER 16

A insley awoke moments before the alarm sounded. She leaned over and turned it off and then stayed in bed a few extra minutes, her thoughts lingering on Jackson and what had occurred between them last night.

There was no doubt about it. The man knew his way around a woman's body. He had explored her in ways no man had ever done. Not only had Jackson touched her physically, but he had touched her soul. She looked forward to spending more time with him and learning what would please him. She realized last night had been about him catering to her needs and making her comfortable, and she loved him for doing so. Having his love emboldened her, and she wanted to show him the depth of her feelings for him. She also wanted to learn what would arouse him and make him happy and looked forward to their next physical encounter.

She hadn't minded him using a condom, but she was going to ask him to forgo doing so the next time they were together. He had mentioned his age a couple of times and how he wanted children. So did she. She didn't see the point in them waiting to start a family when it was a priority for both of them.

Energized by the thought of having Jackson's babies, Ainsley quickly got ready and headed down to the bakery, attacking her list and getting items into the ovens. Gus arrived before Gloria and Sheila as he always did, and while they made donuts and cinnamon rolls, she told him she had news.

"You're going to marry that lawyer, aren't you?" he asked.

"Yes, I am. And I would like you to make the groom's cake."

Gus grinned, his pleasure obvious. "You would trust me to do that, Ainsley?"

"I can't think of anyone I would want to make it more than you, Gus."

He nodded thoughtfully. "Chocolate, I'm assuming? Most groom's cakes are chocolate."

"Yes, that will be fine. Jackson wants me to make our wedding cake. It will be my gift to him."

Gus rubbed his chin in thought. "What do you want on the groom's cake? I want to personalize it."

Ainsley was at a loss as to what to tell him. For a moment, panic seized her heart and squeezed hard. What did she really know about Jackson? Yes, he was a good man. He'd been brought up right by Boo. He was an attorney. He was only beginning to like sweets, but she didn't know all the little things that a fiancée should know about the man she was going to marry. She had no idea what his favorite color or movie might be. She had no idea what his favorite food was or his favorite memory.

Why was she even marrying this man?

They had rushed into it, and Ainsley regretted it.

Then she decided to push the doubt aside. She

didn't need to know all those little things about Jackson. They had a lifetime to learn every small detail about each other. What she did know was he loved her, and she loved him. That was the most important thing.

"All I can tell you is that I love him more than I thought possible, Gus. I'm leaving the cake's design in your hands."

Her second-in-command nodded thoughtfully. "I'll work on it, Ainsley. Do you want me to tell you what I'm doing, or would you rather it be a surprise?"

"Either. I'll be working on our wedding cake. That'll take up a lot of my time. That reminds me, we will be getting married not this coming Monday, but the next one. I'm going to need you to take the weekly order and purchase everything at Costco and the specialty outlet on that Monday. I'll give you use of my SUV. Can you do that for me?"

"I don't have a car. I haven't driven in a long time," he said quietly, flushing a dull red. "Not since that night. You know the one I'm talking about. I don't even have a driver's license anymore. My cousin drops me here each morning. Or I ride my bike."

"We can find someone to drive you. I'll bet Sheila would be happy to do so. She's always asking for ways she can help out more."

Gus reached over and placed his hand over hers. "You know I haven't had a drink since that night."

She saw how serious his expression was. "You told me so, and I believe you, Gus."

"I have a confession to make. I've never told anyone. Not even my attorney. But I wasn't driving the car that night, Ainsley. I had gone to my daughter's piano recital that afternoon. I was sober and had been for twenty-three days. She was so happy I came to hear her play even though her mom and I had split up a few years earlier. Seeing that look on her face, I wanted to always to keep that smile there," he shared. "I had decided that I wanted to see her and my son on a more regular basis. Then it all went to hell in a handbasket."

Ainsley put her hand atop his. "What happened, Gus?"

"My baby brother came to see me that night. He had been drinking. I understand now that alcoholism is a disease. That it can run through families. My dad was a drunk and his dad before him, too. I became one—but I was ready to give it up—for my kids. I had caused my ex-wife and them a world of hurt. I finally understood that I could make a change in my life. But Bobby, he was in a bad place. I tried to get him to stay over, but that meant sleeping on my floor. He didn't want to. I told him to let me drive him home, but he refused. I finally said I would ride with him and sleep on his sofa. I thought being in the car, I could help watch his speed. Make sure he didn't do anything foolish.

"I was wrong."

Gus shook his head sadly. "He always took chances. Even as a kid. He was the one who climbed the highest trees. Waded out into the ocean the farthest. That kind of thing."

She squeezed his hand. "What happened?"

"It doesn't matter now," he said sadly, tears starting to stream down his cheeks. "We crashed. He killed a dad and daughter and hurt the mother. Bobby had knocked up a girl. That was what he had told me that night. He'd been drinking to celebrate it. He was going to ask her to marry him."

Gus brushed away the tears. "He had a chance to

be a better man to his kid than I had been to mine. I told him I would take the blame—if he got clean. Killing someone scared him into being sober, Ainsley. Bobby hasn't touched a drop since then. He married that girl. They have two kids now. He's a good man and has a good life."

Her heart broke for Gus. He had taken the blame for his brother's actions, which had cost him his own kids.

"You should tell your son and daughter this, Gus," she urged.

He shook his head. "I don't think they'd believe me. They've thought ill of me for so long now. They've moved on. At least what I did gave Bobby a chance to be the husband and father I'd never been."

"Where is he now?" she asked.

"California. He got a job offer with a freight line. He's a terminal manager now. I haven't seen him since I went to prison. We stay in touch, though."

"You sacrificed a lot for him."

"It was worth it. Bobby's made a good life for his family, Ainsley." He pulled a handkerchief from his pocket and blew his nose. "Thank you for the faith you've had in me. Not just in making this cake, but in hiring me. Giving me more responsibility. Everything."

Gus stood abruptly and left the kitchen, going to the restroom. She realized he needed a bit of time to pull himself together. When he returned, they went back to work as if his confession had never occurred. She was thankful that he had trusted her enough to tell her the truth. She only hoped one day he could tell his children the truth.

Gloria and Sheila arrived, and Ainsley also shared her good news with them, explaining when the wedding was and that Jackson and she would delay their honeymoon because of him starting work at his new practice and tourist season approaching.

"But I will need help getting ready for that week's order."

Sheila volunteered to drive Gus to Seattle to pick up what the staff would need that week. They took a few minutes talking over ideas for the wedding cake's design, and then Ainsley told them it was time to get to work.

Once things slowed down later that morning, she played with various ideas and finally hit upon how she would craft the cake.

She checked her e-mail around noon, eager to see if Jackson had forwarded Pete's bid for the work on Clancy's place. It was in her inbox, and the number, which she assumed was reasonable, still made her wince. She knew Willow and Tenley wouldn't have recommended Pete unless his prices and work were good. She had seen the results at both her friend's houses and knew Pete's crew would do a nice job. The thought of spending that kind of money, though, boggled her mind. The fact that she wouldn't be contributing to it bothered her even more.

Ainsley called Jackson. He picked up after the first ring.

"Hello, Beautiful."

She smiled to herself. "Hey, you. I just saw Pete's estimate for the work. It's a lot, Jackson. I think we need to scale back. Only choose a few projects to do now."

"I've taken care of it," he assured her. "We're not biting off too much. Pete is going to start tomorrow."

"Even before the sale is concluded?" she asked worriedly.

"I spoke with Clancy for almost half an hour this morning. We agreed upon a price for the house. I drew up the papers and e-mailed the docs to him. We'll close by the end of the week. We both feel comfortable allowing Pete inside to begin the work. Rylie's meeting me at the house now to talk about which furniture to remove. Which she can put on consignment and which we should give away because it's too worn."

Jackson had shared with Ainsley what pieces he had in storage and what he would like to bring up to the Cove, as well as what items of Clancy's they might need. She trusted her cousin and knew Rylie would help advise them on how to handle everything.

"We can sit and work with Rylie about what we need to order after she's seen the place."

"This is going to cost a lot, Jackson. And I'm not contributing anything."

"We talked about this, Ainsley. Right now, you need to put your money back into the bakery. A marriage isn't always a fifty-fifty partnership. Sometimes, one person gives more than the other, whether it's financially, physically, or emotionally. We're doing this for us. I'm not worried. Neither should you be."

"All right," she said, understanding what he said in theory but still feeling she fell short.

"Have you been thinking about our wedding cake?"

"I have," she said, excited about the prospect. "Are you wanting it to be a surprise?"

"No. I know it's a lot of work, and I want to hear about each step of the way."

"I'll share the design with you tonight. You can help me make any adjustments."

"I'm looking forward to that. Want to have dinner?"

"Yes," she said, happy to know they would have time together.

"I'll pick something up and be at your place at five-thirty, okay?"

"That's fine. Oh, did you go to the courthouse?"

"I did. I'll tell you about my visit over dinner. I can't wait to see you."

"Same," she said, a part of her still not believing this wonderful man was hers.

"Ainsley? I love you. Don't ever forget that," Jackson said.

"Hearing that, I'll probably float through the rest of my day," she said, laughing. "I love you, Jackson. I love you so much."

She ended the call and told Gus she would take over the kneading of the bread. The motion soothed her and gave her time to finalize the design for their wedding cake in her head. When she finished working the dough, she put pen to paper and drew up what she envisioned.

"Gus, come look at this."

He came and listened as she walked him through the design. When she finished, she saw the huge grin on his face.

"That'll be the best damn wedding cake ever, Ainsley," he declared. "You'll need to put it on the website."

She often replaced photos on the bakery's website, updating it regularly to showcase what new items she tried.

"I hope I can pull it off," she said.

"Have faith in yourself," Gus told her. "You'll do it."

Ainsley couldn't wait to show her sketches to Jackson.

CHAPTER 17

G erard McGreer looked into the mirror and saw his transformation was finally complete.

He had become Anthony Abbott.

He had done exactly what his attorney had told him to do. The day Gerard was found not guilty, he had filed the petition online to have his name legally changed. His second move had been to Google L.A.'s top plastic surgeons. Cost didn't matter. He had made plenty of money on the dark web, as well as slowly and methodically taking small amounts from numerous accounts from places he had worked over the years. It was done on a rotating system so that it would escape notice. He had shut down all of that once he had been indicted by the grand jury for rape and murder, not wanting any of his extracurricular activities discovered while he was awaiting trial.

Still, he had oodles of money in numerous offshore accounts, as well as stashes of cryptocurrency under various names. That meant he could book the best plastics man available. He had been told when he called Dr. Knott's office that there were no openings for consultations for three months, time he wasn't willing to waste. The brief time of his incarceration had taught him to live to the fullest every possible moment.

He politely asked to be placed on Dr. Knott's waiting list in case an opening occurred, while scheduling an appointment for the beginning of May. The receptionist told him he would be notified by the scheduling department if anything did open up.

Once he hung up, he immediately hacked into the plastic surgeon's practice. The first thing he did was move himself to the top of the waiting list. The second thing was to check the next day's schedule to see who had consultations with Dr. Knott.

He discovered it was a surgery-only day, as was the next one, which worked to Gerard's benefit because it gave him two days to create an opening in the schedule. He selected the name of the first appointment and then researched everything he could about Timothy Thompson, who held the slot. By the end of the day, he knew more about Timothy than the man's family or employer ever did. It was a piece of cake to break into Timothy's house. His alarm system was a simple one, and Timothy slept in a separate room from his wife, due to his excessive snoring. Mrs. Thompson had complained about it enough on social media, citing her husband's upcoming surgery with the renowned Dr. Knott to have the problem repaired, including a new nose job.

The couple, in their late forties and childless, did have carbon monoxide detectors, but he removed the batteries from them. Many people were careless when it came to smoke or carbon monoxide detectors, forgetting to replace the batteries yearly, or neglecting to put any in altogether. He did the same for the smoke detectors and would let the authorities think whatever they would of that.

He checked each bedroom and found both occupants asleep. Since carbon dioxide was odorless, colorless, and tasteless—and the pair was asleep—they most likely would not know what hit them. Even if they did awaken, they would be disoriented, with a pounding headache, nausea, and an accelerated heart rate. They wouldn't be thinking clearly enough to know to get out of the house. Before he started a fire in the fireplace, though, he slipped into each bedroom, making certain both Thompsons were asleep and their doors open. The accountant's snores were so loud that Timothy could sleep through an L.A. earthquake with ease—along with his imminent death.

It only took a few moments to photograph his subject. Timothy was the true kill. His wife was merely collateral damage, and so Gerard wouldn't photograph her. He enjoyed looking at pictures of his various victims. Usually, he took them before, during, and after death occurred. This time, though, he couldn't expose himself to the carbon monoxide and would have to make do with photos of the sleeping Timothy before he succumbed to the poisoned air. With Timothy being asthmatic, he would be even more susceptible to the carbon monoxide being released into the air.

Returning to the den and its wood-burning fireplace, he closed the flue and started a fire. Chances of carbon monoxide poisoning were much higher with a wood-burning fireplace, which he had seen on social media posts. He shook his head, thinking how much of people's lives had become open books, thanks to various outlets where people posted regularly. It had saved him time, knowing he could easily bring about their deaths using their own fireplace against them.

The fire burned cheerfully in the grate as the smoke started backing up into the room. He quietly slipped from the house, his first kill since his trial almost textbook in nature.

The deaths of the couple were featured on the noon news the next day.

The morning after the deaths were reported, he gladly took the call from the person who scheduled Dr. Knott's appointments, telling him of an opening at eight-thirty tomorrow for his consultation. Gerard eagerly accepted it and met with the plastic surgeon the next day.

He had been honest with the doctor, telling Dr. Knott that he had been unjustly accused of a horrendous crime and how it had ruined his life, complaining how he would never be able to work again because employers would Google his name and read about the trial, which had been splashed across headlines across the country and displayed prominently on every Internet news site. He did tell Dr. Knott how he had already petitioned to have his name changed, which was the first step in separating himself from the crime, but that he also required a new look. He fed into the plastic surgeon's ego, telling Knott he was the only person who could help save Gerard's life by creating a new face for him.

Fortunately, Dr. Knott told him only a few adjustments would be necessary to give him an entirely new look. Digital photographs were taken of his current face, with particular attention paid to the nose area. Knott used computer software in order to manipulate the photographs, giving Gerard a better idea of the results. The surgeon walked him through rhinoplasty and how he would alter Gerard's nose. They also agreed to chin surgery, in order to balance his profile.

The surgeon assured him this would give him an entirely different look.

He had decided he would merely shave his head since he was prematurely balding, but Dr. Knott asked him about hair implants, which appealed to Gerard's vanity. They required little effort on the surgeon's part, and it would allow him to keep a headful of hair. He readily agreed to everything the physician mentioned and impressed upon Dr. Knott how he wanted these changes done as soon as possible. He told the doctor he could change his patient's life—literally save it—if he operated on him as soon as possible.

Having already done a deep dive into Knott, he had a suspicion of what might follow next. Gerald offered to double the surgeon's fees if Knott agreed to operate immediately. He hoped he wouldn't have to kill again to get moved up on the good doctor's operating schedule. While he enjoyed killing, he didn't want to waste precious time doing so, because it would have to be a fast kill. He preferred savoring them. Timothy Thompson had been a necessary exception.

Dr. Knott readily agreed to move Gerald to the front of the line—at triple the usual fees.

He took a few moments to pretend to consider it and then agreed, thinking the man greedy. Gerard decided to let Dr. Knott operate and handle the follow-up appointments. Then he would eliminate him, as well as remove all records of Gerard having been a patient of the plastic surgeon.

Over the next three months, he had the surgery and gradually healed. The first few days he experienced the slight bleeding and drainage of mucus and old blood. Dr. Knott had not only packed his nose internally for a week, but he had also taped Gerard's nose with a splint for protection and further support.

His swelling had been less than most, according to his physician.

Other things had moved smoothly, as if Fate reached out and kissed him. Despite Jackson Martin's warning of a crowded docket, the court had ruled within six weeks to grant Gerard's name change to Anthony Abbott, and he had placed the appropriate notices in the obscure newspapers recommended by the court clerk. He had been worried that some eagle-eyed reporter would see these notices in the major daily newspapers, which is why he had been upset upon learning of the publication part of the process and how the notices had to appear for four weeks in a row.

Everything had gone through accordingly to plan. Legally, he was now Anthony Abbott. He thought his new name had a regal ring to it and matched his new face. He had seen Dr. Knott today, with the plastics man dismissing him, saying his job was now done. Knott had complimented him on his new look, that of no glasses. A month earlier, he had undergone LASIK surgery, correcting the nearsightedness which has caused him to wear glasses. Without the heavy frames —and with his new nose and chin—Gerard McGreer no longer existed.

He smiled into the mirror, admiring the dental work he had undergone two weeks ago. He had done so under Anthony's name, having his teeth capped, giving him a brilliant smile. He had practiced for hours in the mirror, perfectly an easy smile which would disarm others. He would let the oral and eye surgeons both live because they had no way to link Anthony to the old name and face of Gerard McGreer.

But Dr. Knott was another matter.

He had spent the past couple of months learning

the plastic surgeon's routines and knew he had a gambling problem, which is why Knott had squeezed his patient for the additional fees. He knew now that Dr. Knott owed over four hundred thousand in gambling debts. He had also taken out second mortgages on his L.A. home in Bel Air. And his secondary homes in Aspen and Malibu. He decided to leave enough clues so the police would believe that in desperation, Dr. Knott decided to end his life due to the massive debts, rather than have the criminals he owed do so for him.

Composing a beautiful suicide note for Knott, he had explained in it how Knott was in debt and how the thugs he owed had threatened to break both his hands if he failed to pay by a certain deadline, which had arrived. The note explained that surgery was his reason for living, giving back to those who needed his skills in order to make for a better life. Gerard thought it some of his finest work.

He printed out a copy of the suicide letter now, folding and placing it inside his pocket, along with the barbiturates he would mix in alcohol for Dr. Knott to down. It would be a combination of Nembutal and Seconal which, according to the Internet, would be quite effective.

Using a throwaway phone, he called for a rideshare, the account attached to a fake credit card. Anthony walked two blocks for his pickup, making a mental note to dispose of the phone and wipe the credit card account from the rideshare company. The driver of the mid-sized sedan dropped him six blocks from his true destination, his storage facility, which held all kinds of treasures. Entering it, he climbed into the dark, eight-year-old sedan he used for his work. It was a Chevrolet, nothing flashy to draw attention. He regularly changed the license plates.

He drove it now to Bel Air and parked three blocks from Dr. Knott's residence. He had found the floor-plan, along with recent pictures, through a sloppy real estate agent who hadn't taken down any of the photos since Knott had purchased the home two years earlier.

The alarm system presented no challenge because Dr. Knott had already halted payments to the security company, telling them that he was going through a rough patch and promising to take up payments soon if they would leave the equipment in place.

Entering without a problem, thanks to flimsy locks, he stopped in the surgeon's study and claimed a bottle of Glenmorangie Grand Vintage 1990 Single Malt Whisky, cited as one of the best available. He had already crushed the barbiturates into a fine powder and now poured it into the bottle, which was three-quarters full, capping it and sloshing it thoroughly so as to mix the drugs well.

Next, he sat at the Dr. Knott's desk, powering up the computer. No password was required, which he thought sloppy on Knott's part, but it made his job all the easier to do. He pulled out the paper from his pocket and, opening a word document, typed the let-ter, reading it softly aloud to see that no typos were present. A man like Knott would want his suicide note to be meticulous and error-free.

He hit *print* and the printer softly whirled, spitting out the single page, which Anthony then signed, having practiced the physician's signature until he had perfected it. He left the printed copy in the center of the desk and even left the computer on in order to help the police and the coroner establish the time of death.

The basics taken care of, he now headed upstairs to the primary bedroom. The surgeon lived alone, his third divorce behind him. The numerous divorces and alimony and child payments had been another drain on Knott's income, as had been his lavish lifestyle.

Stepping into the darkened bedroom, the only light he saw was from a clock sitting atop a bureau. It read two minutes until two. He moved to the bed and heard the soft snores of his doctor as he placed the whisky bottle on the nightstand. With his gloved hand, he turned on the bedside lamp.

Unfortunately, Dr. Knott slept with a sleep mask, and so the light had not disturbed him. Gently, he nudged the surgeon's shoulder several times until Knott awoke with a start. He pushed the mask back to where it rested on the top of his head and blinked rapidly several times, his face showing confusing and then surprise as his groggy mind identified who stood next to the bed.

"You?" asked the plastic surgeon. Understanding then dawned on the man's face.

It didn't surprise him. The doctor was, after all, quite bright. Bringing the pistol he had brought into view, he said, "I would like to thank you for the remarkable work you did on me, Dr. Knott. I am thrilled with the results. You have an amazing talent and a wonderful bedside manner. However, we are going to need to bring our relationship to a close."

The plastic surgeon visibly trembled, yet he gazed steadily into his intruder's eyes and said, "There's no need to do that, Anthony. You are a new person, thanks to my handiwork."

"I am," he agreed pleasantly. "Now, pick up the bottle and drink. Call it a toast to your final, lasting success."

"If I refuse?" Knott asked defiantly, sitting up, bracing his back against the headboard.

He took a step forward and placed the cold muzzle of the gun directly against the good doctor's forehead. "Then I will pull this trigger," he promised quietly. "Of course, that would only be after hours and hours of exquisite torture. While you are an expert at changing a person's looks, I, on the other hand, am an expert in bringing pain and humiliation to others. I could share with you all that I will do to you. I'm very good at the details, as well as the big picture, as they say. In the end, though, know that you will have suffered such agony that you will beg for death."

Dr. Knott slowly nodded, obviously resigned to his fate. All in all, he thought the surgeon was taking things quite well.

"I've written a lovely suicide note for you," he explained. "I've already printed it out in your office downstairs. I signed it myself. I must say, my forgery skills are improving. If the police think to have it reviewed by a handwriting expert, they most likely will find any shakiness or hesitation could be attributed to you already having taken the barbiturates waiting for you in your Glenmorangie."

"Would you like me to go to the office or remain here?" the surgeon asked dully.

"Oh, here is fine," he said cheerfully. "You're the kind of man who would want to go easily, falling asleep against your luxurious Egyptian cotton sheets. I did choose the best bottle of whisky you owned, hoping that would make you happy."

His tone then changed from cheerful to dead. "Now. Drink, Doctor."

With shaking hands, the plastic surgeon retrieved the bottle from the nightstand, unscrewing the top and placing it on his nightstand. Knott took a long pull on the whisky and placed the bottle in his lap, sighing.

"I suppose if I have to go, this is the way to do so. You must know of my debts."

"I do. Drink again," he urged, more gently this time.

It took twenty minutes for the physician to consume all the alcohol. At the end, he was so sleepy that the bottle fell from his fingers to the floor. A bit splashed onto the carpet, while a small trace amount remained inside the bottle.

Gerard took several pictures and then turned off the light, thinking Knott would have done the same. Gently, he pulled the sleep mask back over his surgeon's eyes.

"You really did a nice job, Doctor. I thank you."

He walked out of the bedroom. From now on, he would think of himself as Anthony.

And begin a new chapter in his remarkable journey.

CHAPTER 18

Ainsley was the last to arrive at Eats 'n Treats. She caught sight of Tenley waving from a booth in the back and headed that way, pleased to see that Gillian Roberts was also present. Gillian slid from the booth and gave Ainsley a tight hug.

"Congratulations, my dear. You are getting a real winner in Jackson, but he is getting a marvelous partner in you."

"Thank you, Gillian," she said. "I know Jackson looks upon you as family because you had a hand in helping to raise him, along with Boo."

Ainsley slid into the booth, and Gillian followed. Everyone greeted her, and Tenley said, "We've already ordered for the entire table. We know you probably still have lots to talk about with Jackson, and we wanted this meeting to go as quickly and smoothly as possible."

"Thank you all for being here tonight. For always being here for me," she said from her heart. "I look upon each of you as dear friends and my chosen family."

The server set down iced teas and waters for

everyone and told them their appetizers would be out soon.

"Let's get down to the good stuff," Rylie said. "Do we know the time of the wedding?"

Willow said, "I actually called Jackson before coming here. He said he had arranged with the Barton County clerk for the ceremony to be a week from this coming Monday at three o'clock that afternoon."

"Perfect," Tenley said. "We'll have time for the ceremony and pictures afterward, and then we can all return to Boo's and get things set up." She looked to Ainsley. "Have you decided what you might like us to serve? And whom you'll invite?"

Ainsley pulled up a list of guests on her phone which she and Jackson had worked up. "I have the list. I'll text it to everyone here so that you all have access to it." She did so. "As far as food goes, we will have two cakes, both our wedding cake and a groom's one. I've entrusted Gus to make the groom's cake, and he was thrilled to be asked to do so."

"Can you tell us a little about the wedding cake? I assume you'll be creating it," Gillian said.

"I'm going to leave that as a surprise. Only Jackson and I will know its design before that day. Maybe Gus, because I'll need him to help me transport it to Boo's. As far as food goes, though? I'm all about finger foods and ease. You know me, I could make a meal out of appetizers."

"Speaking of appetizers," Willow said as their server returned with a large round tray filled with food, setting down plates of nachos, wings, fried mozzarella, and eggrolls.

Ainsley chuckled. "This is exactly the kind of things I love to eat and would like to serve at our reception."

"Carter had some ideas," Tenley began, pulling out her phone and bring up a list. "He wants to make all the food as his contribution to your big day. I'll help him. I've learned lots from him, and I'm turning out to be an excellent sous chef."

Tenley began detailing the appetizer ideas Carter had come up with, including mini-sliders, prosciutto-wrapped persimmons in goat cheese, shrimp cocktail shooters, and fried mac-and-cheese bites.

"It all sounds wonderful to me," she told her friend. "I say give Carter free rein and let him come up with any or all on your list. And if he can get a few vlogs from it, more power to him."

As they nibbled, Ainsley agreed to every suggestion her friends made. Willow said she and Dylan would provide the wines and champagne. Gillian offered to arrange the bridal bouquet and flowers for the serving tables at the reception, asking Ainsley what her favorite flowers were and promising to incorporate them into the bouquet and arrangements she would create.

Rylie asked, "What's there for me to do? I suppose I can help pull together an outfit for my cousin. If I recall, you only have two dresses in your wardrobe, both black. I'm sure Jackson saw one of those when he took you to the Old Coast Pub House."

"Yes, please take me shopping. Even though it won't be a ceremony where I march down an aisle, I want you to stand up beside me and sign the license as one of our witnesses."

"I'm having all the fun at this wedding," Rylie said. "First, the shopping for a dress and shoes. Then I get to help furnish the lovebirds' new house. How is that going?"

"Pete e-mailed an estimate for the various jobs

that we discussed as we walked through the house with him. Jackson and I will talk things over this evening and decide which renovations to move forward with." Ainsley glanced at Willow. "Jackson's decided to move into my apartment while construction is going on. We thought it would be more convenient to leave the house open instead of Pete's crew having to work around us."

"You are always welcome to stay at Boo's," her friend said. "Dylan and I expected that you would until the house was finished." Then Willow smiled, a wicked gleam in her eyes. "Unless you're intending on having lots of raucous sex that would disturb our sleep."

They all laughed, and Ainsley joined in, saying, "I hope we do. Actually, Jackson has made me feel so cherished in that regard."

"He's always been a gentleman," her future sister-in-law said. "I can imagine how much he will treasure you as his wife."

Willow's cell buzzed. She glanced at it and smiled. "It's Sloane. I haven't heard from her in almost two weeks. Mind if I take this?"

"Put her on speaker," Tenley urged. "Let's make her a part of our celebration."

Ainsley nodded her approval, and Willow answered. "Hey, Sloane. I'm with the girls at Eats 'n Treats, and you're on speakerphone. What's up?"

"Hmm. A weeknight dinner with the girls? Is something going on?"

Willow responded, "Yes, remember I mentioned meeting a friend from the Cove in Paris. You came in the weekend right after Ainsley left for Oregon, ready to start her bakery."

"Yes," Sloane said. "You've bragged enough on Ainsley's desserts."

Ainsley spoke up. "Hi, Sloane. It's Ainsley—and we're here celebrating my engagement to Jackson."

"That's fantastic," Sloane said. "How did you meet? Was it on one of his visits to the Cove, or did you get together in L.A.?"

"I grew up in the Cove, so I've always known who Jackson is. I'm a little younger, though, and didn't quite run with his crowd when he lived here."

"She's five years younger than my brother," Willow chimed in. "He's practically robbing the cradle."

Sloane laughed and Willow added, "Jackson has moved back to the Cove. He's taking over for a local attorney who is retiring. Jackson and Ainsley hit it off right away, and they'll be getting married in a couple of weeks. I wish you could be here for the wedding."

"I do, too," Sloane said, a hint of sadness in her voice. "I miss you, Willow. You and Tenley. Frankly, I'm jealous you're both there without me and that you've made some wonderful new friends."

"Come visit us anytime," Tenley suggested. "It's a wonderful place. Who knows? You might fall in love with the Cove and want to stay."

"I don't think the network would like that. Besides, I'm far too ambitious to settle down in a small town."

"Where are you now?" Willow asked.

"I'm on the move. About to get on a plane to Madagascar within the hour. I'll be doing a week-long series of stories from there. I just wanted to touch base and hear your voice before I left. Tenley being there saved me a call to her. And it was good to hear about your celebration. Congratulations again, Ainsley. I hope we'll meet someday soon."

"I'm glad you called," Willow said. "Please try to

take some time off after this assignment and come visit. It would be amazing to see you in person."

"I'll do my best," Sloane promised. "Gotta go. Give my congrats to Jackson. Hugs to him and Ainsley. Bye."

"Stay safe," Tenley called out.

They finished their meal and with the reception now planned, Ainsley felt good about her wedding day. Rylie asked when she would like to go dress shopping, and she said, "Let's see if we can go Monday after Jackson and I purchase our wedding license. Are we going into Portland? I could do my usual bakery supply run while we're there."

Rylie nodded. "No to the bakery run. I'll meet you at the courthouse so we can head straight to Portland from there. That way, Jackson can return to the Cove. And you're off on Tuesdays. You can get supplies then. Monday is going to be all about you."

Hugs were exchanged, and Ainsley walked back to the bakery's rear door, finding Jackson's car sitting there. He got out and came to her, enveloping her in a warm embrace.

"I'd kiss you—but I don't think I'd stop once I started. I'll save that for when we're inside," he teased.

They went upstairs to her apartment and settled on the sofa, Jackson pulling her into his lap. As promised, he spent a good half-hour kissing her. By the time he stopped, they were both out of breath.

He slid her from his lap so that she sat next to him. "Tell me about your dinner with the girls. What got decided?"

Ainsley ran through the various appetizers they would have and told him Gus had agreed to bake the groom's cake. Briefly, she shared what the older man had told her about having decided to stay sober and then the horrific accident occurred, Gus taking the blame for his brother's actions.

"Why would he do that, especially because he had decided he wanted to do better by his kids?" Jackson asked, puzzled.

"Bobby's girlfriend was pregnant," she explained. "I think Gus thought it might be too late for him to have the relationship he had always wanted with his own children—but that he could give that gift to his younger brother. From what he told me, Bobby's stayed sober and is a great husband and father."

"Poor Gus. I'm glad he was able to share this with you. You've believed in him from the start. Giving him the responsibility of baking the groom's case lets him know just how much faith you have in him."

Jackson smoothed her hair. "What about our wedding cake? Did you have any time to play with designs?"

"I did." She leaned forward and retrieved a manila folder from the coffee table, opening it and showing him her sketches.

"These two are for a waterfall cake. And these three would be used for a painted cake. Do you have a preference?"

Jackson studied the sketches, placing them on the coffee table and moving them around. He finally pointed to one. "They're all terrific, but I like this one the best. How would you make it?"

Briefly, Ainsley went through the process of painting a cake, explaining the difference between the frostings and telling him they would do a taste test to see which one he preferred.

"Fondant is easier to work with, but not as many people like its taste compared to buttercream. While buttercream is more difficult in a painted cake, the design would turn out well using either."

He dropped a sweet kiss on her lips." Considering I'm marrying a master in the dessert department, you probably would enjoy that challenge. I don't need to taste anything. Run with whichever you think will make for the best cake."

"Do you want to at least taste the fillings? I was thinking about vanilla, raspberry, or coconut, but I'd like your opinion."

"You know me. I'm just awakening to the tempting world of sweets. I'll like whatever you choose. You can surprise on this part."

She placed the folder on the coffee table again and leaned into him. "Let's talk about the house. Give me the scoop."

"I spoke to Clancy for over an hour today. He and Myra have found the house they wish to purchase. Their bid was accepted, and they've set a closing date already. As far as his house in the Cove goes, we settled on what I think was a very fair price. I told him what Pete thought it was worth and the amount of work we planned to put into it. He threw in all the furniture he'd left, saying we could keep or sell it."

"That's very generous of him."

"Clancy is a great guy. I drew up the papers this afternoon for the sale and purchase of the house and e-mailed the docs to him. He said he will look over them tonight and send them back signed, first thing in the morning. I'll head over to the bank in Salty Point tomorrow morning and by the end of the day, we'll be homeowners. Our very first home together."

"Hopefully, our first and last," she said, "thinking of the extra money we'll be sinking into it. What have you told Pete to work on?"

"He understands that the kitchen is first on our list. It's a gut job and will take the longest. He'll have samples for you to look over. Backsplash. Cabinets. Colors. And I told him you already knew which appliances you wanted to put in. I also met him at the house late this afternoon, and we pulled up several sections of carpet in different rooms. The floors beneath the carpeting are beautiful, Ainsley. I'm not quite sure why Clancy had covered them. Of course, it might have been the owner before him who did so. It might have been a preference of Clancy's or his wife's. Regardless, Pete said a light sanding would get them into excellent shape."

Jackson talked about the rest of the work being done and how Pete was balancing their house with another two streets over, one where he was adding on an extra bedroom and converting a garage into a man cave.

"How long does he think it will take?"

"He thinks between four and six weeks. His crew has already started on the other house and he can pull additional firemen on their days off to begin work on ours. He'll move back and forth between the two, supervising."

She thought a moment. "Did you agree to everything on Pete's list?"

Her fiancé nodded. "I decided it would be a good investment of both time and money to have everything we wanted done completed at the same time. That way, our lives won't have to be disrupted in the future, and we wouldn't have to move out or have workmen work around us." He kissed the top of her head. "I don't want it to be a few years down the road and us, with a kid or two, having to move in and share space at Boo's with Willow and Dylan and their family."

He paused. "Willow told me they are waiting a year before they'll start trying for a baby. I think we need to talk about our timetable."

Ainsley faced him, framing his face in her hands. "I wanted to address that very topic tonight." She swallowed. "I know this may be bold, Jackson. We probably should take a little more time to get to know one another better, but we're both eager for children. What better way to learn about each other than by starting a family?"

His smile lit up the room. "Trial by fire, I suppose. All kidding aside, Ainsley, you've made me a very happy man. I won't have to keep borrowing condoms from Dylan for too much longer, much less buy a box of my own."

She gave him a lingering kiss. "What do you say, Jackson Martin? Why don't we start trying for a baby right now?"

CHAPTER 19

Ainsley finished getting ready and then stepped from the bedroom, seeing Jackson scrolling through his phone, looking handsome in a dark blue sports coat and tie.

He glanced up. "Ready?"

"I am," she told him. "But I do feel a few nerves zipping through me."

Rising, he came to her, slipping his arms around her. "Well, we are about to go apply for our marriage license. It's a pretty big step in a relationship. I'll admit I'm a little nervous myself."

"You're still certain about this, aren't you?" she asked, anxiety now filling her. "About us?"

His response was to dip his head and give her a very thorough kiss, one which left no doubt as to his feelings as she clung to his shoulders to steady herself.

Breaking the kiss, his gaze met hers. "I have never been more sure about anything in my life, Ainsley. I love you. I want to spend the rest of my life with you. Let's go jump through the hoops it'll take to do so legally."

They went downstairs to his car and left the Cove, heading for the Barton County courthouse.

On the way, she asked, "When are you meeting with Clancy today? I know he was supposed to land sometime yesterday afternoon."

"We're set to meet at one this afternoon. Really, there won't be much to discuss. We've already closed on the house, and I was also able to send him the documents which allowed me to purchase his law practice. Everything has been signed and properly filed. Funds have been transferred, as well. Today is more about Clancy clueing me in on a few clients and their personal stories. I do have some questions, based upon the files I went through last week. I've made a list of them. It shouldn't take long."

Jackson added, "Clancy also got married while he was down in Houston. He and Myra decided to go ahead and do so while they were there so her family could attend. Myra has stayed in Houston, while Clancy has come back to the Cove to tie up all loose ends for the both of them."

"Will he be around next Monday for our wedding and reception?"

"He won't be staying that long, but he's wished us the best. I think after today, Clancy wants to slip away quietly. He wouldn't want to take away any attention from us."

"But he was supposed to have a huge birthday celebration in the Cove this summer. We'd already discussed what he wanted his cake to look like. I've got the drawings done. All he and Myra needed to do was choose the cake's flavors."

"Maybe we can talk him and Myra into coming back for one."

They arrived at the courthouse at eight-thirty on

the dot and went inside, heading for the county clerk's office. Since the building had just opened, they were the first in line to see her.

"Good morning, Bertha," Jackson said. "I'm back with my fiancée. This is Ainsley Robinson."

The clerk, who looked to be in her early fifties and still very attractive for her age, smiled and offered Ainsley her hand.

"I tasted some of your cupcakes not too long ago," Bertha said. "My sister was having a fiftieth birthday party and instead of a cake, she wanted to have a variety of cupcakes served instead. I tried a German chocolate one and also a chocolate almond fudge. You are quite the baker."

"Thank you so much. I remember your sister coming in. We had fun coming up with the different flavors and frostings. I hope she had a good time."

Bertha chuckled. "My sister has always had a good time. She's on her fourth husband and they left last week on a six-month cruise. She's always had a zest for living. But let's get down to business. May I see the ID that you brought?"

She and Jackson handed over their IDs, and Bertha gave them a tablet with a document loaded onto it for them to fill out. They went to two nearby chairs and entered their information. It didn't take long to complete the application, and Jackson handed it back to Bertha, who returned their IDs to them.

The clerk looked over their responses and then smiled brightly. "This will do the trick. Give me a few minutes, and I'll have the license generated for you."

True to her word, Bertha presented them with a marriage license less than five minutes later. She handed it over to Jackson.

"It's good for two months, as you know, but I still

have you on my calendar for three next Monday after-noon. Is that still the plan?"

"Yes, Bertha. Thank you for everything you've done. I guess we'll see you a week from today."

They said their goodbyes and left the county cour-thouse. Ainsley looked around and didn't see Rylie's SUV. She had told her cousin to meet them here around nine, in order to give them time to obtain their marriage license.

"If you're looking for Rylie, she's not going to pick you up here," her fiancé said, escorting her back to his car.

Disappointment filled her. Ainsley had been looking forward to shopping for her wedding dress.

"She's meeting us in Portland instead."

"Why?"

Jackson gave her an enigmatic look. "You'll see."

They drove into Portland, traffic light this Monday morning, unlike what it would become in the next few weeks as tourist season hit the Oregon coast. Jackson seemed to know exactly where he was going, and Ainsley sat back, trusting him. She looked down at their joined hands, still not quite believing that they had fallen in love so quickly and would soon be man and wife.

Jackson pulled into a parking place, and Ainsley glanced up, seeing they were at a jeweler's. She had forgotten all about rings.

He came and opened her door, helping her from the vehicle, and they went inside. The store was empty except for a man who greeted them by name.

"Ah, you must be Jackson and Ainsley," he said jovially. "I'm Burt, the owner. Clancy Nelson tells me you are looking for wedding rings."

"Yes to the rings," Jackson said, "and an engagement ring, as well."

She shook her head. "No, Jackson," she protested. "I don't need one. In fact, I won't even wear my wedding ring while working in the bakery. A simple band will do for me."

"You don't have to pick out anything flashy," he told her, "but you *are* getting an engagement ring. You can wear both after hours."

Ainsley thought how her mother hadn't received rings at her wedding and was happy that Jackson wanted to provide both for her.

Burt led them to a display case of wedding bands and engagement rings.

"I've known Clancy a long time," the jeweler said. "He told me to take care of you. You're a baker, Ainsley?"

"Yes. I don't want to be kneading pastry or bread dough and lose my ring doing so."

"Might I make a suggestion then?" Burt asked. "Since you will only wear your ring after you close your shop each day, you might want to consider soldering the engagement and wedding rings together so they are one. It would be easy to slip on and off that way."

"I like that idea," she told him.

"Then let's look at what you might like."

The jeweler pointed out different cuts of various diamonds. Her eye was drawn to one he referred to as marquise. She asked to try a few on and liked the look of the marquise better than the others.

Glancing up, she asked Jackson, "What do you think of this one?"

He lifted the hand she wore the engagement ring

on and kissed its knuckles. "I like it. Let's find a band that it looks good with."

Burt made a few more suggestions, and once more Ainsley tried on a few wedding rings, slipping the engagement ring atop them each to see how they paired together.

"That's the one," she said in unison with Jackson, and they both laughed.

"Obviously it is, since you both agreed," the jeweler said, removing the rings from her finger. "Let me measure now to obtain your size for a good fit."

He made a few notations on a pad and then set her rings aside before pulling out a tray of bands for Jackson to try on. The jeweler pointed out three he thought would be suitable, and Jackson tried on all three.

"I like this one," he said. "It seems to match your band." Looking to Burt, he said, "This is the one."

Again, the jeweler slipped the ring from Jackson's finger and measured, jotting down notes to himself.

"Would you like anything inscribed inside them?"

Jackson looked to her. "That's a nice idea. What would you like?"

She thought a moment. "How about next Monday's date? And maybe our initials."

Her fiancé nodded. "I like it."

Burt wrote down the date of the ceremony and their initials on his note pad. "I can do this work now since you don't live in Portland," he said. "It won't take long. Less than half an hour. Would you care to wait and then try them on? That way, I can make any necessary adjustments."

"Yes, we have the time," Jackson told him. "I think we'll head next door to the coffee shop and have a cup before we return."

They went to the shop on the east side of the jewelry store and ordered lattes. As they sipped on them, Ainsley saw Rylie pull up. Quickly, she texted her cousin and watched as Rylie got out of the car and then glanced at her phone. Ainsley waved through the window, and Rylie joined them inside the coffee shop.

"Since you met us here, I gather you knew about ring-shopping."

"Jackson texted me last night because he knew we were going dress-shopping today. He said you needed to find rings and that Clancy had recommended a jeweler to him."

"They should be ready by now," Jackson said. "Let's go try them on."

The jeweler greeted them as they entered the store and opened one of two small ring boxes sitting on the counter.

"Shall we try the lady's first?" Burt asked.

Ainsley held out her left hand and allowed him to slip the ring onto her finger, thinking the next time this happened, it would be her groom who did so.

She held out her hand, inspecting it, then turning it toward Rylie. "What do you think, Cuz?"

"I love it!" Rylie exclaimed. "I really like how the two rings are actually one, just like the two of you will be."

Ainsley pulled the ring from her finger and then looked inside, seeing the date and their initials inscribed with hearts on both sides of the inscription.

She smiled at Burt. "The hearts are a lovely touch."

"I hoped you would like them," he said with a smile.

While Ainsley placed her joined rings back into the box, Jackson tried on his band, declaring the fit to be perfect. He removed his ring and put it back in its box, closing the lid.

"If you wouldn't mind ringing these up separately, Burt," Ainsley said, "I would like to pay for my fiancé's ring."

The jeweler chucked. "No payment is necessary. Clancy said the rings would be his gift to you both since he won't be able to attend your ceremony."

Her gaze turned to Jackson's, and he shrugged. "I would argue if anyone but Clancy did this. He has always served as a mentor to me. I know this is something he would want to do for us. If it's okay with you, that is."

"I think it's a beautiful gesture," she said, tears brimming in her eyes at the old man's generosity.

They left the store, with Jackson taking both ring boxes. Ainsley was worried she might lose his while out shopping.

He walked them to Rylie's car and opened the passenger door for Ainsley. Before she got in, he cupped her cheeks and gave her a long kiss.

"That's to remember me while we're apart today," he told her.

"We need to do something special for Clancy," she said. "Maybe we could cook dinner for him this evening."

"We could—but where would we seat him? Your apartment is not set up to entertain even one guest. Unless he wants to balance his plate on his knees while sitting on your sofa, which has seen better days. How about we take him to the Old Coast Pub House instead? I can call for a reservation." He paused, a twinkle in his eyes. "And not for eight o'clock."

She chuckled. "I like that idea. How about six?"

"I'll tell him at our meeting this afternoon. We can

also hit him up tonight about him and Myra returning for his birthday celebration. In fact, we could host it. The back yard is huge and perfect for entertaining, especially with the screened-in porch. It would be a nice way to thank him for all that he's done for us."

"I agree." She tugged on his tie, bringing his lips down to hers again for a final kiss.

"I'll see you at the apartment," she said.

"Deal."

Ainsley climbed into the SUV, while Jackson closed the door, turning and heading toward his own sedan.

As Rylie backed out from her parking spot, she said, "If it weren't you, I would be totally disgusted by the excessive PDA. But having known you our entire lives, I think it's pretty darn awesome. One suggestion, though," her cousin continued. "Once we find your dress and shoes today, we'll leave them at my house. In fact, I would like for you to spend Sunday night at my house and get ready for your wedding there. I'll drive you to the courthouse so Jackson won't see you on your wedding day until three that afternoon."

Ainsley leaned over and hugged her cousin. "That sounds perfect. You've always had a way with hair. I'd love for you to style it. How do you think I should wear it?"

"That will depend upon the dress you choose. I've been looking online and think I've found the absolute perfect one." Rylie turned right at the corner. "Trust me. You're going to look fantastic in it."

Two hours later, Ainsley had tried on seventeen dresses, including the one Rylie thought would look good on her. She hadn't thought to wear white, but Rylie said a wedding was a wedding and pointed out an entire section in the bridal boutique that was labeled *Courthouse Weddings.* In the end, she decided on the first one she had tried on, the one Rylie had called and had the clerk put on hold for them. It was an A-line sheath, tea-length, an off-white silk with a cowl back that dipped low, adding a dramatic flair.

Trying it on again and looking into the mirror, she knew she looked good. Probably the best she ever had.

"You are positively glowing," Rylie said. "And the skirt has a nice swing to it. Perfect for dancing."

"I'm not much of a dancer," she reminded her cousin.

"But I'll bet Jackson is. And he would be happy to take his new wife dancing if she wore this."

Fortunately, the boutique also stocked shoes, and Rylie chose a pair with chunky, three-inch heels which were the same shade as the wedding dress. Surprisingly, they were chic and comfortable. Even if they hadn't been, Ainsley would have chosen them. They looked as if they had been made to be worn with this dress.

They talked nonstop on the way back to the Cove, the dress bag lying in the rear of the SUV, the shoebox next to it. Rylie dropped her off at the bakery, and as Ainsley walked up the stairs to her apartment, she thought she had never been happier.

She couldn't wait to see what marriage between her and Jackson would be like.

CHAPTER 20

Ainsley was soaking in a tub, about to get out, when her cell rang. She leaned over the tub's edge to pick it up, seeing it was Jackson.

"Hi, you," she said huskily.

"Hey. I missed you last night."

She sighed. "I missed you, too. But I'm with Rylie on this one. I don't want to see you until the ceremony today. Not that I buy into that 'bad luck to see the groom on your wedding day' bit, but I think the anticipation will be good for us."

"Agree. I took out some of my frustration with Gage this morning. Did our usual training session, using the barbells out of the back of his truck. Then we ran three miles."

"I hope you didn't use up all your energy," she said, her meaning clear by her tone.

He laughed. "I plan to keep you up all night, future Mrs. Martin. And I mean *all* night."

Ainsley shuddered, thinking of Jackson's hands on her, doing the marvelous, delicious things that made her body come alive.

"I'll hold you to that, Mr. Martin. Did you do anything else this morning?"

"Went to the office. Drew up a quick will for a client in Salty Point. She came by and signed it. I'll get to the courthouse early and file it before our ceremony."

"You better not be late."

"Trust me, I won't be. I did go by the house to check on the progress. Pete was there. It's really coming along, Ainsley. Pete thinks we'll be in it sooner than he anticipated."

She had met with Pete and selected everything from the farmhouse sink she wanted put in to the handles on the new, soft-close kitchen cabinets. She had worked with Rylie on the shades of paint for various rooms and on the bathroom makeovers. By the time Pete's crew finished, the Nelson home wouldn't be recognizable. It would have transformed into the Martin household.

"Any estimate on when work will be completed?" she asked.

"Pete had said four to six weeks. He's now saying three to four. That's entirely thanks to Carter, you know."

Not only was their friend catering all but the cakes for the reception, he had donated an entire week of his time to work on their house, convincing a few of his firefighter friends to do the same.

"Carter is a good friend. I can't wait to taste everything he's made for our party," she said.

"How about you? What did you do today?"

"I put the final, tiny finishes on our wedding cake. Gus helped me load it into my SUV, along with the groom's cake. He is so proud of his cake, Jackson, and he should be. It turned out better than I could have imagined. If my instructors at l'Ecole Lenŏtre had seen it, they would have hired him on the spot."

"I'll be sure to find Gus at the reception and compliment him. Are you pleased with the cake you made? The last I saw, it was really coming together."

"I am."

Ainsley had baked three tiers, using an English garden as her theme. The dominant colors in the floral cake were varying shades of pink and mauve, with the green stems and leaves. On the middle tier, she had lettered the line, *You will forever be my always.* Jackson hadn't seen the quote, and she was eager to view his reaction. She felt it was her best work to date, and Gus had reminded her to photograph it so that the picture could be placed on the Buttercup Bakery website. She did so, also including his groom's cake, photographing it from several angles.

It had surprised her when Jackson told her Gus had contacted him for ideas to incorporate into the groom's cake. At first, Gus had thought to make the theme sports-related, but after talking to Jackson, Gus had told Ainsley he had changed his mind. He didn't share with her what he designed and baked, and she had only seen the finished product this morning when they drove both cakes over to Boo's house.

It had been all about Paris—and had taken her breath away.

Gus told her that Jackson had said he had never left the country before, and he wanted to travel with Ainsley at some point, especially to Paris, knowing she had spent a formative part of her time in the City of Lights.

The rectangular sheet cake had been a suitcase, with a US passport in the upper left corner and two wedding rings in the lower one. The center of the cake had been a showstopping Eiffel Tower, with the right side having the Seine flowing from top to bottom. Gus had etched their names in the water of the famous river and had a couple strolling alongside it.

The cake had been spectacular, and she had burst into tears on the spot. Fortunately, she was dressed in sweats and wore no makeup at that point. They took the cakes inside Boo's house, and Willow also began to weep, telling them she had never seen such beautiful art on two cakes.

"I can't wait to see them both," Jackson said, bringing her back to reality. "I'll let you go. I know you need to get ready. I love you, babe. I can't wait to stand up and make our vows."

"I love you," she said, her throat thickening with unshed tears.

Ainsley climbed from her bath and dried off, opening the door to let out the steam from the bathroom. She slipped into her wedding lingerie, a delicate bra-and-panty ensemble that were mere wisps of lace, and then threw on a robe over them, leaving the bedroom to find Rylie. Gillian had arrived, looking chic in a pearl-gray suit.

She hugged the older woman, who said, "Your bouquet is in Rylie's refrigerator. I spent the morning arranging the flowers I picked up. All of them are now at Willow's. She helped me set them out throughout the house. And I saw the cakes!" Gillian's eyes lit up. "Oh, you and Gus outdid yourselves."

"Thank you for taking on all the floral arrangements, Gillian. I'm so happy to have you be a part of our wedding and celebration."

"I'm delighted to do so, Ainsley. I thought the world of Boo, and I feel I am her eyes and ears today, watching over Jackson and Willow now." She cupped

Ainsley's cheek. "Boo would be so pleased that you and Jackson are marrying. Boo always had a lot of faith in you, Ainsley. She told me you were as much of an artist as she was, albeit in a much different medium."

Ainsley hugged Gillian, grateful for having this woman in her life, especially since her mother and Boo wouldn't be here today.

Rylie entered the room. "We need to get you ready," her cousin said, looking smashing in a navy mini, which showed off her legs. "Gillian is going to do your makeup. I'll take care of your hair."

"I hope that's all right with you, dear," Gillian said.

"You always look so pulled together, Gillian. I would be happy to have you handle my makeup. Just be sure you're using waterproof mascara," she joked.

Twenty minutes later, Ainsley looked at her image in the mirror. "I'm... beautiful," she declared. "Thank you so much, Gillian. You're going to have to teach me your tricks. You did this so quickly."

"I think your glow is due more to being so much in love than my makeup job. Let's get you into your wedding dress so that Rylie can work her magic."

Ainsley shed her robe as her cousin retrieved the dress. Once she donned it, she turned, looking at it from various angles in the mirror.

"Oh, my, you look fantastic in that, Ainsley," praised Gillian. "Jackson won't know what hit him."

Rylie pursed her lips in thought and then said, "I had wanted to go with soft, sexy waves, but we really do need to show off the back of this dress. I think an updo will be perfect."

She seated herself in the chair before the mirror again.

"You can watch every step of the way," her cousin

told her, brushing Ainsley's locks until they shone and then beginning to braid and artfully twist sections of hair.

As she watched Rylie at work, joy filled her. Yes, she was sad her parents had not lived to see her wedding day, but she hoped to be as happy as they had been in their marriage. They had struggled with money throughout it, but their hearts had been full of love for one another, as well as for her, giving her a wonderful example of what a marriage should be like.

Rylie finished her work and gave Ainsley a hand mirror. She stood and used it to inspect the back and sides of her hair. Having her hair up showed off her long neck, making it appear elegant, and the deep cut of the dress' cowl, which draped her slender back to perfection. She placed the mirror on the vanity and gently hugged her cousin so as not to wrinkle her dress.

"You did an incredible job, Rylie. You not only have a great eye for furniture and how to put a room together, but I only hope I can return the favor someday soon. Maybe Jackson has some hot lawyer friend that will decide to chuck it all and move to the Cove and become his partner. Then you'll fall madly in love with one another and have half a dozen babies."

Rylie laughed. "Not happening, I'm afraid."

Ainsley clasped her cousin's hands. "You will find someone to love," she promised. "And when you do, it will be magical. And forever."

Gillian said, "We better leave for the courthouse soon. You don't want to be late for your own wedding."

Rylie retrieved the shoes that matched the wedding dress, and Ainsley slipped into them, thankful again for how fashionable and comfortable they were.

"One last thing," she said, retrieving her purse and slipping out her mother's earrings. "This way Mom will be with me. Dad, too, since he gave these to her."

As she placed the earring's stem through her lobe and fastened the back to it, her eyes misted with tears and she blinked them away.

They all went to the courthouse in Rylie's car. Ainsley was grateful for the sunny day and the fact there was little to no wind. They entered the courthouse and cleared security, heading to the county clerk's office. When they arrived, Dylan was waiting to greet them. He took Ainsley's hands in his and kissed her cheek.

"My almost sister-in-law looks incredible."

"Thank you, Dylan," she told him.

"Bertha asked one of the judges if she could conduct the ceremony in his chambers so it would be a little more private. I'm happy to escort you there, and if you let me, the short way to Jackson once we enter the room."

Dylan looked to Gillian and nodded.

The older woman stepped forward. "Dylan graciously asked if I could also help take you to your groom since your parents aren't here to do so."

"I can't think of a better pair to walk me to my man," Ainsley said, her throat thick with emotion.

"Let's get this show on the road," Rylie declared, and they went to the bank of elevators.

When they arrived at the judge's chambers, they paused in his secretary's office. Rylie went through the doors first, pausing to glance over her shoulder.

"Take a minute to compose yourself. I love you, Cuz."

Ainsley slipped one hand through the crook of Dylan's arm and placed her bridal bouquet in that hand as she slid her right hand through Gillian's arm. Taking a deep breath, she slowly expelled it and then nodded.

"I'm ready."

They entered the judge's chambers, and she heard the strains of Vivaldi's *Four Seasons*, spotting Tenley holding up her phone, the music coming from it. She smiled at her friend and then turned her attention toward her groom.

Jackson wore a dark pinstripe suit with a white dress shirt and red tie. He had asked Ainsley what her favorite color was, and she had responded that it was red, noting how she loved the vibrancy of the color. Jackson wearing the red tie might be a small detail, but it let her know how in-tune he was with her. Dylan and Gillian guided her the short length of the office and handed her off to Jackson. He slipped his left arm about her waist as she clutched her bouquet, the sweet smell of roses and sweet peas wafting up to her.

Leaning over, he brushed a brief kiss against her temple. "You look beautiful," he said softly.

Rylie came and stood to her left, and Willow went to stand by her brother's side, Jackson having designated her as his best person. Tenley, Carter, Gage, and Gillian formed a semi-circle behind them, and Tenley slowly lowered the volume of the music until it faded away. Ainsley turned her attention to Bertha, who smiled at them.

"Are you ready?" the county clerk asked.

"Yes," they responded in unison, and Bertha began.

Ainsley had been to other weddings and had heard the same words spoken before, but this time the significance in them moved her. Her heart beat rapidly as she listened to Bertha's melodic voice, thinking how much she loved Jackson and what a wonderful life they would experience together. Bertha nodded and Ainsley handed her bouquet to Rylie, turning and facing Jackson, who threaded his fingers through hers. He repeated the vows the clerk uttered, his gaze never leaving hers, tenderness in his eyes. She repeated the same vows, blinking back a few tears, eager to keep these sacred promises over a lifetime to the man she loved.

Willow handed her brother a ring, and Jackson placed it on Ainsley's finger, promising his love and devotion over the years to come.

She turned and accepted Jackson's ring from Rylie and repeated the same sentiments, sliding the gold wedding band onto her groom's finger. He clasped her hands in his, and they listened to the final words as Bertha confirmed they were now man and wife.

Her new husband's lips touched hers for their first marital kiss. In it, Ainsley felt the promise of the life they would live together, full of love and joy and plenty of laughter.

Jackson broke the kiss, and she saw the tears in her husband's eyes, as well as his love for her shining through.

"I love you, Mrs. Martin," he said, a satisfied smile spreading across his face at addressing her that way.

"I love you, Mr. Martin," she replied pertly

Then Jackson pulled her to him again for a longer, deeper kiss.

When he finally broke it, he squeezed her hands. Turning to the county clerk, he said, "Thank you, Bertha, for performing our ceremony and finding us a private setting for our wedding."

"Happy to do so, Jackson," the older woman replied, an indulgent smile on her lips.

"Let me get a shot of you two together with Bertha," Gage said.

Gage took the photo and several more after it, having been dubbed their official photographer. He added some of her and Jackson alone and others with various friends and family.

Gillian touched Gage's sleeve. "You need to get in a few of these," she told him, taking the camera from him.

Gage almost seemed reluctant to do so, and Ainsley knew how shy he could be.

"Get over here, Gage," she ordered, "or you'll never get any chocolate out of me again."

The former Navy SEAL grinned and hustled toward them. "You said the magic words, Ainsley Martin."

Ainsley Martin...

She really liked the sound of her new name.

Gillian took a few photos, and then Bertha insisted that Gillian join the others, while the county clerk snapped a few shots.

"We've taken up enough of your time, Bertha," Jackson said. "Again, thanks for making today special for us. And remember, when you get off work, you're invited to our reception at my sister's house."

"I wouldn't miss it for the world," the county clerk said.

They left the judge's chambers and went outside to the various vehicles. Naturally, Ainsley went with her new husband. Once they were inside it, he framed her face in his hands and kissed her, a slow kiss which brought instant heat to her belly.

"It's hard to believe, but we did it." His thumbs gently caressed her cheeks.

"It seems a little surreal, doesn't it?"

"All I know is I am the happiest man on the planet. We're going to have a wonderful life together, Ainsley. Yes, there will be ups and downs. A few fights along the way, where we both believe we're right—but we'll learn to compromise. I feel as if today is the first day of the best part of my life."

Jackson kissed her again, an achingly tender kiss which showed her just how much he cherished her. Ainsley knew they were two of the lucky ones and that they would live their lives in love.

CHAPTER 21

Anthony was on a natural high.

He had made his first kill since being brought to trial—and it had been the sweetest balm, feeding his soul.

He went through the pictures again, reliving and savoring each moment. He had deliberately waited to kill again, in part to prove to himself that he could do so. He needed to control the beast. Not the other way around. This kill hadn't been prolonged or messy, a different sort of necessary destruction to protect the new him.

Methodically, he had changed several things in order to remain a free man. He had a new storage unit now. A new used car and sets of license plates to place on it. He determined new ways to stalk his victims, though he was ready to return to his typical kill—tall, slender blonds.

Because she had been one...

He supposed in the long run he had mommy issues, just as many killers had. In his case, however, they were also sister issues. At least that's who he had first thought Anita was. His sister. He had been raised with the single sibling, and she had never been affectionate toward him. Anita was thirteen years older than he was, which had made it easier to pass off her baby as her baby brother instead.

His first kill had been the man who had impregnated Anita.

Their father.

It had been his first murder, not soon after he had learned the ugly truth from the woman he believed to be his mother. She had turned to drink and gradually, over the years, had become a sloppy drunk, one with loose lips. Her drinking was done at home, and she would become quite maudlin. Anthony had believed she held some secret that she kept from him. Perhaps it was a certain look in her eyes, or the way he would catch her studying him every now and then. He waited and one night, deep in her cups, he got her to talking about the past. About her strange relationship with her firstborn. Anita had left the house when Anthony was almost five and she about to turn eighteen. Their father had reported her as a runaway, but the police had done little to track a girl of that age.

In her drunken state, dear old mom had finally admitted to him that he was her grandchild. That his sister had been his mother—and that she blamed her own mother for not protecting her. For not preventing the incest which had occurred in their house.

Anthony—formerly Gerald—had been fifteen at the time. He knew his mother wouldn't remember the drunken confession, but he felt loathing for the woman before him. It angered him that she hadn't done more to save her own flesh and blood from a monster. As far as his father went, Anthony had never had much of a relationship with him. Joe McGreer was interested in boxing and NASCAR racing and had an average IQ. He resented and belittled Gerard, calling him a fucking nerd and four-eyes. Gerard excelled in school, particularly math and computer sciences. He tested off the charts. At twelve, he was already hacking into businesses and moving money around for his own private use.

That night of revelations from his grandmother changed the trajectory of Gerard's life. He was on the cusp of leaving the McGreer house for Cal Tech, which was giving the boy genius a full ride to the university. With his new knowledge, he was suddenly interested in tying up loose ends before he left for college. Crime had always fascinated him, and he devoured crime novels and podcasts, as well as watching every movie and TV show which dealt with forensic science. He scoured websites and had already learned to think like a criminal, feeling certain urges within him. Dark urges waiting to escape and flourish.

His grandmother died that night, but not by his hand. She had stumbled into the kitchen, mumbling to herself, as he retreated to his bedroom. As usual, Joe McGreer was out late doing who knows what. When Gerard went to the kitchen two hours later in need of a snack, he found his grandmother's body on the floor, quickly piecing together what had happened as he saw exactly where she had struck her head on the edge of the linoleum counter, falling to the ground, breaking her nose. He didn't move the body as he idly wondered if the first blow had killed her or if she'd drowned in her own blood.

He deemed this divine intervention because her accidental death would help him to put into motion a plan he had already been working on since their conversation that night.

Dialing 911, the operator had asked him what his

emergency was. Gerard turned on emotions of fear and extreme anxiety, playing his part to perfection. With just the right amount of hysteria in his voice, he had told the dispatcher he had come to the kitchen for a late-night snack and had found his mom lying on the floor in a pool of blood. Unresponsive. He had begged the woman to send help, going to first unlock the door and then returning to wait by the cooling body.

The first responders had arrived within four minutes, entering the house and coming to the kitchen, where he sobbed loudly. They checked his 'mother's' body. One of them comforted him as best she could.

His father arrived home just as the body was being transported to the ambulance, and the plans he had made changed abruptly. His parents didn't have friends, only each other. They were barely civil toward one another, but the police wouldn't need to know any of that. Gerard decided his father would be so despondent over his wife's accidental death that he would commit suicide tonight.

It was a thing of beauty by the time Gerard finished.

At seven the next morning, he once again called emergency services, hysteria rising in his voice, making his words almost unintelligible. The 911 operator quickly dispatched a team to their house, and his father's body was found in the bathtub, wrists slit, the knife and empty bottle of his wife's Ambien on the floor near the tub on the tiled floor.

Social Services came for Gerard, and he explained how he was about to leave for college in four days. His news surprised them, seeing the skinny, slight teenager who looked much younger than his fifteen years. He had researched legal emancipation and had thought about filing for it, though that would no longer be necessary. After spending a few nights with a foster family in Burbank, he was released from the state's custody and allowed to Uber to Pasadena. Cal Tech's offer had included tuition, room, and board, and he took advantage of all three that first year, trying to blend into college life as best as a gawky, geeky fifteen-year-old could.

By his second year, he had leased an apartment online with the first of many aliases and moved in. The apartment manager either turned a blind eye or didn't bother to keep up with the tenants living in each apartment, as long as payment came in each month. He made certain it did so, and Anthony graduated from Cal Tech with both his bachelor's and master's degrees and all the tools he needed to succeed both professionally and personally.

He lined up the first of many excellent jobs, but he postponed the start date of his initial employment by a month. They wanted him badly enough to wait the extra few weeks. Work could wait—because he had found Anita McGreer and wanted to speak to her.

He had no idea what he would say to her. She had left so long ago that he only had a vague image of her. His dad had burned every photograph of her after she had run away. She had never contacted her family. No card, letter, or phone call ever came. Gerard supposed he was merely curious about her. He certainly felt no connection to her. She had spent little time with him before she left the McGreer household.

Anita was a waitress in a second-rate diner in Bakersfield, struggling to make ends meet. She had arrests for drug possession and prostitution but now seemed to be clean. He actually had plenty of money and could easily give her some, making her life easier. He just didn't know if he wanted to do that.

Going to the diner where she worked, he watched her over a couple of hours, seeing how hard she toiled at the dead-end job. She waited on him, and he never spoke more than a few words to her, not wishing to reveal his identity to her in a public setting. She was in her early thirties and looked a good twenty years older, stick-thin and with greasy hair. He didn't quite feel sorry for her. He had learned that he didn't seem to feel the same emotions that others did. Research had revealed to him that he was a psychopath, hitting markers which included possessing no pity or remorse and experiencing no fear.

He already knew her address from his online explorations into her life and followed her home at a discreet distance when she left the diner after her shift ended.

She unlocked the door and was entering her efficiency when he called her name. Anita had turned, fear in her eyes at a stranger being this close to her in the wee hours of the morning.

"I'm your brother," he had told her, and then corrected himself. "No, your son. Gerard."

He didn't know what he had expected her reaction to be, but she flinched—and then revulsion filled her face.

She had surprised him, shoving him hard, telling him to get away from her. That she still had nightmares. That she wanted nothing to do with him because he was a reminder of the worst years of her life. How she had been molested over and over, finally becoming pregnant and forced to give birth to her own father's child.

Anita accused Gerard of being just as evil as their

father had been and that she wanted nothing to do with him. She hurried inside and started to slam the door in his face when he threw a hard punch that connected with her throat. She crumpled, falling to her knees, her hands flying to her throat as she tried to gasp for air. He stepped around her, dragging her body back into the room, and closed the door. Watching her, it was apparent he had broken her windpipe. Watching her die brought him even more pleasure than having killed the monster they both called their dad.

He didn't know if he had expected redemption, but he surely hadn't wanted her rejection. In that moment, a deep hatred took hold of him—and the seed planted would grow with each subsequent death. The death of women who resembled Anita. His mother.

Anthony shook his head hard, withdrawing from the memories of a decade ago. He had fed the beast within him, committing regular rapes and murders of women who looked like his mother. Anthony realized she had rejected him from the beginning. That no bond had existed between them. She had merely been the vessel he had grown in, the one who had birthed him, giving him life. He liked to think of himself as the Angel of Release, granting his chosen ones a release from this life and all its ugliness.

Putting aside his camera, he went back to his mental To-Do List. If anything, he was a man—and murderer—who liked to be prepared. Though his latest kill had been meticulous, planned better than any previous ones, he knew there was always the tiniest possibility he might slip up as he had before. Because of that, he wanted to have Jackson Martin's phone number in his contact list. It had surprised him a bit how his attorney had been a bit off-putting when he had tried to line up Martin in case of any future charges. Martin had said it would depend upon the caseload he and his partner had at the time. Gerard supposed they weren't necessarily in the repeat representation business. Still, Jackson Martin was a brilliant attorney, one who had shredded prosecution witnesses on the stand. His closing argument was masterful, and Gerard knew if he were ever charged with a crime again, Martin was the only one who could represent him.

He opened his tablet to search for Martin's information so he could enter in it into his new cell phone. He didn't bother wasting his time learning numbers. He had no friends, so very few people were listed in his contacts. Googling Watterscheim & Martin, he was surprised what came up instead.

Watterscheim & Flannigan.

Intrigued, Anthony clicked on the legal site and went to the *about* tab, which listed both partners, Bill Watterscheim and Richard Flannigan, as well as various office staff, all of whom he recognized. No mention of Jackson Martin anywhere on the site.

He didn't see the brilliant lawyer leaving the profession. Perhaps he had a falling out with Watterscheim and began his own firm. Gerard scoured the Internet but only found two Jackson Martins who were attorneys in California. One was located in Chula Vista and practiced family law. The second had law offices in Sacramento and specialized in divorces.

Where the hell had his Jackson Martin gone? And why?

This was damned inconvenient. Not that he was going to be caught again anytime soon, but Gerard had a burning urge to locate the man who had kept him from prison. Well, the attorney accounted for ninety percent of the case's outcome. The terror pregnant Juror Number Four must have experienced seeing her dead cat also played a factor. He had met a junkie when he'd first been arrested. They had shared jail space at county lock-up. In their conversations, it came out that the man enjoyed torture. A lot. Anthony had thought he could use the felon and had contacted him through a clever system he had designed involving disappearing texts. He'd also sent Juror Number Four messages using it.

The junkie had leaped at maiming the cat. Anthony made certain a payment of five hundred dollars was sent to him before and again after his work with the juror's pet. The drugged-out felon was the only link between Anthony and the cat. He had planned to eliminate him once he won his release and found it wasn't necessary.

The man had OD'd the day the verdict came in, most likely using some of his new cash to score the heroin that killed him.

Idly, he wondered if Juror Number Four had approached Jackson Martin. If she had, nothing would have changed. Gerard couldn't be retried on the charges, thanks to double jeopardy. But if she had shared with Martin what had happened to her beloved cat and the text message which no longer existed, had that scared off his attorney?

He always thought Martin knew he was guilty. As a professional, he had never asked his client about his innocence or guilt. He had done the job Anthony—actually, Gerard—had paid him to do. It bothered him, though, that Jackson Martin was among the missing. That warranted a call to Watterscheim & Flannigan.

Using one of his many burners so there would be

no way to trace the call back to him, he dialed the number.

"Law office."

"Yes, this is Sam Johnson. I would like to book an appointment with Jackson Martin. He represented me a few years ago when I—"

"I'm sorry, sir, but Mr. Martin is no longer with the firm. Mr. Watterscheim is still a partner, however, and Mr. Flannigan is also available."

"Is he a partner like Mr. Martin was?" Anthony asked, a touch a naivety in his voice.

"Yes, Mr. Flannigan bought out Mr. Martin's share of the partnership. I'm sure either Mr. Flannigan or Mr. Watterscheim would be happy to represent you in your upcoming matter."

"Oh, I'll have to think it over. Mr. Martin did such a wonderful job in court. I'm a little reluctant to be represented by another attorney. I suppose you can't share with me where his new office is."

"Mr. Martin left the state, Mr. Johnson. He wouldn't be available to serve as your attorney."

"I see. Is he still practicing law? I certainly hope so. It would be a shame to lose someone so talented."

"Mr. Martin is now practicing in his hometown. Maple Cove, Oregon."

Bingo.

"You don't think he would consider coming back to California?" Anthony added a touch of a whine.

"No, I'm afraid not." She paused. "Can I set up an appointment for you?"

Anthony went ahead and made the appointment for the non-existent Sam Johnson, giving the receptionist the burner's number. When the client didn't show and the phone number proved to be a dead end, the matter would be quickly dropped.

Immediately after disconnecting the call, he searched for Maple Cove, Oregon, finding it was a coastal town about an hour west of Portland. He pulled up pictures of the area. A map of the town. Reviewed the Chamber of Commerce's website, where the only attorney listed was a Clancy Nelson.

Anthony then typed in Jackson Martin and Maple Cove—and hit a treasure trove.

His attorney had been quite the scholar-athlete, finishing first in his high school class and lettering in three sports. He skimmed the stats of games Martin had played in and how he won an academic scholarship to the University of Southern California.

Then his search led him to a new website. That of Maple Cove's newest attorney. Jackson Martin's handsome, smiling face looked back at him. Perusing the website, he saw the services offered and thought it a shame for such a brilliant lawyer to be stuck in a small town. He found an online story in a local newspaper which reported the retirement of Clancy Nelson, who had practiced in Maple Cove almost six decades, and how his law practice was being taking over by former hometown hero Jackson Martin.

He did a thorough search of Martin's name, adding Oregon and Maple Cove to those searches. He discovered his attorney had sat for the bar and passed it at the same time he'd earned the right to practice in California, so maybe Martin had always planned to return home. Maybe the retirement of this community leader and assuming his practice was too good to pass up.

Then he stumbled across an interesting tidbit. A marriage license which had been filed with the Barton County courthouse. It seems Jackson Martin had recently married an Ainsley Robinson. Quickly, he went back to some of the Maple Cove sites because he re-called seeing that name.

Yes, there she was, listed as the owner of the But-tercup Bakery by the Chamber of Commerce. He changed his search, suddenly interested to find out everything he could about Jackson Martin's new bride. They had certainly married quickly. Anthony won-dered if they had been engaged for a lengthy period or if she had been a former girlfriend of Martin's whom he'd connected with when he returned home.

He clicked on the chamber's listing of Buttercup Bakery, and the Robinson woman's website came up. Scrolling through the site, his mouth began to water at the scrumptious pictures. It seemed Ainsley Robinson —now Ainsley Martin—was an incredible artist as far as sweets went.

Then he clicked on the about tab, bringing up her picture and bio. Reading the information, a slow smile spread across his face.

Ainsley Martin was a blond. And just the type he loved to kill.

CHAPTER 22

Anthony pulled the Chevy into a parking spot along the Maple Cove square. He had been here two days now, staying two towns away in a Crescent Cove bed-and-breakfast. He had put trackers on both Jackson's and Ainsley's vehicles and become familiar with the area and their movements. He had studied the Buttercup Bakery website and decided he would see if he could meet with Ainsley about a wedding cake, to get to know her. Usually, he didn't meet his kills in person before their playtime together. He stalked them from afar, only learning of them through their online presence. Social media was a godsend for information about a person. People put up the most personal aspects of their lives, down to what they ate for breakfast each morning and where they vacationed.

He now entered Sid's Diner, which he knew to be the heart of this small town. A woman greeted him, the tag on her blouse revealing her name was Nancy.

"Table for one?" she asked.

"Yes, please. A booth if you don't mind me taking up that much room."

He glanced around the diner. It had been crowded when he had driven by early yesterday morning, but he had waited until almost nine o'clock on a weekday, and the crowd had thinned considerably.

"Not a problem, sir," the older woman said. "Right this way."

She led him to a booth in the center of a wall of booths, and he slid in, accepting the menu she offered him.

"I always like to ask for a personal recommendation when I'm eating somewhere new. What do you suggest I try?" he asked, a technique he used to disarm strangers.

"We have a good egg man on the grill. His over-easy eggs and bacon are terrific. He also makes excellent hash browns and biscuits."

"I'm sold," he told her, practicing his smile. "I'll have a little coffee to go with it."

She smiled warmly. "Be right back."

Anthony watched her put in his order as he quickly observed the others seated in the diner. She returned, bringing a pot of coffee, pouring him a cup.

"New in town? Or passing through?"

He knew small town residents were a nosy bunch, and this woman typified them. She would be the kind to have her finger on the pulse of the community and spread gossip faster than a brushfire.

"Thinking about moving to the area," he said genially. "My fiancée and I enjoy the ocean. She's from a small town and would like to move to one near the water. We both work from home, and so we're really free to settle wherever we wish. We'll be getting married soon. I'm here scouting out things, including finding someone to bake our wedding cake."

He dropped the last nugget, knowing Nancy would

take the bait and give him information not necessarily found on the Buttercup Bakery website.

The woman said, "I have just the place for you. Buttercup Bakery. The owner, Ainsley Martin, attended a fancy pastry school in Paris. She's a local girl who used to sell cookies before school sporting events when she was barely a teenager. I can say, bar none, Ainsley makes the best desserts I've ever tasted—and that includes the pie at my diner. You should check out her website. Better yet, I'm sure Ainsley would be happy to speak to you about your cake. Why, she's a newlywed herself, you know. Married a boy who was also raised in the Cove. Jackson practiced law down in L.A. a good number of years, but he's back now. We're so happy he's returned."

She left, and he began listening to the conversations from the table to his right and the booth behind him, trying to glean any additional information. He had gone to the town library yesterday and accessed their digital files, learning everything he could about Jackson Martin. His attorney had been a hometown hero in several sports and had won a prestigious scholarship to USC. His new wife had also grown up in Maple Cove. Her parents were both deceased, but she had a cousin who operated an antiques store, also located on the town's square. The tracker he had placed let him know that Jackson had visited a house twice, which Anthony had discovered had belonged to his grandmother, a renowned sculptor. Jackson's sister, also an artist, now lived in the house, along with her sheriff husband. Anthony had stood in the woods next to this house for hours yesterday, watching people come and go, including Jackson and Ainsley, who carried in suitcases.

Anthony wondered how long they would be

staying there and hoped to find out soon. He had discovered through perusing the local town newspaper that Jackson had only recently bought the practice of a Clancy Nelson, who had practiced law in the town for over six decades. Anthony didn't know if this had been a sudden decision or a planned one. If planned, it upset him that Jackson had never mentioned it when Anthony was asking about using the law office's services in the future.

His server brought his breakfast to him. Nancy was right. The eggs were some of the best he had eaten, and the bacon was cooked to crisp perfection. The biscuit was light and fluffy, and he finished it quickly, asking for an additional one when she filled his coffee mug again.

As he continued to eat, he listened to the talk around him. He didn't learn anything useful, but he knew that sometimes stray bits of information could be put to good use, so he filed away everything he heard.

Nancy brought him the bill, and she was the one who rang him up near the door, proudly telling him she was the owner of the diner and hoped he would return soon, bringing his fiancée.

Anthony thanked her and strolled toward Buttercup Bakery. It was now half-past nine, and the morning rush at the bakery definitely had ended. He supposed business picked up when tourist season began in the summer. Right now, he knew from the website that the bakery was closed on Mondays and Tuesdays but would add Tuesdays back to its hours come June. Today was a Wednesday. He would ask for a wedding cake to be baked not for this weekend but the next. He didn't want to give Ainsley a reason to turn him down.

He entered the bakery, deciding on his new alias as he approached the counter. He recognized both women working it from their pictures on the website. There would also be an older gentleman in the back who was a fulltime baker, and Anthony assumed Ainsley was busy back there, as well.

The woman in front of him was being waited on by the older clerk, Gloria. Sheila, the younger of the two workers motioned toward him.

"What can I get you?" she asked with a friendly smile.

"I was hoping to make an appointment to see your owner." He smiled the practiced smile, knowing he disarmed Sheila with it. "You see, I'm getting married soon and need to see about a wedding cake. Nancy at the diner sent me over here."

"You've come to the right place," Sheila assured him. "Let me see if Ainsley can visit with you now."

Sheila moved to an open door and said, "Ainsley? Do you have time for a wedding cake consultation?"

Anthony couldn't hear the response, but Sheila turned back to him and nodded. "She said five minutes. Can I get you a cup of coffee while you're waiting? On the house, of course."

"That would be nice," he said. "And let me have a bear claw to go with it, if you don't mind. I'll pay for it."

He set a five-dollar bill on the counter. Sheila waved it away. "Happy to treat you. Have a seat, and I'll bring both to you."

There were only four small café tables in the bakery, and he took the one in the far corner. He studied the items in the display cases, his mouth watering, thinking Ainsley Martin was a very talented woman.

He thought so even more after he bit into the bear claw, which Sheila had presented to him.

Moments later, the object of his interest stepped through the opening and joined him.

Taking a seat, she offered her hand and said, "Hello, I'm Ainsley Martin, the owner of Buttercup Bakery. I hear you're in the market for a wedding cake. Congratulations."

He smiled, finding himself not having to act. Genuine warmth shone on her face, and he responded to it.

"I'm Charles Chapman, but I usually go by Charlie. I'm getting married in ten days." He did his best to look sheepish. "I'm having to handle all the details myself because my fiancée teaches English as a second language in Tokyo. She'll be ending her term and returning to the US for good. We want to get married pretty much as soon as she arrives, which is why I'm taking care of the wedding."

"I'm a newlywed myself," Ainsley confided. "What kind of wedding are you having, and how many people are invited?"

"It's going to be small," he replied. "Only family and a few friends. About two dozen total. We'll get married at a courthouse and have a small reception in her cousin's home in Crescent Cove. That's where I'm staying now."

He had decided to name that place, knowing it was close enough to Maple Cove for it to make sense that he would come here for his cake, and yet he hoped she wouldn't press him too much on names or details.

"I'm happy to help you, Charlie," she said brightly. She opened the sketchpad she had placed on the table and asked, "Are you thinking a single layer. Two tiers? Round or oblong?"

"I… I'm not sure what I want," he admitted. "Maybe I'll know it when I see it?" he asked hopefully, playing the clueless fiancé.

She chuckled and pulled her phone from her pocket. "Let me bring up the Buttercup website, and you can see examples of cakes I've baked. We'll find a few you like, and then I can draw something to your specifications."

Ainsley handed him her phone and started talking about the various cakes, nodding so he would scroll to the next picture.

"Phone call, Ainsley," Gloria called out. "It's Mrs. Jacobs again. She's wanting a change to the cake for her husband's fiftieth."

"I'll be right back, Charlie. Keep looking."

The moment her back was turned, Anthony searched her contact list, finding Jackson's new phone number and committing it to memory. By the time Ainsley returned, he handed her the phone and tapped the photo displayed.

"I like this one. It's not too large, but I like the two different levels and how they're stacked."

"Good choice," she praised, claiming the pencil again as she began to sketch on her pad.

He watched, fascinated as the cake came to life on the page.

"This is a little different than the picture, but it captures the essence of it," she told him, putting the finishing touches on the drawing.

"I noticed the cherry blossoms. They are all over Japan. Becky and I have traveled the country extensively while she's been there. She would really like having cherry blossoms incorporated into the cake's design."

"I'm glad to hear that. I was hoping you'd say so.

Are you comfortable going ahead and placing your order? Or would you like to think about it? Talk it over with Becky?"

"I don't need to think about it, though I would like to snap a picture of your sketch and the cake on your phone."

He took out his own phone and photographed both as she said, "Since the cake you chose is on my website, you can direct Becky there first and then show her the sketch and how I'll alter things slightly to personalize it for your wedding."

She got up and went to the counter, removing a business card from the holder it sat in and handed it to him. "Website is listed there. Also the bakery number. And I'll jot down my cell, as well."

Picking up her phone, she opened her calendar. "You said ten days? That would be not this weekend, but the next."

"Yes. Becky lands on a Thursday. I've checked on the State of Oregon website and found we can apply for our marriage license and have the three-day waiting period waived if we pay an additional fee. She gets in that morning, so we'll go directly to the county clerk's office and apply. I figure she'll need to catch up on sleep the rest of Thursday, and then Friday will be spent getting ready for the wedding on Saturday. She already found a dress in Tokyo. We also bought our rings there during my last trip to visit her, so that's taken care of. I've got the other details covered."

He grinned, ready to drop another personal nugget, which would seem friendly and possibly might draw out a mention of Jackson Martin. "We're both Mickey Mouse fans, so we'll go down to Anaheim and spend a few days in the L.A. area with the mouse. Neither of us have been there before. We're looking forward to it. I just hope after Disneyland I can find a nice restaurant to take her to."

"My husband worked in L.A. for several years. I can ask him if he can recommend a restaurant to you."

"Oh, would you? That would be terrific."

"Do you have time to wait a few minutes?" she asked. "I can print out the contract for you to sign, and you can put down a deposit on your cake. It will include a taste testing, which you'll have to do on your own, I'm afraid, since I'll need to know the flavors in advance."

"No, you're the expert. I'll leave all that up to you. We like pretty much anything sweet."

"Then let's talk flavors and icings," she said, giving him a few recommendations and even going to the display case and pulling a few slices of cake from it so that he could sample a few flavors, as well as try different kinds of icings. Together, they settled on a white almond cake with a ribbon of raspberry running through it and cream cheese icing.

"I think you've made a wonderful choice, Charlie. I have an apartment upstairs, which I've recently turned it into an office. Come on up and let me print out the contract for you and we can go over the details."

He smiled broadly. "That would be great."

Anthony followed her through the kitchen, seeing the older man pictured on the website kneading bread. They went up a set of stairs and into the tiny upstairs apartment. It had enough room for one person, but two would be pushing it.

It would be perfect, though, for what he had in mind after hours. Absolutely perfect.

She offered him a seat and then went to a desk, typing in a few commands. The printer soon began to whir.

"You said you recently got married yourself. So, did you live here before your marriage?" Once again, he knew enough to fill in the spaces with conversation in order to keep someone at ease.

"Yes, I did. All the stores on the square have second levels. A couple of people live in them or rent out the apartment. Some use the extra space as storage. My cousin, who owns Antiques and Mystiques on the square, uses hers as an office. I decided to do the same. I liked it because it's quiet. No one living on either side."

Again, another nugget that let him know this would be the room where he would enjoy bending Ainsley to his will.

"Where did you and your husband move?" he asked, think it a natural question. "Somewhere nearby? Becky and I love the water. With her having family in Crescent Cove, Maple Cove might be a nice alternative. You know—being close—but not *too* close." He chuckled.

"We are renovating a house we bought just a few blocks from the square. It should be ready in a couple of weeks. Until it's ready, we've moved in with my husband's sister and her husband. We'll be staying with Willow and Dylan until we get the go-ahead from our contractor to move into our house. I can tell you the Cove is a wonderful place to live. Salty Point is nice, as well."

"I work from home, so it doesn't really matter where we live. She's a little burned out from teaching, though, and will probably take a break." He smiled. "Who knows? We might go ahead and start a family. We've been dating forever. Six years."

Ainsley smiled softly. "Jackson and I want to do exactly the same thing."

She placed a hand against her belly, and Anthony wondered if she might already be pregnant and didn't even realize it yet.

He signed all the papers she put before him and asked, "Do you mind if I put down a cash deposit?"

"Cash works for me," she said with a smile. "The rest of your balance is due the day before the wedding. The cake will be finished by then. Your contract calls for us to deliver it to your venue."

"Oh, I could pick it up. You don't have to go to that kind of trouble."

She shook her head. "I'm a bit possessive about the wedding cakes I bake. I want to make certain they are delivered to the site without a problem."

"I like the fact that you are meticulous," he said. "I, myself, am the same." He smiled. "It has been a pleasure meeting you, Ainsley. I look forward to seeing how our cake will come to life."

Anthony also looked forward to the private time he would spend with this woman.

CHAPTER 23

Jackson closed the file he was reviewing. It still amazed him how quickly and easily he had settled into life in the Cove after having been gone fifteen years. He knew many of the people who lived here and was getting to know others who had come after he left for California as he took on Clancy's former clients, making them his own.

He glanced at his watch and saw it was almost five o'clock. He and Ainsley were supposed to have dinner with Carter and Tenley tonight at five-thirty. After living all those years in L.A., to be able to leave work, claim Ainsley, and drive to the Clarks' and be seated at their table ready to eat in half an hour was nothing short of miraculous. He hadn't realized how stressful life in L.A. was, and he couldn't be happier to be back in his hometown, practicing law, with the woman he loved by his side.

He didn't know what gossip in the Cove had been regarding their whirlwind romance and marriage, and frankly, he didn't care. Jackson had never been happier in his life. He only wished he would have thought to come home years sooner. Of course, Ainsley wouldn't have been here then. She would have been working in Portland or Seattle or attending pastry school in Paris. He supposed the fates had aligned and brought him back to take over Clancy's practice at the perfect time.

Closing the file, he left it on the desk and rose. His eyes fell to one of Willow's paintings hanging on his office wall. He had commissioned it from her, willing to pay whatever her going price was. His sister had insisted upon making the painting a gift to him. The scene portrayed was the view standing at the bottom of the steps at Boo's place, looking out at the Pacific Ocean. He still remembered the moment he stood there with Ainsley and the picnic they had shared on the beach. It was the day he declared his love for her. He would say that was the best day of his life, but every day with Ainsley proved to be better than the one before.

Jackson locked the office and went to his car, driving the short distance to Boo's house. He and Ainsley had decided to move in with Willow and Dylan a few days ago. Ainsley's apartment above the bakery simply didn't have room for the two of them. At six-three, he barely fit into the shower. The lack of closets and storage space had also proved to be a major problem.

Instead, he had helped her convert the apartment into her office during her two days off, bringing over a desk from the house they'd purchased, as well as a few tables, lamps, and two comfortable chairs. The pitiful excuse for a sofa was long gone. With office space above the bakery now, she could use it not only to keep her records and plan orders but also meet there with clients for consultations. Rylie had helped arrange everything and had even printed out several enlarged photos of cakes and other sweets she had created and framed the photographs, placing them on the walls.

They would live with his sister and brother-in-law until the construction had been completed at their house. He entered Boo's and found it to be quiet. Dylan would be home from work soon, barring any emergencies, and he supposed Willow was working upstairs in her studio. Jackson went to his childhood bedroom and found Ainsley sitting on the bed, slipping into a pair of boots.

He went to her and framed her face with his hands, bending and giving her a slow, sizzling kiss. After he broke it, she grinned at him.

"Are you trying to keep me from making it to dinner on time?" she teased.

"It's a thought," he said, kissing her once more. "But I don't want to disappoint Carter and Tenley."

She slipped on her other boot and stood. "Ready if you are."

"I don't need to change. Sports shirt and slacks should be fine." He sighed. "Casual Friday is every day in the Cove."

They went downstairs to his car and drove the short distance to the Clarks' home.

Carter answered the door, a dish towel draped over his shoulder. "Tenley's on the phone with Sloane. She'll join us shortly."

He led them to the kitchen, where all kinds of wonderful scents lingered in the air. The island was covered with a veritable feast of appetizers.

Carter held out a hand. "This is dinner. I know it's Ainsley's favorite kind of meal."

Jackson watched as his wife's eyes lit up. "This looks incredible, Carter. Even better than what you made for our wedding."

Tenley entered the kitchen. "Inspiration struck my lovely husband after he provided the finger foods for your reception." She hugged Ainsley. "And I helped with several of these. Carter might make a cook out of me yet."

"What is everything?" Jackson asked. "I know if you made it, it'll be good. But I'd love to know what I'm putting into my mouth."

Carter started at the top of the island and went clockwise, detailing each appetizer's contents. "Beef sliders with onions. Stuffed mushrooms. Berry skewers. Meatballs. Pollo asada tacos. Caprese crostini. Pulled pork sliders. Bacon-wrapped dates. And deviled eggs."

"Even if I have one of everything, I'm going to be full," Ainsley warned. "But it will be a good kind of full."

"Grab a plate," their host said. "Try one of each if you would. I don't expect you to like everything, but I value your feedback."

They spent a few minutes making their plates before carrying them to the large dining room and taking a seat.

"I helped with some of the prep work," Tenley told them, "but for the most part, my job was to film Carter while he put together these appetizers."

"Tenley was right," Carter said. "Preparing food for your wedding party inspired me to investigate appetizers more. I really see the potential of a book in them." He laughed. "Maybe you should get married again and have another reception. That way, I could try out all these recipes on a larger scale."

"But you're already working on a cookbook," Ainsley noted. "The one which is supposed to come out when Tenley's first book does, before Thanksgiving."

Carter grinned sheepishly. "I know. And that cookbook is going really well. But I believe that people are staying in more nowadays. Doing more entertaining at home. Appetizers are a big part of entertaining. I believe a cookbook focused solely on them would be viable. I haven't decided how to break it down yet. I could by the kind of cuisine. Italian, Mexican, that kind of thing. I could go the sweet versus savory route. Or I could break it into food groups. Appetizers that feature meat, dairy, fruits and vegetables. It's all in the beginning stages, but I wanted to get some of my thoughts down and have some taste testings to give me guidance on the direction I want to take the book."

As they ate, they provided feedback to Carter, who took notes with his right hand and ate with his left.

"This is all fantastic input," Carter said. "Maybe Tenley and I can host the next Game Night, and it can be an all-appetizer one."

"Let's don't forget we haven't had a Game Night since before Ainsley and I got married," Jackson interjected. "That means I'm still owed my winning dessert."

Tenley chuckled and said, "Then we'll steer Carter away from too many sweet appetizers so everyone will have room for whatever Ainsley concocts."

They sipped on a glass of wine after finishing, a new blend Carter and Tenley had discovered while at a local vineyard the weekend before. The couple both talked a little about the books they were working on. Their agent had encouraged their respective publishing houses to publish Carter's cookbook and the first of Ainsley's fantasy trilogy the same week, and the pair would do a book tour together near the end of the year.

"How are you settling in to your new office, Jackson?" Carter asked.

"I familiarized myself with all of Clancy's files now. I've made calls to the bulk of his clients, reaching out and letting them know I've taken over his practice. I did send an e-mail to that effect, but I'm also trying to talk to everyone by phone—or in person, if they choose—in order to get to know them and their needs. I wrote up a will today, and I'm representing one of the mayor's kids on a misdemeanor charge in court next week."

Ainsley smiled at him. "He'll have to break out a tie for that. I believe Jackson has enjoyed dressing more casually to go to work each day."

"My dry-cleaning bill used to be sky-high," he admitted. "Of course, that included my laundry, as well. I never had time to do it."

"How is living with Willow and Dylan working out?" Tenley asked.

"You know Willow," Ainsley said. "She makes everything easy for those around her. We're trading off on the cooking for dinner."

"Willow told us not to think of ourselves as guests but as family," Jackson added. "That means doing our own laundry and cleaning our bathroom. I don't mind that a bit. It's nice to have time to do the small stuff."

Carter nodded. "I know what you mean. Although I loved being a firefighter, it's nice to be able to manage my own schedule now. Tenley feels the same."

"I sure do," his wife said. "I don't miss the days of dressing up and going in to work, often putting in many hours after I was supposed to be off the clock."

"Do you have a writing schedule?" Jackson asked her.

"It varies from day to day. I do feel I get my best work done in the morning when I'm fresh. I write until noon, and then I break for lunch with Carter. He also has been writing and planning and prepping mornings, so that in the afternoons we can film his vlogs."

"Have you heard anything about the pilot you shot a few weeks ago?" Ainsley asked.

"Not yet," Carter told them. "The waiting is hard. Hopefully, we'll hear something soon. If it doesn't work out, it's not meant to be in the cards at this point, and we'll pursue it down the road."

"I told him that the vlog is really fulfilling that role," Tenley said. "Carter has already got fantastic feedback through it. I try and monitor the comments once a day and pass along suggestions from people."

"Some of them have even given us ideas for dishes we should try," Carter said. "I'm open to suggestions from any and everyone. Are you gearing up for your busy season, Ainsley?"

"It is right around the corner. June will be here before we know it. I did get an order for a wedding cake today."

"Oh, who's getting married?" Tenley wondered. "Anyone we know?"

"No, it's a guy new to the area. Anthony Abbott. He's living temporarily in Crescent Cove with his fiancée's family. She teaches ESL in Japan and will be returning to Oregon late next week. They're getting married a week from this Saturday, and Anthony wanted me to do a small cake for the wedding he's throwing together. Since the fiancée has been living in Japan and Anthony's visited her often, I thought to incorporate cherry blossoms into the cake since Japan is famous for them."

Jackson listened as his new wife described the cake she had designed for her new client. Pride swelled within him, knowing how talented and creative she was.

"We better call it a night," Tenley said. "I don't want you or Ainsley to start yawning on us."

He laughed. "My late nights in L.A. are a thing of the past. I'm still training with Gage three days a week. We were meeting at five but backed it up to four-thirty. I'm actually getting up at three with Ainsley now and drinking a protein shake while I skim the overnight news and my e-mails. I guess it's like being married to a morning TV show anchor with the hours we keep. We're in bed between eight and nine every night, and I've grown to like it quite a bit. I feel I'm more productive. That, and not having to fight the sprawl of L.A. traffic. It was reason enough to move back to the Cove."

He took Ainsley's hand and brought it to his lips, kissing it tenderly. "That—and this woman."

They left their friends' house and returned to Boo's, where Jackson slowly undressed Ainsley, kissing every inch of bared flesh. He made love to her, savoring her scent and the feel of his skin against hers. He turned her so that her back was to his chest, and he wrapped himself around her as a human blanket.

"Mmm," she said sleepily. "This... you feel... heavenly. I wonder if we made a baby just now."

He kissed her nape. "I hope so. Go to sleep, babe," he urged.

Almost immediately, Jackson heard Ainsley's soft, even breathing, knowing she had dropped off to sleep.

He thought about a few of the items on his to-do list for tomorrow.

Then something tugged at him. Something he couldn't put a finger on. He mentally walked through his day and couldn't figure out what troubled him. He decided to shrug it off. If it were something important, it would come to him.

Jackson buried his face in Ainsley's hair and drifted off to sleep.

CHAPTER 24

Ainsley was icing pastries when she caught the tang of Jackson's cologne. Seconds later, his arms went around her from behind, and he nuzzled her neck.

"Good morning again," he said huskily, turning her so she faced him and giving her a kiss.

He was leaving this morning to fly down to L.A. and meet the moving van at his storage facility. They had talked about what furniture he had which they could place in their new home this coming Monday. Pete's crew—in part, thanks to Carter's work on their house—had finished ahead of schedule, and they would do a final walk-through tomorrow afternoon once the bakery closed. Jackson had already arranged with Rylie to bring a few pieces to her shop for consignment.

She looked up and saw Willow standing in the doorway and said, "Thank you again for agreeing to drive Jackson into Portland for his flight."

"Not a problem," her sister-in-law said. "It's nice to spend some time with my big brother. Besides, I don't have a set schedule, so it's easier for me to get away for a couple of hours. I don't mind going into Portland because I'm stopping by an art supply store for new paints and canvases after I drop him at the airport. It was perfect timing."

"You still will pick me up when I get in tonight?" Jackson asked her. "I'm scheduled to land a little before six."

Ainsley nodded. "Yes, I'm going to go into Portland a little early to do my usual Monday stock-up run. That way, we'll have that entire day devoted to moving into our new house. Since Antiques and Mystiques is closed on Mondays, Rylie has promised to be there to help out in any way she can."

"You can always call on me, too," Willow added. "That's the beauty of working for myself."

Jackson looked around. "Is that my box?"

"It is," she told him.

"Ooh, are we taking goodies for the road?" Willow asked, rubbing her hands in glee.

"No, this is for my old partner and the office staff in L.A. I told Bill I would drop by to say hi once I handled everything with the movers and was headed back to LAX for my flight home. I wanted to show off my wife's talents."

He scooped up the box.

She reached for two small sacks sitting on a nearby counter and handed them to Willow. "These are for the two of you. Breakfast in the car. I also told Gloria to make up two lattes when you came in."

Willow opened one sack and inhaled deeply. "Mmm. I love a road trip when there's food involved, especially pastries you've made."

Jackson kissed her again. "I'll see you tonight." His eyes fell to the wedding cake she had finished early this morning. "That is a thing of beauty. For the wedding tomorrow?"

"Yes, it's the cake for Anthony Abbott and his bride. Since it's small, I can drop it off myself in Crescent Cove and then head up to Portland for my shopping."

"Let's get on the road, Bro," Willow said. "You claim the lattes for us."

Her husband kissed her one last time and grinned. "See you soon."

The rest of her day flew by, and she said goodbye to her staff a little after three. Gus had boxed up the wedding cake for her and now carried it to her car.

"Are you sure you don't need my help delivering this cake?" he asked as he placed it in the back of her SUV, securing it so it wouldn't be jostled during the drive.

"No, you see how small it is. I'll drop it off and then head up to Portland. Tomorrow morning, you can help me unload the supplies from the car, though. We probably won't do so after we get home tonight."

"I can do that," Gus told her. "Tell Jackson hello."

Ainsley went upstairs to her office and took a quick shower, washing the sweet smells of the bakery from her and dressing in fresh clothes for her husband. She added a touch of lipstick and was about to head out the door when her cell rang.

She didn't recognize the number but with Jackson being out of town, she decided to answer it.

"Hello?"

"Is this Ainsley Martin?" an anxious voice asked.

"Yes, it is. Who is this?"

A muffled sound occurred, and then, "This is Anthony. Anthony Abbott. I'm almost to Maple Cove. I've come to get... the cake."

"I told you that I would be delivering it," she said gently, hearing how upset he was. "In fact, it's already in my car now. I was about to leave."

"Don't," he said, urgency in his voice. "I'll get it."

"Then you'll need to come around to the alley behind Buttercup Bakery," she said, worried at how he sounded and guessing the wedding was off. "I'll meet you out back. We can transfer the cake to your car, then I need to get on the road. I'm picking up my husband at the airport in Portland."

"I'll be there... in less than five minutes."

Her client hung up without a goodbye, and a wave of sadness swept over her. This had only happened on one other occasion, a couple canceling their wedding at the last minute. The bride and her mother had shown up at the bakery, both in tears, the bride hysterical. She had caught her groom in bed with her maid of honor two days before the wedding. Ainsley had baked all three tiers and had iced the bottom layer by the time they arrived. The mother of the bride told Ainsley to send her the bill for what was owed. She had told the mom their deposit would cover supplies and time she had already spent, not wanting to add to their heartache.

Now it looked as if another wedding wouldn't take place.

She made her way downstairs and unlocked the rear door leading to the alley, propping it open in case Anthony changed his mind and wanted to leave the cake behind. She could always slice it and sell those tomorrow and try to turn a little profit from the disaster. She went to her car and unlocked it, tossing her purse onto the passenger's seat and opening the tailgate to her SUV.

A car rounded the corner and pulled in two spots

down from hers. Anthony Abbott got out, a bottle in one hand and two champagne flutes in the other. He slammed his door using his foot and came toward her.

Frowning, she said, "I see you are upset. Can I do anything for you?"

"You can drink a toast with me and celebrate the fact that I dodged a bullet," he said flatly.

She really didn't want to have a drink since she was about to get on the road to Portland, but she didn't want to upset him further. She could take a sip or two and then send him on his way.

"Come inside the bakery," she suggested.

He brushed past her and she hit the remote so the car would be locked and her purse safe before following him inside. He had already uncorked the champagne and was pouring some into a glass. He moved to the other flute and filled it, as well, handing it to her.

"I should have known," he muttered, tapping his flute against hers and taking a drink of the champagne.

The bubbles tickled her nose as she did the same and then held it in her hand, watching him to see what explanation he might offer her.

His gaze met hers, anguish in his eyes. "She doesn't want to marry me. She's going to marry someone else." He took another drink, and she took one more sip before setting her flute on a nearby table.

"The thing is," he continued, "I know him. I thought he was my friend." He cursed softly and then downed the contents of his glass. "I guess it's better I found out now than us going through the ceremony and her cheating on me with him."

"I agree," she said. "I know you are in a world of

pain now, but in the long run, you'll be happy you didn't commit to marriage with her."

"Do you think there's someone else out there for me, Ainsley?" he asked, his gaze intense.

"I hope so," she said encouragingly. "Right now, though, you're going to need to take time to heal. You don't want to start up another relationship quickly."

She blinked a few times, her eyes suddenly feeling heavy. Her bottom lip also felt as if it were going numb. An odd feeling rippled through her.

He took a step toward her and picked up her abandoned flute. Bringing it to her lips, he urged, "Drink."

She did so, draining the glass, as if she had no will of her own or control over her movements. She began to grow dizzy and said, "I need to sit down." The words sounded faraway and slurred to her ears.

"Why don't you come upstairs and rest a minute?" he said, his voice solicitous and yet sounding odd.

She tried to focus on his image, but it kept shifting.

He slipped an arm about her waist and draped her arm over his shoulder. They began moving toward the stairs.

Suddenly, she found herself in a chair, not remembering how she got there. Nausea filled her. She was going to be sick. She tried to push herself up to reach the bathroom. But her hands didn't cooperate. She looked down and saw they were somehow bound together. Confusion filled her, and she tried to stand without their help but couldn't seem to move. Her whole body tingled. She made a noise, knowing she was about to throw up, but a mixing bowl appeared in front of her. She vomited into it. The bowl moved away, and she glanced up as someone dabbed her mouth with a handkerchief.

It was... Anthony Abbott...

He smoothed her hair, tucking a lock behind her ear.

"What?" she asked groggily.

"There was no Becky," he told her quietly. "No wedding."

"No... wedding?" she echoed, disoriented.

"No, Ainsley. It was all a ruse. To meet you."

"Why?" was all she could get out, her thoughts clouded, fear pooling low in her belly.

"I wanted to meet the woman my attorney married," he said brightly. "You see, I was one of Jackson's clients."

Even though her brain seemed fogged, she knew instinctively who this man was.

"You're... the one. His last client in L.A. The one he got off."

"Ah, I didn't know I was the last one. I only knew Jackson had left California and come to his hometown. Had that been the plan all along, Ainsley? Were you engaged while Jackson defended me?"

She was having trouble forming thoughts, much less putting words together, but she knew to give no more information to this monster. Ainsley pretended to say something and then closed her eyes, hoping to buy time.

That was the last thing she remembered.

CHAPTER 25

Jackson landed at LAX and was glad he would only be in town for the day. With no bags to claim, he called an Uber and was soon on his way to the storage facility. He went inside the office when he arrived and arranged to give up the space by the end of the month. He went to the unit and unlocked it, walking through the small space. He didn't know how many of the clothes packed away in the numerous boxes he would wear since many of them were suits, dress shirts, and ties. Still, he would have them brought to the Cove and see what he truly wished to keep before he gave away anything. He had gone through a list of the furnishings he had with Ainsley and Rylie and knew which pieces would go to the new house and which ones would go straight to Rylie's store for resale.

The moving van arrived, and he greeted the movers. The driver handed him a tablet, and he quickly read through the paperwork before signing.

The driver reclaimed and skimmed over it, saying, "I see we are making two stops. One at a house, and one at a store? Same town."

"Yes. I can tell you which furniture goes to which place, so if you want to group the pieces going to the house with all of those boxes and deliver it before you go to the store—or vice-versa—I can."

The man nodded. "Direct us on what to do then, Mr. Martin. I have tags that will designate what goes to which stop."

With Jackson's guidance, the movers loaded their van, keeping the two groupings apart. When the final box left the storage unit, he pulled down the door and went out to the truck.

"Delivery is scheduled for this coming Monday," one of the movers told him. "Is that correct?"

"Yes, it is."

The movers climbed into the van and left the property as Jackson called for another rideshare to take him to his former office. He had the box of pastries with him, eager to show off his new wife's artistry.

He got antsy with all the traffic, once again grateful that he had left L.A. behind. He read the national news daily and found himself turning to a few California newspaper websites, skimming them to see if his former client, Gerard McGreer, had been arrested. The case—and the client—had left a sour taste in Jackson's mouth. He thought of the last day, just before McGreer's verdict came in, and how the accused was already trying to line up Jackson and the firm in case something else happened and he was charged with a crime again. He shuddered at the thought, hoping no other innocents would be violated by McGreer.

He arrived at his former workplace and was greeted warmly by their receptionist.

"How are you, Cindy?" he asked as she moved from behind the desk and gave him a big hug.

"We've missed you, Jackson," she said. "Flannigan is doing a great job, but no one could ever replace you."

Their paralegal appeared with a stack of files, placing them on Cindy's desk, and giving him a hug.

"Come on back to the conference room," she said. "Bill and Flan are working on a case, but they know you are stopping by."

Jackson followed both women back to the familiar conference room, placing the box he'd brought on the table and shaking hands with Bill Watterscheim.

"It's good to see you, Bill," he declared. "You're looking good," his former partner told him. "And we're swamped with cases. Sure you don't want to come back?"

"Not on your life," he said, laughing. Then he turned and greeted Richard Flannigan. "Hey, Flan. How are you fitting in at Watterscheim & Flannigan?"

"Best decision I ever made was to buy you out, Jackson," the attorney said. "Have a seat."

They gathered around the conference table, and Jackson opened the box he had brought. Both women oohed and ahhed over what was inside.

"These are from my wife's bakery," he said proudly.

"Let me grab some plates and napkins," Cindy said, hurrying from the room.

Bill eyed the contents. "If they taste half as good as they look, I'll know why you married Ainsley so quickly."

They spent an enjoyable half-hour catching up, their two private investigators also making an appearance and claiming pastries from the box.

Jackson consulted his watch. "I'm going to need to head out in order to make my flight home."

"You were just here for the day?" Bill asked.

He nodded. "I have to be back because tomorrow we're doing a walk-through in the home we purchased. We had some work done to it, and we're meeting the contractor to make sure everything is up to speed before we move in on Monday."

Everyone rose, and Bill offered Jackson his hand. "It was good to see you, buddy. Yes, I was pissed that you left, but Flan here has been a terrific replacement. Thanks for recommending him."

"Do you have a rental?" Flannigan asked.

"No, I just Ubered everywhere. It's easier."

"Why don't you let Cindy take you to the airport?" Bill offered. "Friday afternoons are a little slow. We can cover the phones."

"I can do that," their paralegal piped up.

Jackson looked to Cindy? "Do you mind?"

"Not a bit." She grinned. "Because I have no plans of coming back here once I drop you off. Any excuse to try and beat the traffic."

They left the office, climbing into Cindy's Honda, and heading toward the airport. He asked her about her twin boys, who were eight, and who lived and breathed baseball. In turn, she asked him about his new life in Maple Cove, and he readily shared with her.

Just before they reached the airport, she said, "One of your old clients called not too long ago."

A since of dread filled him. "It wasn't Gerard McGreer, by any chance?"

"No, it was Sam Johnson. He said you had represented him before, and he was pretty disappointed that you had left the firm and the state. He went ahead and booked an appointment but stood us up. When I tried to call the number he left, it was a dead end."

"You said Sam Johnson?" he couldn't remember a client by that generic name, but then again, he had had hundreds of clients over the years. "I guess I've had too many clients. His name doesn't ring any bells for me."

Jackson told her he was flying Southwest, and Cindy pulled up at the terminal to let him out.

"Thanks again for the ride," he told her. "Say hello to your family for me. And come see us sometime. The Oregon coast is beautiful."

"I wish we could, but summer means baseball tournaments. That's where my vacation days will go. Maybe someday."

Jackson got out of the car and went into the terminal, claiming his boarding pass and getting through security with no problems. He walked to his gate and saw the flight was on time. Taking a seat, he decided to check in with Ainsley.

Then he changed his mind and called the office, their paralegal answering.

"Hey, it's Jackson. Cindy mentioned to me that one of my old clients—a Sam Johnson—recently called and was looking for representation."

"I remember her saying that. He was a no-show."

"I don't remember him, and it's bothering me a little. Would you mind checking and seeing what charge I represented him on? That might jar a memory for me."

"Give me a minute," she said.

He heard her long fingernails clicking on the computer keyboard and then a pause.

"Hmm. I don't see a record of a Sam Johnson. Is it possible you represented him when you were on the other side of the table? Maybe the DA's office brought a case against someone, and he was the victim your office represented?"

"I don't know," he said guardedly. "Thanks anyway. It was good see you."

"You, too, Jackson. Take care."

He hung up, racking his brain, not able to recall a Sam Johnson, much less any case with a Johnson. He was usually good at names and had excellent recall of people he had represented. Why could he not remember this person?

It slammed into him, so hard that it seemed like a physical blow. Jackson couldn't breathe.

Anthony Abbott.

He finally remembered where he had heard the name. And it wasn't when Ainsley had mentioned she was baking a wedding cake for an Anthony Abbott. No, it was the name Gerard McGreer had thrown out when he was talking about changing his name after the trial.

Panic swelled within Jackson, choking him, making his hands tremble violently. It wasn't a coincidence that Anthony Abbott had come to Buttercup Bakery. Jackson's gut told him there was no such thing as coincidence. That a man of the same name had not miraculously appeared in the Cove, needing a wedding cake baked.

He tried to still his shaking hands as he called Ainsley. She was supposed to deliver the Abbott cake to Crescent Cove. He needed to stop her from doing so.

After three rings, her phone went to voice-mail. Looking at the time, she was either in Crescent Cove by now or should be on her way to Portland.

Fear seized him. he tried to calm himself as he dialed his brother-in-law's number.

Dylan answered on the first ring. "Hey, Jackson. Still in L.A.?"

"You've got to find Ainsley for me," he said tersely. "She's in danger."

"Tell me everything," Dylan urged.

Quickly, Jackson told him of his last client in California who had been accused of rape and murder and how he'd been found not guilty.

"It struck me when he tried to line me up for future representation, even before the verdict was read, Dylan. After it was, one of the jurors approached me, claiming she had been threatened to vote not guilty.

He explained the circumstances, how his client was tech savvy, and the messages had disappeared from the juror's phone, which but she had found her dead cat as a physical warning.

"It was the straw that broke the camel's back for me in wanting to leave L.A. I knew in my heart Mc-Greer was guilty."

"What does he have to do with Ainsley?"

Jackson gripped his phone. "McGreer told me he wanted to start a new life. He asked me how to go about changing his name legally. I told him how to do so, and he mentioned a name to me. Anthony Abbott. I didn't remember until now. Ainsley has a client by that name, living in Crescent Cove. She was to deliver a wedding cake to Abbott this afternoon when the bakery closed before coming to Portland to pick me up."

He had watched people boarding the plane and knew he would need to get on it soon. "I've got to board now, Dylan. You've got to find Ainsley. I called and voice-mail picked up. I haven't been able to reach her. just saying those words caused apprehension, worry, and dread to run through him.

"I'm on it," Dylan told him. "Text me your flight number and ETA. I'll have one of my deputies, Raymond Garcia, pick you up and get you back to the Cove as soon as possible."

"Thank you. Please. Find Ainsley. Keep her safe."

Jackson rose and joined the dwindling line, boarding the plane, and then texting Dylan his flight info. As the plane rolled away from the gate and he turned off his phone, Jackson had never felt more helpless his entire life.

CHAPTER 26

Jackson stood next to Ainsley's car, which was parked behind Buttercup Bakery. He called her cell and, as expected, heard the ringing inside the car. Dylan had located her locked SUV, with her purse and the cake she was to deliver to Crescent Cove, inside it. The bakery was also locked. Dylan and his deputies had scoured the square, talking to all the tenants on it, especially the ones on the side of Buttercup Bakery, asking if they had seen Ainsley in the alley with anyone or seen any vehicles they did not recognize. They had struck out. No one had seen a thing.

Dylan had notified his counterparts in Crescent City and Salty Point, giving them the heads up on Ainsley's disappearance and the possible connection to Gerard McGreer, now going by Anthony Abbott. Deputy Linda Goodnight was a whiz with computers and had located McGreer's petition to change his name with the State of California. She had also found the notices he had posted in public newspapers.

A squad car pulled up, and Deputy Oswald Jones got out, as did Gus. The baker rushed to Jackson's side.

"I'm sorry, Jackson. I just didn't know. The guy

didn't set off any alarm bells with me. You'd think he would have, me being a convicted felon and having spent enough time around men like him."

Jackson said, "Don't blame yourself, Gus. It's not your fault. But we need to compare notes on this Anthony Abbott and his appearance. If he changed his name, I have a feeling he might have also altered his physical appearance."

Dylan stepped forward. "I pulled up a few pictures from his trial. Ones that appeared in newspapers in L.A." He turned his phone toward Gus. "Is this the man who came in the bakery?"

Immediately, Gus shook his head. "No. He looks nothing like the man we saw."

"Give us a description then, Gus," Dylan urged. "As detailed as possible."

Gus closed his eyes tightly, his face scrunching up in thought. "Abbott didn't have that receding hairline. In fact, he had a head full of hair."

"Could've been hair transplants," Jackson murmured. "What else, Gus?"

"His nose was different. Thinner. And his chin was stronger. More... square." Gus opened his eyes and looked at the picture again. "He didn't wear glasses. And I can't tell what his teeth look like, but this Abbott fellow had a good smile."

"Then he's had dental work done," Jackson noted. "Probably had them capped. Maybe contacts or LASIK because I know he was extremely nearsighted."

Gus nodded vigorously. "His smile was... so easy."

"Gerard McGreer is a psychopath," Jackson said flatly. "He would have practiced that smile to disarm others."

Dylan said, "Salty Point has a guy who's a decent sketch artist. I'll contact their chief. Gus, would you be willing to go over there and work with him on a sketch?"

"Anything you need," Gus said fervently. "Ainsley means the world to me. She believed in me when no one else did. We've got to find her."

Dylan signaled Deputy Garcia and asked him to drive Gus to Salty Point. He fired off a quick text and then looked to Jackson. "We're doing everything we can."

Dylan's phone rang and he answered it, tersely asking a few questions before hanging up.

"That was Crescent Cove. They think they found where Abbott was staying. At a B&B. But he was using the name Sam Johnson. He checked out this morning. Nothing left behind. The woman who runs the place has already cleaned the room thoroughly. She did give a description of Johnson to the police. It matches what Gus told us."

"He used that name when he contacted my former law firm in L.A.," Jackson said.

His thoughts wandered to his defense of McGreer. What McGreer had done to his victim. A mix of anger and regret filled him, having gotten his client off so he could terrorize others again.

Including Ainsley.

"I'm going to go back to the station," Dylan told him. "I'll call you the minute we have any kind of break in the case. Do you want me to have someone take you home?"

"No, I think I'll stay here in town."

"Are you sure?" Dylan asked. "Willow is at home. I know she wants to comfort you in any way she can."

"No one can comfort me," Jackson spat out. "My wife is missing! For all we know, she could already be dead." He wheeled, storming down the alley.

Immediately, he regretted his outburst. He knew Dylan and his deputies were doing everything they could to find Ainsley.

Returning to his friend, he said, "I'm sorry. I'm teetering on the edge."

Dylan placed a hand on Jackson's shoulder and squeezed. "I understand, buddy. If Willow were missing, I would be out of my mind."

"I'm going to go sit in the gazebo," Jackson said. "I need time to think. Maybe I know something about McGreer, and I don't even know I know it yet. Something that might help us find Ainsley."

He walked down the alley and turned, moving toward the center of the town's square. Climbing the steps to the gazebo, he sat on the bench. Tears stung his eyes.

What would he do in a world without Ainsley?

No, he couldn't think like that. He had to remain positive. Yes, Gerard McGreer had taken Ainsley, but Jackson knew there had to be more to it. More to play out. Somehow, his gut told him that McGreer would want Jackson involved.

His phone chimed, and he pulled it from his pocket to read the text. His blood ran cold.

Don't say anything to anyone. I see you are alone. Return to the alley behind the bakery.

As Jackson stood, the text dissolved, leaving no trace of it. That was confirmation enough of who sent it to him. McGreer had done the same to the juror he'd terrorized.

He returned the way he had come, his gait even, rounding the corner and heading down the alley again. As he did, another text came in.

Rear door is now unlocked. Come through and lock it. Apartment upstairs also open. Come in and join the fun.

His gut soured reading McGreer's words, and once more, the words disappeared from his screen. Jackson reached Buttercup Bakery and entered, closing and locking the door. He wanted to quickly search for some kind of weapon but didn't want to show up armed and endanger Ainsley any more than she already was.

He went to the door that led to her apartment and found it also unlocked. Mounting the stairs, he paused a moment at the top to collect himself. He had to outwit a killer. Both Ainsley's life and his were on the line. He would not let her down. He would not let her die. If it came down to it, he would sacrifice himself if it would mean she could live.

Jackson turned the knob and pushed open the door. Immediately, he caught sight of Ainsley, who sat in one of the two chairs in front of her desk, her wrists bound together.

Gerard McGreer stood behind her, his gaze locking on Jackson's. One hand fondled her breast in an obvious attempt to rile Jackson. His other held a gun to her right temple. Ainsley didn't seem aware of either. Her eyes were glazed. Her jaw slack. It was obvious McGreer had given her some kind of drug.

He took a few steps forward and called her name. She didn't even look in his direction.

"Stop," McGreer commanded.

"What did you give her?" he demanded, coming to a halt.

McGreer shrugged, giving Jackson the easy, practiced smile Gus had mentioned, showing off the new set of teeth. "Rohypnol. Ainsley doesn't even realize you're here. She won't remember some of the things I do to her as you watch. But once it wears off? She'll feel plenty."

"Don't touch her," he warned, his voice low and deadly. "She hasn't done anything to you. I'm the one you want. Isn't that right?"

His former client shrugged. "You're merely a bonus, Jackson." McGreer's smile turned pure evil. "Did I scare the big, bad attorney from practicing law in California? Did that sweet little pregnant juror tell you I threatened her?" McGreer paused, his smile pure evil. "Do you have *any* idea what I'm capable of?"

Jackson braced himself. "I know exactly what you can do. I saw your handiwork in the photographs the DA entered into evidence. I'm only sorry I got you off."

McGreer clucked his tongue. "You shouldn't be. You were fucking brilliant. I'm brilliant myself. I was only sorry I got careless that one time and was charged." He beamed. "Because I've raped and killed many times, Jackson. All blonds, just like your pretty little wife here."

"Why?" he asked, wanting to keep McGreer talking while he tried to think of a way to stop him.

"Why? It doesn't matter. I'm a product of incest, so I suppose that makes me a little crazy to begin with." He stared hard at Jackson. "But I like to think I'm crazy like a fox."

"You've already made a major mistake," Jackson told the killer.

"What?" McGreer asked, his brow furrowing.

"You should have stuck with the Sam Johnson alias. The one you used when you contacted my former law practice. The one you used in Crescent Cove. You didn't use it with Ainsley, though. You gave her your new, legal name. Anthony Abbott. I think you wanted to get caught."

"Actually, I wanted to see if you would recall that's who I said I would become," the killer said, though

Jackson could see alarm flare in the man's eyes. "I was testing *you*, Jackson. And you failed miserably. If you would have remembered, you would have known your sweet piece of ass here was in danger."

"That name is burned now. The police know it. They'll be looking for you. Both the woman who ran the B&B where you stayed and one of Ainsley's employees have already given the authorities an excellent description of what you look like now."

A flicker of annoyance crossed McGreer's face. "I don't really need the Anthony Abbott name," he said, a bit too hastily. "But I do like my new look. Shedding my glasses after so many years was liberating. Getting a decent nose and teeth also felt pretty damn good."

"They're working with a sketch artist now," he told the killer. "Your face will soon be over all the different news outlets."

"Fuck," McGreer said, his face growing red.

"You don't have time for Ainsley to come around. You need to get out of here now, McGreer. Abbott. Whatever you want to call yourself. Get a head start. Flee the Cove. I won't call anyone. All I want is to take care of Ainsley."

Jackson took two steps forward. Panic appeared on McGreer's face. "Stop. Now."

He did so, knowing he was closer than before. Almost close enough to lunge at McGreer. But the psychopath still held a gun to Ainsley's head. Jackson couldn't risk it going off.

"I'm sure you have money socked away. Lots of it," he said encouragingly. "You're a smart guy. The best there is at tech. You could get out of the Cove. Disappear for a while. Grow a beard. Shave your head bald. Have a little more plastic surgery. You might like your new look even better than this one."

"I could," McGreer mused before a dazzling smile lit his features. "Then come back for Ainsley someday. When neither of you would expect it."

He didn't understand the killer's fixation with Ainsley—and Jackson couldn't risk this man returning and taking his wife from him.

Jackson had to end this. Here and now.

He spotted what he hoped would do the trick. It would mean moving quickly. It might mean getting shot. But he needed to draw McGreer's attention—and gun—away from Ainsley, who was too drugged to help herself.

McGreer reached into his pocket and tossed something onto the desk. A pair of handcuffs.

"Put them on," the madman ordered. "Cuff your right wrist first." He glanced around. "Then lock the other one around the handle of the stove over there."

Jackson took two steps and reached the desk. If he wanted, he could even touch Ainsley. He picked up the handcuffs and slipped one around his right wrist as instructed, clicking it into place. Glancing up, he saw McGreer had finally turned the gun away from Ainsley and now pointed it at Jackson.

Just as he'd hoped.

He turned to go and then spun quickly, grabbing the vase of flowers that sat on the desk. He launched it at the gunman, heaving it hard, harder than any pitch he'd ever hurled at a batter. It struck McGreer in the face. The gun went off, the sound incredibly loud in the small apartment. A searing pain burned Jackson's shoulder as he lunged for the killer, knocking McGreer off his feet and landing atop him.

Jackson jammed his arm against McGreer's throat, pinning him to the ground. He reached for the killer's right wrist and gripped it, slamming it against the ground three times before McGreer released the gun. It was just out of his reach. Jackson didn't dare release McGreer's wrist. Already, the psychopath tried to buck him off, punching Jackson's side with his left hand.

He felt his strength begin to ebb, the pain in his shoulder now on fire. He couldn't let this man live. McGreer was too great a danger to Ainsley.

Then the punches ceased and Jackson's eyes flew to his right. McGreer had grabbed a sharp piece of glass from the shattered vase. Before he could try and slice Jackson with it, Jackson lunged for it, grabbing McGreer's wrist in both his hands as it moved toward him. Leveraging his weight since he was on top of the killer, he was able to turn it back toward McGreer.

And moved it to his throat.

Jackson pushed with all the strength he had, McGreer pushing back in their deadly struggle. Then a crazed laugh sounded from the killer and he went limp. The glass plunged deep into his throat. Blood spurted. Jackson scrambled to his feet, his shoulder in agony. He glanced down and saw the bloodstain spreading. He grew lightheaded and leaned against the desk, pulling out his phone. He didn't want to dial 911. Instead, he called Dylan directly.

"We're above the bakery," he gasped. "Need an ambulance." His gaze fell to the floor, where Gerard McGreer's frozen gaze stared at the ceiling. "McGreer's... dead."

The phone slipped from his hands. He didn't try to retrieve it. Dropping to his knees, he placed his hand on the wound in his shoulder and pressed hard. His other hand took Ainsley's.

"It's all right, babe. We're going to be all right."

EPILOGUE

PARIS—FIVE MONTHS LATER

Jackson awoke, his shoulder stiff as usual. Ainsley snuggled close to him, her warmth a balm to his body and soul.

He had been lucky. In so many ways.

The gunshot wound he'd suffered had led to soft tissue damage and massive bleeding, though no bone had shattered. Fortunately, Carter had been with Dylan when Jackson called for help and rushed to the bakery. With his EMT experience, Carter had been able to get the massive bleeding under control before the ambulance arrived to take both Jackson and Ainsley to the emergency room. Carter rode with them, giving the EMTs instructions and keeping Jackson calm.

His only concern had been for Ainsley.

Fortunately, the effects of the Rohypnol wore off, leaving her a bit groggy and confused for a day. At least, that's what Willow had shared with him. He had been in surgery and recovery, unconscious during those hours. By the time he was awake and aware of his surroundings, Ainsley was by his side. She, like many victims of Rohypnol, didn't recall anything that had happened between her and McGreer that day. It was all a blank. She had lost the entire week leading up to that fatal day, which Jackson thought was a blessing in disguise.

His wife did experience a tremendous amount of guilt, though, allowing Gerard McGreer into their lives. It was Tenley who had convinced Ainsley to go into therapy to work out those issues. She had seen a therapist for three months after the incident and now had come to terms with what had happened.

Jackson wasn't charged with killing McGreer, or Anthony Abbott, his legal name when he died. It was a clear act of self-defense. While Ainsley had encouraged Jackson to also speak with a therapist, he had no issues to resolve. No anxiety or nightmares. No depression or anger, all normal feelings which could be caused by such a traumatic event. Jackson had done what he needed to do to save his wife's life.

And he would do it a thousand times over if he had to.

Fortunately, his friends had taken the reins and worked a set of miracles for them. By the time he left the hospital, it was to return to their new, furnished home. Rylie and Gage had done the walkthrough with Pete, approving the work the contractor had done, and Rylie and Willow met the moving van that Monday. When Jackson and Ainsley returned home, it was to a house filled with furniture arranged to their taste. The refrigerator and pantry were stocked. The linen closet filled. Their clothes hung in the closets and were placed in the drawers. Beds were made. And to their surprise, Willow had hung one of her paintings over the fireplace and placed one of Boo's sculptures in their den.

They didn't change a thing.

Carter had provided meals for a week, bringing them over hot and fresh. He had also stocked the freezer with another week's worth, and they ate off that, as well. Jackson did rehab with his shoulder and continued to train with Gage, though their regimen had changed somewhat because of his injury. It continued to morph based upon Jackson's progress.

He and Ainsley had settled into a routine once more. The bakery had its busiest summer since its opening. His law practice continued to attract new clients. They had even been able to hold Clancy's birthday at their home on the Fourth of July.

Now, though, they were on their delayed honeymoon.

Jackson had thought from the beginning to bring Ainsley to Paris once tourist season on the Oregon coast ended. He had never been abroad and knew how much the city meant to her. They had left for two weeks in France, some days staying in the city, others taking day trips to places such as Versailles, Mont St. Michel, and Normandy. They had hit all the usual tourist attractions. The Louvre. Notre-Dame and the Eiffel Tower. The opera house and Arc de Triomphe. They had also gone to museums and markets. Out-of-the-way bistros and cafés. He had become a fan of *pot au feu* and *coq au vin*, and also desserts such as *tarte tatin* and *mille-feuille*, and Ainsley promised to make him both pastries once they returned home.

Today, they would finish up their stay with a tour of the Paris catacombs and a final stroll—with a bit of shopping—along the Champs-Elysees.

Jackson felt his wife begin to stir. Moments later, she pressed a kiss to his chest.

"Good morning, Mr. Martin," she said sleepily.

"Good morning, Mrs. Martin. And Baby Martin," he added, not bothering to hide his grin.

He placed his palm against her belly, only now with a slight bulge. She was twelve weeks along today, and they would tell their family and friends of the pregnancy once they returned to the Cove.

"Do you hope for a boy or a girl?" she asked.

"Either." He grinned. "Maybe it's both."

She laughed, a sound that brought joy to him. Jackson kissed her. The kiss heated up, and soon he was making love to the woman who had changed his life for the better. He loved to hear all the sweet noises she made as she came. Most of all, he enjoyed cradling her in his arms when they finished. He had never felt closer to anyone than he did Ainsley in those moments right after they made love together.

"I don't think it's twins," she said. "They don't run in my family. Do they in yours?"

"Not that I know," he replied, nuzzling her throat. "I'm just thrilled to be a dad. And your husband. Those are the best roles I'll ever play."

"I hope he or she has your athletic ability. And my baking smarts, of course."

He chuckled. "Now that would be a perfect child. I hope he or she has your blond hair."

"And your sunny smile. I think I fell in love with your smile even before I fell in love with you," she told him.

Jackson looked down at his wife. "You make me want to smile all the time."

He kissed her deeply, knowing their love—and family—would grow in the coming years.

READ LYRICS OF LOVE –
BOOK 4

If you loved Jackson and Ainsley getting their HEA—with a little help from all their friends at Game Night—you'll want to read *The Lyrics of Love, Book 4 in the Maple Cove series!*

Ainsley's cousin Rylie takes center stage in a tender romance that will tug on your heartstrings, as the Maple Cove Game Night group embraces Nash, a newcomer to the Cove.

Country superstar Nash Edwards retreats to Maple Cove to lick his wounds after a nasty divorce, determining he'll never marry again. He meets antiques dealer Rylie Robinson—and their encounter has him rethinking what he wants in life.

Rylie is approaching thirty, and her friends are marrying and starting families. She yearns to do the same, fighting her attraction to Nash. Rylie's not interested in casual sex with a man who doesn't trust women.

Will Nash realize Rylie is the best thing that has ever happened to him—or will his stubbornness keep them alone and apart for good?

A Bit of Heaven on Earth

A Knight for Kallen

SECOND SONS OF LONDON:

Educated by the Earl

Debating with the Duke

DUKES DONE WRONG:

Discouraging the Duke

Deflecting the Duke

Disrupting the Duke

Delighting the Duke

Destiny with a Duke

DUKES OF DISTINCTION:

Duke of Renown

Duke of Charm

Duke of Disrepute

Duke of Arrogance

Duke of Honor

MEDIEVAL RUNAWAY WIVES:

Song of the Heart

A Promise of Tomorrow

Destined for Love

SOLDIERS AND SOULMATES:

To Heal an Earl

To Tame a Rogue

To Trust a Duke

To Save a Love

To Win a Widow

<u>THE ST. CLAIRS:</u>
Devoted to the Duke

Midnight with the Marquess

Embracing the Earl

Defending the Duke

Suddenly a St. Clair

<u>THE KING'S COUSINS:</u>
God of the Seas

The Pawn

The Heir

The Bastard

<u>THE KNIGHTS OF HONOR:</u>
Rise of de Wolfe

Word of Honor

Marked by Honor

Code of Honor

Journey to Honor

Heart of Honor

Bold in Honor

Love and Honor

Gift of Honor

Path to Honor

Return to Honor

Season of Honor

<u>NOVELLAS:</u>

Diana

Derek

Thea

The Lyon's Lady Love

ABOUT THE AUTHOR

A native Texan and former history teacher, award-winning and internationally bestselling author Alexa Aston lives with her husband in a Dallas suburb, where she eats her fair share of dark chocolate and plots out stories while she walks every morning. She enjoys travel, sports, and binge-watching—and never misses an episode of *Survivor*.

Alexa brings her characters to life in steamy historicals, contemporary romances, and romantic suspense novels that resonate with passion, intensity, and heart.

KEEP UP WITH ALEXA
Visit her website
Newsletter Sign-Up

MORE WAYS TO CONNECT WITH ALEXA

9 781648 392627